BRANDON

OTHER TITLES BY MELODY ANNE

BILLIONAIRE AVIATORS

Turbulent Intentions
Turbulent Desires
Turbulent Waters
Turbulent Intrigue

BILLIONAIRE BACHELORS

The Billionaire Wins the Game
The Billionaire's Dance
The Billionaire Falls
The Billionaire's Marriage Proposal
Blackmailing the Billionaire
Runaway Heiress
The Billionaire's Final Stand
Unexpected Treasure
Hidden Treasure
Holiday Treasure
Priceless Treasure
The Ultimate Treasure

UNDERCOVER BILLIONAIRES

Kian
Arden
Owen
Declan

ANDERSON BILLIONAIRES

Finn
Noah

BRANDON

AN
ANDERSON
BILLIONAIRES
NOVEL

MELODY
ANNE

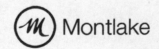 Montlake

Published by Montlake, Seattle

www.apub.com

Amazon, the Amazon logo, and Montlake are trademarks of Amazon.com, Inc., or its affiliates.

ISBN-13: 9781542017060
ISBN-10: 1542017068

Cover design by Letitia Hasser

Printed in the United States of America

This book is dedicated to Sarah Huff. I'm so grateful for strong women like you in my life. Your love, strength, and raw determination are an inspiration for us all. Oh, and maybe, just maybe, we'll bring ya with us on the next Canada trip. :)

PROLOGUE

"It's beginning to look a lot like Christmas . . ."

Several heads turned, and a few people chuckled as the deep baritone voice belted out the first line of the song seemingly every person around the world hummed, sang, or whistled as the warm weather turned cold and December crept up before anyone was ready.

"How are you doing today, Mr. Anderson?" Chloe Hitman asked as she wiped a cloth across the pristine wood counter in front of Joseph Anderson. She clearly could see he was in a mighty fine mood this cold December first.

He had big plans for Chloe. She was a fighter, but for anyone to think they could battle him was downright laughable. Joseph had yet to fail when he truly wanted something. And he was sitting at the bar of Chloe's beautifully redone restaurant with a plan of action.

He was in the mood for a wedding.

"I'm wonderful," he told her. "Now you tell me—what did you do with these counters?" he asked.

She grinned, the smile lighting up the dimly lit place. She'd owned it for only about six months, and she'd already made magic happen. It was difficult to get a table without reservations . . . unless you were Joseph Anderson, of course.

"I went to this amazing wine bar in Oregon, of all places, and saw a counter with lights embedded in it. I knew I had to make it happen, so voilà, here it is," she said. She'd been involved in every single detail of this place, and it showed. She took pride in all she did. That was why Joseph wanted her, and only her, to finish up his kitchen at the veterans center that he'd been involved in each step of the way.

"It looks like constellations," he told her as he looked a bit closer.

She clapped her hands. "Exactly!" she exclaimed. "I wanted something unique that would fascinate people."

"So you want to keep them sitting here for hours?" Joseph said.

"Yep. I want them to have a great experience from the time they walk through the front doors until they step back outside. I want them to feel they can sit here all night."

"I love the way you think," Joseph said as he pulled out a cigar.

"Now, Joseph, I know you don't often hear the word *no*, but you know there's no smoking inside," she said with a chuckle as she shook her finger at him.

He sighed as he held the fine cigar in his fingers.

"Of course I know that. I just like to hold it while I sip a fine glass of scotch," he said.

She chuckled. He truly had picked well when he'd chosen her. She was a true gem.

"It would be amazing to live a life without rules. I can't imagine what it feels like," she said.

"I follow the rules," Joseph assured her. "I just tend to make up my own as well."

That got another laugh from her. "I can't imagine what this world would be like without rules," she said. "As much as I complain about them, I do appreciate law and order."

"And if there weren't rules, it wouldn't be any fun to break them," Joseph said.

"That's a very good point," she said. "Now, let's get down to it. What has you in my place on a Thursday night? You're a busy man, and I'm surprised to see you all alone."

"Am I bothering you?" he asked.

Her eyes widened. "Not at all," she quickly assured him. "It's always a pleasure to visit." Then she smiled. "Though I *have* been warned about you."

His smile fell away as his eyes narrowed. "Warned?" he said.

She laughed, not at all falling for his usual tricks. He might have to be a little more cautious around this one. He liked it a lot.

"Yes, I've been warned that you like to meddle in people's lives. And I've definitely been told when you're acting all innocent is when you're the most dangerous."

She placed a hand on her slender hip and gave him a smiling challenge. He was truly going to enjoy taking her down. He couldn't even imagine what fun her and Brandon's children would be. They were both smart, funny, and beautiful. Those kids were going to be a delight.

"The fact that I enjoy helping out those I care about has nothing to do with meddling. I just like to get things done, and I pick the best of the best to accomplish that. Does my track record for success say anything less?" he challenged.

She sighed. "No one can say you don't have the golden touch."

"Exactly!" he exclaimed as his fist hit the counter, making the person to his right jump in her seat. Chloe laughed again.

"Don't be scaring my customers," she warned. She stepped over to the woman and refilled her drink. Joseph hadn't had this much fun in a while. He was definitely going to be hanging out at this place more often.

She came back and refilled his scotch. He pulled out the contract he'd been carrying with him for a while.

"You've done amazing with this place. Now it's time to give back to the community," he told her.

She warily eyed the document before meeting his gaze, challenge in her eyes.

"I told you I don't have time to do the kitchen at the veterans center," she said.

"And I told you I want the best. Look what you've done with this place in less than six months. Don't you think the poor men and women who've served our country deserve what only you can give them?"

"Playing on my heartstrings?" she questioned.

"I'm just wanting to give back," he said as he took a sip of his drink. It was damn fine.

"Why do you want me to do this so badly?" she asked. And he knew right then that he had her. He leaned back, feeling pretty dang good about it.

"I told you—I only hire the best."

"Fine. I'll read the contract," she said, and he grinned. But she held up a finger. "I *said* I'd read it. That doesn't mean I'm committing to it."

Before Joseph could reply, Chloe's shoulders tensed as her gaze was directed behind him. He knew that look. He was curious to see what had brought out the expression.

Joseph turned to see a very attractive, well-put-together woman approaching. She glanced his way before her eyes focused once more on Chloe. She moved to them and gracefully sat down on the stool next to Joseph.

He instantly liked the woman. Joseph had always told the masses he got a feel for a person within the first few seconds, usually before any words were even spoken. It was all in their attitude and the way they held themselves. He admired confidence and drive. This woman had them in spades. The resemblance between her and Chloe told him she was most likely her mother.

The day just kept getting better and better.

"Hello, Chloe," the woman said in a polished, autocratic voice. She was used to getting her way and used to people listening to her. She looked slightly familiar, but Joseph couldn't quite place her.

"Hello, Mother," Chloe said, her shoulders stiff. There wasn't a lot of warmth between the two of them, but Joseph still liked the woman. He could see respect and love there but also a wall. There was a story here he truly wanted to learn.

"Mother, this is Joseph Anderson. Joseph, this is my mother, Genevieve Hitman."

"It's a pleasure to meet you, Mrs. Hitman," Joseph said as he held out a hand.

"Please, call me Genevieve. The pleasure is all mine," she smoothly said.

He smiled. "Now I know why you look so familiar," he said. "You own the culinary school. I can't believe it's taken me this long to put it together." He frowned for a moment. He liked to know everything about the people surrounding him, and he should've realized who Chloe's parents were long ago. That was foolish of him, but in his defense, Chloe never spoke of her parents. He wanted to find out why.

"Yes, my husband and I do," she said.

"Do you want a glass of wine?" Chloe asked.

"Yes, darling," Genevieve said. Chloe didn't ask which kind. She obviously knew what her mother drank.

Chloe pulled out a fresh bottle of red and began pouring while Joseph faced her mother. He had so many questions but didn't know where to start. That was a first for him.

"What brings you out to our small town?" Chloe asked as she set the glass in front of her mother.

"I haven't seen you in a month," Genevieve said, the words sounding like a bit of a scolding. It was well placed, in Joseph's opinion. A child should visit their parents much more often than monthly.

"I'm sorry, Mother. I've been swamped with the restaurant," Chloe said.

"It seems to be doing well," Genevieve said. Though she was barely looking around. Even as she said this, she looked at the counter and frowned. "Do you have a rag?"

Chloe sighed as she grabbed a rag and began to wipe the counter. "I've got it, darling," Genevieve said.

Joseph noticed how Chloe clenched her jaw, but she handed over the cloth, and Genevieve wiped over the area Chloe had just swiped, then proceeded to clean the entire counter in front of her.

"A clean surface is the first step in all preparation of food," Genevieve said.

"Yes, I know, Mother. You've said that since I was a child," Chloe said as she took the rag back.

Chloe looked at Joseph again. "Along with owning the school, my mother is also a world-renowned food critic. She can make or break a new facility."

Genevieve laughed before taking another sip of her wine. "I wouldn't say I have that much power," she said. But Joseph had a feeling she did indeed have it. He could see it by the way she carried herself.

"And what does your father do?" Joseph asked.

Chloe smiled. "He's a chef and has a line of high-end restaurants."

"That's quite the combination," Joseph told her. "Did you always want to go into the family business?"

Chloe's shoulders stiffened. "This is my restaurant, not one of my father's."

Those words made her mother frown. "Your father always wanted to go into business with you," she said. It was obvious this was a point of contention between them.

"It's always wonderful to have the kids work with us, but also it gives me enormous pride when I see my family members striking out on their own," Joseph said.

"Sometimes a wiser person knows when to strike out and when to join," Genevieve said.

Interesting, Joseph thought. He liked this woman. He could see her character beneath the very uptight demeanor. He wanted to know more.

"Are you going to offer me a menu?" Genevieve asked.

"Is it for a family visit or for your paper?" Chloe asked.

"You know it would be unethical for me to comment on your business. Of course, I'd be biased."

Chloe gave a smile that didn't reach her eyes. "No, Mother, I don't think there'd be any bias at all," she said as she pulled out a menu.

Joseph would've never thought Chloe's mother would be who she was. Chloe was full of warmth and a lot of vinegar. Her mother looked as if she didn't often, if ever, let go and smell the roses. He wanted to dive in and learn so much more about them.

And he would.

In his later years of life Joseph had learned he didn't need to be in a hurry. Slow and steady truly did win the race.

"As much as I want to sit here and keep visiting, I have an appointment I can't miss," Joseph said as he threw down an exorbitant amount of money for his couple of drinks. Chloe tried to protest, but he ignored her as he stood and looked at Genevieve. "It truly was a pleasure. I look forward to next time."

"Me as well," Genevieve said.

Joseph leaned in, then slid the papers closer to Chloe, letting her know he hadn't forgotten about his reason for being there. She took them with another long-suffering sigh.

"Thank you for coming, Joseph. Remember that I just said I'd look at them. This is in no way a done deal." He smiled at her before turning and walking away.

She could say whatever it was she wanted. He knew he'd won. He might as well start planning the wedding to his nephew to save time later. Then by this time next year he could be holding a new grandniece or grandnephew in his lap while the Christmas presents were being opened.

Yes, it truly was beginning to look a lot like Christmas, and as long as a mystery was there to be solved and love was in the air, he was getting exactly what he wanted each and every year.

CHAPTER ONE

Was time anyone's friend? Brandon Anderson wasn't sure. They said time healed all wounds. That was partly true. It was sort of like that scar on his leg from when he'd had a perfect grand slam. He'd slid into the base after sending three of his teammates home. The ball had hit the catcher's mitt as he'd done his best to knock the guy over.

And he'd been the victor, securing their national championship 12–11. His teammates had carried him on their shoulders from the plate as blood had dripped down his calf. He hadn't even realized the injury would get him six stitches until the adrenaline had slowed. But the scar remained to this day.

Time marching on was like that. He'd lost his mother, the single-most devastating day of his life. It had been two years, and there were times he'd still feel such an ache it took all he had not to shed a tear. But then he'd have moments of remembering something amazing about her, and he'd smile so big his cheeks would hurt.

He'd also gained a family on that tragic day. He knew it had been his mother's way of letting her sons know they'd never be alone. Even in her dying moments she'd been sacrificing, giving to her children. That was who she'd always been. That was who she was now that she was in heaven. She'd gone too soon, but there was no way she'd be forgotten.

He'd been angry for a while, but his sense of humor and love of life had been what his mother had loved most about him—according to her. He wouldn't dishonor her memory by changing who he was.

During that first year after Brandon had lost his mother, he'd made mistakes—several, in fact. But then he'd met Chloe. He smiled as he thought about the spitfire of a woman who'd made it more than clear she wanted nothing to do with him.

Brandon had always loved women, from the time he'd been in first grade and talked one of his classmates into holding his hand. He'd loved all girls until he'd become a man; then he'd loved women. They were everything he wasn't, and nothing made him happier than making one smile.

But Chloe was unlike any woman he'd ever met before. She was confident and sexy, funny and stubborn. She'd intrigued him, and the second she'd told him not to get any ideas, it had been like a red flag waved in front of a bull. He'd wanted to win her over. He wasn't a man to take by force. No, he'd much rather win her with charm. He had no doubt he could do it.

There was a part of him that felt guilty to live his life and find happiness when his mother couldn't do the same. But when he did feel bad, he knew he was doing what she'd want him to do, and she would smack him over the head if she knew he was living half a life because of grief.

When Joseph Anderson had told him he wanted him as the electrician for the veterans center, he'd been honored. Not only had Brandon served as an air force pilot, but he was getting to know his family, and working closely with them was the best way to do it.

There had been a part of him that had thought about turning it down, because from the time he was young, he'd been determined to make it on his own, without help from his family. As a middle child in a sea of brothers, he'd always tried to find his identity without being just a brother.

It might have appeared to the rest of the world as if he was nothing more than a carefree boy in a man's body who was more interested in making the room laugh than earning an honest day's wages, but what people saw on the surface wasn't always what lay beneath.

He worked hard and had done so his entire life. There were always ideas brewing in his head, and he'd never been willing to settle for second best. Sure, he liked to laugh, and he loved to live life to the fullest, but he wanted to stand out, to make a name for himself.

The veterans project was just too amazing for him to pass up. It was a cause he stood for, knowing he had his freedom because of those who'd sacrificed the most. And then it had the added bonus of working close to home.

When Joseph had said he wanted Chloe to design the kitchen, Brandon had been beyond thrilled. That meant the two of them were going to be working closely together. The kitchen was the heart of any place. And with the sparks that flew between him and Chloe, that was going to be one steamy room.

He smiled as he strolled down the street to Chloe's restaurant. She'd made magic happen with that place. She'd turned it from ordinary to beautiful. It was *the* place to go to in town now.

He knew Joseph had presented her with the offer to do the veterans center, and he also knew she was fighting it. That impressed him. It wasn't easy to say no to Joseph. Brandon didn't know anyone who ever had. He was sure there had to be people out there, but maybe because they'd said no, they were nowhere to be found, sinking in their careers that had never gotten a chance to take off.

But that brought him right back to Chloe.

Maybe she was the first to say no to Joseph who truly could do it on her own. It made him like her even more. She was confident and talented, and she didn't need anyone to back her name. She just needed her skills and raw determination.

But then again, he knew in the end she would say yes, and they'd be working together very soon. Joseph was pretty irresistible. Brandon hoped he was as well. He'd win the girl. There was no doubt in his mind. He just wondered how long it was going to take.

Chapter Two

There was a pleasant smile on Chloe's lips as she refilled Sal's coffee and asked how his miniature Chihuahua's vet visit had gone. He answered with a grin, his dog tucked safely inside his jacket, her little eyes peeking out at Chloe. Sal Abrams slipped the dog a small bite of his doughnut, and then she disappeared back into the safety of his coat.

Sal was their small-town attorney, and he came to her place daily for coffee and pastries. She'd always adored the man. The entire town did. He was set in his ways, and he'd give his shirt to someone in need. He'd helped Brooke and her sister a lot, and that meant he'd get to drink coffee for free as long as she owned this place.

Of course, he left her such ridiculous tips, which she'd tried to fight him on, it wasn't *actually* free. Someday he might just accept her gift with a smile. But Sal was one of those people who liked taking care of women. She loved that about him. She didn't mind having a wonderful father figure like him in her life.

Chloe had two amazing parents. There was no doubt about it. She didn't talk about them to anyone, because she was determined to make it on her own, without their influence and certainly without their help.

Yes, they were amazing, and yes, the world absolutely loved them. Her mother was a food critic, and she could cut someone down to shreds, all with a professional smile on her face. Chloe had seen people rant and rave and also break down and sob, basically curling up in a ball and giving up, because of the power her mother held.

Her father was the best chef she'd ever known—and his own worst critic. He accepted only perfection in all aspects of his life, including from his daughter. And she seemed to never get it right.

When her parents had begun their cooking school, which had received national and international awards, she'd once dreamed of working there. That had quickly faded as she'd grown. She occasionally taught there, but whenever she worked around her parents, she was a hot mess.

They might not have even realized they did it, but they had never once in her life told her she was doing a great job without adding an aside that would make her feel small. The solution to that was to just not work with them. She loved her parents and didn't want to stop, so she kept as much from them as she possibly could.

She'd heard other people say it was a parent's role to shape and mold their children. She'd been told that the parents who didn't care wouldn't say anything. But she wasn't sure she agreed with that sentiment. Wasn't it good to make your children feel good about themselves? She'd never have kids of her own, but if she had chosen to go that route, she'd decided long ago she'd raise them with love—and zero criticism.

Her relationship with her parents was definitely complicated. But she'd give her last breath defending them as well. Maybe it was why she was her own worst critic. She wanted to be the best, and she never felt as if she was. It was a never-ending cycle.

"Are you still with me?" Sal asked.

She laughed as she shook her head. "Sorry, I got lost in my thoughts for a moment," she told him as she grabbed the pot of coffee and topped him off. "Try this cookie. It's a new recipe I've been working on for a while."

He accepted it and took a bite, his eyes sparkling. "I want every one you have in here," he immediately said before polishing it off in two more bites. "This is the best thing I've ever tasted."

She beamed at him. "I will give you a few more, but I'm testing them out today. Be honest—do you think they need any tweaks?"

He shook his head. "No tweaks at all needed. And no need to test anyone else. I'll take them."

This made her beam. Why couldn't her parents say something like that? She was sure her mother and father would tell her something like "A little less salt" or that there were too many nuts. Something would be wrong with them. Something always was.

"I will make more tomorrow. I guess you'll just have to come back," she told him.

She wanted to continue creating new things to keep people coming. One thing that drove her crazy with any business was when the menu never changed. Her favorite places were always those that brought something new to the menu often. Not just once a year or even once a quarter. If a business wanted to keep her coming back, they had to give her a reason to. They had to make sure she felt as if she'd miss out on something if she even took a week off.

"You know I'll be back every day," Sal told her. He truly was one of her best customers. They chatted for a while longer before Chloe turned.

Then she stopped in her tracks.

Of course it was *him*.

Brandon Anderson was now casually strolling up to her place of business. He walked with confidence wherever he was going. It was something she admired about the man.

And though she'd deny it even on her deathbed, she'd caved in to him . . . once. She hadn't even told her best friends about that night. It wasn't exactly that she felt ashamed. It was just that she had known better.

She'd been feeling down the night of Sarah's wedding. And though she'd let Brandon know in no uncertain terms nothing would happen between the two of them . . . well, somehow she'd woken up in the morning next to the man.

She had done the ultimate walk of shame that morning and was more grateful than words could ever express that no one had seen her. Though she'd made a clean getaway, she absolutely remembered *every single detail* of their time together—and it had been spectacular.

The man *knew* how to please a woman, and she'd been pleased over and over and over again. Chloe had always been a small woman no matter how many Cheetos she shoved into her face. She'd rather have the curves her friends had, but it just wasn't in her genetics. She was grateful she could eat whatever she wanted, since she loved to cook and do multiple taste tests, but she wouldn't mind a bit more junk in the trunk.

But Brandon hadn't seemed to mind her body at all. He'd touched and kissed every single inch of her. Before that night with him, she hadn't known those words could actually be true. But his hands had slid up and down her body as if she were a string on a violin. His mouth had trailed after.

Where she was petite, he was huge. The man had shoulders she could caress all day and night and abs she wanted to run her tongue over again and again. He had a rugged face, but the sparkle in his eyes took away any roughness. She wasn't sure why she was fighting this thing between the two of them.

He'd made it more than clear he wanted more. She could tell herself all day long it was because she wasn't attracted to him, but that would be a lie. She didn't have a traumatic past relationship making her afraid of love. She just didn't want to be a girlfriend. She didn't want to settle.

She'd seen often how amazing a relationship could be in the beginning. Both parties would be putting on their best behavior, willing to do anything for their significant other, but then as time went on and the love hormones began to neutralize, she'd also watched as they stopped pretending, as they each grew more selfish, as the fighting would begin.

Yes, she saw the perfect matches of her best friends. But they were the exception, not the rule. So she'd made it a lifelong mission to never be in a long-term relationship. And that had always worked for her.

Perfection had been her aim her entire life. And there was no way to have perfection in a relationship. The only way to somewhat have it was to never get past the beginning stages where everything was wrapped in a pretty pink bow, where hormones dictated how you saw a person.

Of course, everyone was perfect at the start of a relationship. You weren't able to see flaws in your partner. You didn't want to find anything wrong with them. It was all roses and chocolate-covered strawberries.

In the beginning your makeup was done to perfection, your hair neat and tidy, your clothes wrinkle-free. In the beginning maximum effort was put forth. But once you were comfortable and trusted your partner, that wall of perfection began to crumble, and you let your other half see your flaws.

It was those who had real love who saw those flaws as strengths instead of weaknesses. It was those who saw you through the frosted glass because you were their other half, and there were no such things as flaws in their eyes.

She didn't trust that she could ever see someone in that light. And she certainly didn't trust that a man could see her that way. Maybe Brooke and Sarah had found that. And as much as she wanted to believe they loved their husbands and their husbands loved them, she still wasn't fully convinced the glasses wouldn't one day shatter.

The attraction she felt toward Brandon terrified her. She could completely see herself falling for the man. She could imagine it would be absolutely perfect . . . for about three months. And then inevitably, it *would* all fall apart. When there was as much passion between two people as there was between her and Brandon, it was bound to go up in flames even hotter than most relationships. When those glasses broke, they'd break into a million pieces.

That would be awkward since they worked together. So knowing all of that, she had to be strong. But as he walked toward her, it was much easier said than done. The man was like a giant magnet—and she was definitely magnetized.

By a miracle of sorts, Chloe managed to rip her gaze from him. She quickly walked behind her counter and pushed her way through the swinging double doors into the kitchen, where the ovens were hot and her crew was busy cooking.

Nancy looked up, her smile quickly faltering, making Chloe wonder what it was the woman saw in her eyes. Was it panic, shock, resignation? She didn't know. All she knew for sure was that she was so attracted to this man she didn't trust herself alone with him. She hadn't been able to even look at another man since their night together. If she were being fully honest, she hadn't been able to look at another man since Brandon had strolled into town.

She went through the daily motions of life, worked hard at her place of business, and went out with her friends. But he was *always* on her mind. And even if she could push thoughts of him away during waking hours, there was nothing she could do to stop thoughts of him when she was asleep. He was *that* man. He was the guy you lost yourself in. Chloe wasn't the girl to allow it to happen.

Besides her fear of having anything less than perfection, there was more that could go wrong in a relationship with Brandon. Though Cranston was a small town, she'd bought this restaurant on her own, and she'd made it successful—without the help of her parents. She'd been involved in every detail of the place. And though she wasn't necessarily a wealthy person, she made it just fine on her own. That could all disappear if she were to get in a relationship with Brandon.

Just seeing him walk through her doors had threatened the very fabric of her happiness. He'd consume her. She was sure of it. She might not have experience with men, and she wasn't afraid of them, but she knew he wasn't anything close to ordinary. And when she did decide to play around with men, she looked for the ones who were easily forgettable.

"Chloe, what's happening?" Brooke asked as she entered the room and took a cautious step forward. Chloe had forgotten Brooke had been sitting at the counter visiting with her and Sal. That's how muddled Brandon had made her brain.

Chloe tried to form words as she looked at the worry on her friend's face. Brooke knew sparks had flown between Chloe and Brandon, but Brooke didn't know of their night together. Maybe it was time she confided in her bestie. Maybe they should call Sarah, and the three of them could come up with a plan together. That's how it had always been between them.

Of course, now that Brooke and Sarah were married to Brandon's brothers, she wasn't sure they'd be allies. They might have matchmaking plans in their heads about the third in their trio marrying another brother. It was like a bad Hallmark movie. Okay, if she was being honest in her own head, she could admit she loved those movies. She didn't hate love at all; she just didn't think it was right for her.

"Brandon's here," Chloe whispered. Brooke smiled, and Chloe wanted to call her a traitor.

"Does he have you all hot and bothered? I don't know why you always run from him. You two could light up the city with the electricity that sparks between the two of you. And with him being an electrician, I'm sure he knows which wires to cross." She laughed at her own joke. At least she found herself humorous.

Chloe sighed as she rolled her eyes. That only made Brooke smile even wider. She knew now that at least one out of her two best friends wasn't going to be any help to her. She was doubting her other best friend would do her any good, either.

No matter how many men Chloe had dated over the years, she was normally finished with a guy by date number three. Brooke knew this about Chloe, and it had never been a problem. As a matter of fact, her friends had been impressed with her willpower. Sarah had been pretty similar, actually. Not Brooke. Brooke had been in relationships before. But she was also one hell of a tough woman, and no man had been able to be her equal until Finn. Now her bestie was happier than Chloe had ever seen her before.

"I don't want him," Chloe hissed. "I did have him, though," she added very quietly.

Brooke looked at her again, and then her eyes widened in understanding. The girls normally didn't keep anything from each other, and Brooke wasn't a stupid woman. She was putting the pieces together.

"When?" she gasped.

"After Sarah's wedding," she admitted.

Now it was time for Brooke to be hurt and irritated. "Are you kidding me?" she said, one hand firmly planted on her hip. "You went this long without telling me and Sarah?"

If it had been simply anger in her friend's gaze, Chloe wouldn't have felt so scolded. It was the hurt that was her undoing.

"I'm sorry. I was hoping if I forgot about it, then it would just go away," Chloe said.

"But we share everything," Brooke said.

"I know. I know. But I didn't mean for it to happen," Chloe tried to explain.

"Oh, you just fell onto a bed and ended up naked and sweaty, then?" Brooke said. She was shaking her head at Chloe.

"No, I was *very* aware of my decisions that night. Plus, I was feeling sorry for myself, and he flirts *very* well, and you know—one thing led to another. It had been a really, really, *really* long time."

"I can totally understand you sleeping with the guy. I just don't get how you can keep it from your besties," Brooke pointed out.

"I had to do the walk of shame for the first time in my life. That's how I was able to keep it from you," Chloe said as she threw her hands in the air.

"You know neither Sarah nor I would ever judge you," Brooke said. "We've all done things that weren't our proudest moments, but then we've also always had each other to talk to about it to make ourselves feel better."

"I know. And I probably would've felt better long ago if I'd come to you guys, but I've been hoping he'd just forget about it."

"You aren't exactly a forgettable kind of woman," Brooke said.

"And you are married to his brother. This is a mess," Chloe said.

"If you really aren't interested, then you have to be honest with him. I'm sure he'll respect that," Brooke said.

"He hasn't done anything wrong, exactly," Chloe told her. "He's just always around. And now Joseph is pushing me hard to work on this kitchen, which means we'd be locked together for hours on end." She was tapping her foot in agitation.

"I'm not sure if that's a bad or good thing. I'm confused now," Brooke said.

That made Chloe smile. "Welcome to my world."

"One thing I know for sure is there's not a chance of avoiding him, not in this town, so you either have to be honest with him and tell him to back off or tell him you need time to figure out what you want. I'm sure he'll respect that."

"Do you think a guy would even understand if we told him we have no clue what it was that we wanted?" Chloe asked.

That made Brooke smile. "Nope. He won't understand it at all, but it would give you some breathing room. I really want to see you work on this project. The entire town is rallying behind it."

"As much as I'm frustrated with Joseph, I want to do it. I'm just so stubborn I haven't signed the papers. But I have done some preliminary drawings. I could make this kitchen efficient and amazing. And maybe it would get publicity for this place as well. Though I'm busy now, it's the novelty of a new place in town. I want it to stay busy forever; then someday maybe it can even expand into more cities."

"I think that's a smart business plan. Just tell Brandon to back off and let you breathe, and all of it will work out just fine," Brooke assured her.

"Is that how it worked with Finn?" Chloe asked.

"Finn and I were complicated from the day we met, but in the end it all worked out."

"I don't want to get married," Chloe said.

"This isn't the eighteenth century. You don't have to get married if you don't want to," Brooke pointed out.

"I don't want to fall in love."

Brooke gave her a smile. "I don't think you really get a choice in that."

"You aren't reassuring me," Chloe said. "I've always believed love is a choice. I chose to love you and Sarah. And I've chosen not to love a man."

"I'd say because we're more sisters than besties. And as far as men go, that's because the right one hasn't come along." She looked to the door. "Or he hadn't until maybe now."

"This isn't love. This is just hormones. I'll beat them," Chloe said, more determined than ever before to prove herself right.

"Well, good luck with that," Brooke said as she laughed.

"Look out the door and tell me what he's up to," Chloe said with a growl in her voice. Brooke was of no help at all.

"He sat down at a table. Marcy handed him the menu and appears to be going for coffee." The normality of the moment snapped Chloe from her panic attack. She actually found herself smiling the tiniest bit as she tugged on Brooke's arm to get her attention.

"You have to go find out what he's doing here," Chloe said. "Hopefully it's nothing more than a coincidence, and he's not looking for me at all."

"Considering this is your place, I highly doubt he's just here for the coffee and pastries. Though they are damn fine. I think I've gained ten pounds since this place opened." She sent a glare Chloe's way, as if that was her fault.

"I don't make you eat the food," Chloe pointed out.

"Yes, you do!" Brooke exclaimed. "Since you practically live here, if I want to see you, I have no choice but to come in. And there's no way anyone can walk into this place without getting hungry."

"That's why I bring you here again and again. You stroke my ego," Chloe said.

"Your ego doesn't need stroking. You know what a good cook you are. You got the chef genes, hands down."

She flinched a bit at that statement. She wanted to be good on her own, not because it was in her genetics. She didn't necessarily want to be better than her parents; she just wanted to be best on her own.

"That's most certainly true. Though Sarah has gotten a lot better at cooking."

"Good. Then I never have to," Brooke said, perfectly content to not be a world-famous chef.

"It amazes me anyone wouldn't want to cook. It's so much fun to throw ingredients together and watch magic happen."

"That only happens when you love to do it. I light stoves on fire when I attempt anything fancy."

"That's true," Chloe said with another smile. "And you've done well at calming me. Now you have to go find out what Brandon wants."

"While you hide in here?" Brooke said.

"Yep, I'm totally hiding, and I'm not even ashamed of it."

Brooke disappeared out the doors, and Chloe crept over and glanced through the crack as Brooke sashayed up to Brandon. Brandon looked up with a big smile. Then he stood and gave his sister-in-law a hug.

"Are you stalking my best friend?" Brooke asked with a sly smile. Brandon laughed. Chloe was a bit envious of their easy relationship. Of course, she knew she could have that same relationship if she gave the guy a chance. If she could guarantee friendship only, she might just do that. Maybe her hormones would eventually calm down. Maybe not.

"Do I ever need to stalk anyone?" Brandon asked.

"I wouldn't think so, but here you are . . . ," she said, pointing out the obvious.

"Yep. Here I am. Now are you going to tell me where Chloe ran off to?" he said, giving Brooke an assessing look. It appeared as if he was trying to judge if Brooke was more his sister-in-law or more Chloe's friend. He'd lose. Nobody got in the way of their deep, abiding friendship.

"Well, I hate to tell you this, but she left for the day," Brooke said, thinking on her feet. "Maybe I can help you."

"We both know she doesn't ever leave this place so early," Brandon said, the smile never leaving his eyes. "I bet she's watching this entire conversation, and you're the go-between."

"Whatever do you mean?" Brooke asked, fluttering her eyelashes. "I'd never do such a thing."

Brandon leaned back in his chair, as if he had all the time in the world. Then his lips turned up, and Chloe's breath was taken away. Brandon had a smile that could make the biggest Grinch grin back at him. She was sure the man was very aware of his appeal.

"We both know I spotted Chloe while I was walking in. She disappeared faster than a hooker at the end of her hour, and then magically, you appear. My guess is she's in the back trying to wait me out." He paused for a very long time. "But you should know by now that I'm a very patient man."

Chloe wanted to shout out "Mayday! Mayday! The ship is going down!" Instead, she stayed where she was and tried to have faith in her friend's ability to get information from Brandon or get him out of there.

"I have noticed you're a patient man," Brooke said. "But Chloe is a very stubborn woman."

His grin widened. "I'm very aware of that. I like it."

"What if she just doesn't want to be around you?" Brooke asked.

His smile fell completely away, and Chloe felt instant guilt that she was the cause of that look on his face. She didn't want to hurt the man. He hadn't done anything to her to warrant her rudeness.

"I just want to see Chloe," he finally said. Marcy walked up to the two of them, a quizzical look on her young face as she set down a pastry in front of Brandon. Brandon thanked her and picked up the treat, then took a big bite and sighed. "Perfection as usual," he said.

"You might want to make a graceful exit to show her you're a bigger man than you appear to be sometimes," Brooke warned. "Give her a choice of seeing you or not."

Brandon looked thoughtful for a moment before he chuckled. Then he took another bite of his treat, all without replying. Chloe found herself holding her breath. He finished the pastry and took a large drink of his mocha before looking at Brooke again. Then he stood and pulled out his wallet. He took a few bills out and tossed them on the table.

After picking up his coffee cup, he looked relaxed as he faced Brooke, as if he didn't have a single care in the world. The man probably didn't. He was great looking, was beyond wealthy, and carried enough confidence for a dozen men. He wasn't often denied anything he wanted. This had to be a new one for him.

"Tell Chloe I'll be at my new house," he said. "I won't wait long before I come searching for her again," he added, the words most certainly a promise. "But I'd love it if she came to me instead. We have a lot to talk about."

"When did you buy a place?" Brooke asked with confusion. "Your brother didn't say anything about it."

"That's because I signed the papers on Friday. Today is moving day. I didn't want to say anything until it was a done deal. It's the house on top of Diamond Hill Road."

Brooke whistled. "Wow! Isn't that a bit much for a single guy?"

His grin grew. "I don't plan on being single forever," he told her with a wink before he looked toward the back of the restaurant again. Chloe would swear her heart stopped at his words.

The giant mansion he'd bought had been empty for some time. It needed a lot of work. And Brooke was right—the place was huge, over five thousand square feet. And it wasn't that far from her own place. That made her sweat a bit.

"Wow, I guess we'll be having a housewarming party soon. I've always wanted to see the inside of that place."

"We will indeed. But I'm going to need help making it into a home." His eyes again looked toward the back, and although Chloe was hidden, she felt as if he could see right into her eyes. Did they have a connection? She wouldn't admit it if they did.

"I hope you get everything you want, Brandon," Brooke said. Chloe wanted to shout at her friend that she was the lowest of betrayers.

Brandon just smiled again, turned, and walked out the door as easily as he'd come in. Brooke stood where she was for several moments, and Chloe found herself unable to move. The entire visit had shaken her up.

Finally Brooke turned, and their eyes met through the slit in the doors. Chloe realized she could stop hiding and stepped into the open, signaling for Brooke to come to her. It was better safe than sorry, just in case the man was planning on sneaking back in.

"That was interesting," Brooke said when she approached.

"I heard the entire conversation," Chloe said with a sigh.

"I don't think Brandon is going away until the two of you have a showdown. He isn't the type to tuck tail and run," Brooke said.

"Unfortunately I think you're right," Chloe said with a sigh. "But I certainly don't want to meet with him on *his* territory, and I don't want it to happen here, either. I don't know what to do."

"You could always flee the country," Brooke suggested with a laugh. Her best friend was truly enjoying herself.

"Thanks for the solid advice," Chloe told her with an eye roll.

"Maybe just bed the man again. Hot damn, there were more vibes than usual coming off him. I can now understand why you've been so uptight lately."

"Are you afraid you married the wrong brother?" Chloe asked with a forced chuckle.

Brooke's face turned serious as she looked at Chloe, who was finding it difficult not to fall apart. She pulled Chloe into a hug.

"I love you. Never forget that. And there's no doubt in my mind that I married the man I'm supposed to spend the rest of my life with. Those vibes coming off of Brandon were all for you and *only* you. I think you have him utterly smitten. You're going to have to decide if you want his attention or not. And you're going to have to do it sooner rather than later."

Chloe's stomach tightened at the words. She didn't want to be Brandon's full focus. If she was, she knew she'd be in a minefield with no chance of escape.

"What should I do?" Chloe asked.

"Go and talk to the man," Brooke said. "There's really nothing else you *can* do."

Chloe knew her friend was right. But not today and maybe not tomorrow. She had to get herself together first. She'd never been like this with another man. She didn't want to be like this now.

With that conviction in mind, she decided to take a break. Tomorrow would go better for her—she was sure of it. Tomorrow always made her smile because it meant the possibilities were endless. If a person woke up with a smile, there was nothing they couldn't accomplish. She'd call it a day so a new one could begin. Then she'd be back to herself and able to think more clearly.

With a plan of motion in place, she left the restaurant with Brooke. She'd figure it out. She always did.

CHAPTER THREE

For years Chloe had been coming to her parents' cooking school and working with eager young potential chefs. She remembered the first time she'd stepped into a professional kitchen and how scared she'd been. She was so competitive she hadn't wanted to be anything less than the absolute best.

That was a very difficult task when a person had parents like hers. She'd refused to help at their school when she'd first begun her career. She hadn't wanted them looking over her shoulder and judging her. She'd been judged her entire life, and she hadn't wanted to put herself in a place to feel more of it. But her great love of cooking and helping others had finally won over her stubbornness.

Though she was incredibly busy, she filled in for the other teachers when they were sick or on vacation. This weekend, just when her life seemed to be in the most turmoil of all time, she'd been needed to fill in.

"You're running late," her father said from the office as she tried to sneak by.

"I know. I've got to hurry to make sure everything came in that I ordered," she said as she tried to slide by.

"Your mother's down there now checking the inventory," he told her. "And I haven't seen you in two months now. You can give me five minutes," he said with a raise of his eyebrows.

Chloe nodded as she stopped trying to get away and stepped into the front office, where her father stood behind a counter. This wasn't a typical administrator's office. Her father had told her long ago that if a person wanted to be the best, then they didn't have to have the most skill; they just had to have the most drive.

He'd explained to her when she was very young that he wasn't one of those lucky few who'd been born with a natural ability but that he'd pushed himself by training and practicing every day of his life.

So when he did have to be at the school, he didn't sit behind a desk doing paperwork. He paid people to do that. He stood in his office at a beautiful counter that had all of his favorite kitchen appliances and tools.

Her father never stopped creating. He came up with new recipes and new ways of preparing ordinary foods that made them into coveted dishes. There were still a few secrets he'd been able to closely guard from the greedy hands of those who'd love to bottle and distribute his creations. He did this by keeping the recipe in his head instead of on a computer, where there was a chance of it being hacked.

"It smells delicious in here, Father. What are you making?"

It was so ingrained in Chloe to call her parents *Mother* and *Father* that she never slipped. Most children said Mom, Ma, Pa, Daddy, or any of the other abbreviated versions. But from the time Chloe was a toddler, she'd been taught that it was Mother and Father.

They'd taught her a lot in life about respect. They simply didn't understand children growing up and having children, then allowing those children to disrespect them. They said their life was literally owed to their parents. Some might scoff at that. But the bottom line was that it was true.

They'd also told her that didn't give a parent the right to abuse that privilege and that children were owed respect and dignity, too. A parent didn't have a child for them to become a Mini-Me version of the parent, but to grow into their own person and make a path for the next generation. It was a great line that, if done right, would go on forever.

"Today is dessert day," her father, Donovan—not Donny, not Don, only Donovan—said with a smile. When her father made his sugary confections, she always saw him lighten up. He truly enjoyed creating mouthwatering sweets, which was probably why it was her favorite course to cook as well.

"Ah, food for the soul," she said as she leaned in and peeked in the oven. It appeared to be a sort of cinnamon roll. Though nothing he made could be described so simply as *cinnamon roll*. An ooey-gooey masterpiece was what it was.

The timer went off, and her father moved to the oven and looked inside for a moment before deciding it was time for it to come out. He never opened the door unless he knew it was done. He said the slightest fluctuation of heat could ruin a once-perfect creation.

"I know most people say soul food is country fried, but we all know that the way to anyone's heart is dessert," he said. The smell that had been invading the large space had been stomach-rumbling good before the door to the oven had opened. When the door came down, the smell was enough to drop a person to their knees.

"Please, please, please tell me this isn't a dish that has to sit and breathe," she said, her eyes almost watering she wanted a bite so bad.

He laughed, true joy coming through in his voice. It was the only time she got to see her dad really free. When he was simply creating on his own without eyes on him, his tough exterior fell, and she could see the little boy inside, the person who'd obviously made her mother fall in love with him.

Chloe had seen a lot of reasons her parents had fallen in love. Yes, they were stern and wanted nothing less than perfection from their only child, but when they didn't know eyes were upon them, there was a softness in them she wished they'd show to her more often.

At least she knew she was loved, and at least they'd taught her to be strong and independent. It was so much better than them either not caring at all or not preparing her for the world. When she saw many college-age kids with no idea what they were going to do with their futures, she could appreciate her parents so much more.

"You always have had quite the sweet tooth. It's a good thing you have your mother's metabolism," her dad said. He carefully set the dish down on the counter and pulled out two plates. She waited.

He scooped a generous roll onto each plate, then reached into a dish behind them and settled a mixture of nuts, cinnamon, shaved chocolate, and sliced fruit on top of the already-gooey dessert.

When he was finished, it was picture perfect, ready for the cover of a food magazine. She was sure it wouldn't take long for it to go right there. He made some things for only his restaurants, and some he shared with the world. This would be a world dessert that few would be able to replicate.

Those who thought cooking was as simple as following a recipe didn't truly have a joy of cooking. Most people could read instructions and make a decent dish. But a few select people could create magic.

"All ready," he said. She didn't need any further invitation than that. She picked up her fork and knife and cut her fist bite. She didn't even need a knife, it was so soft and pliant. But that was the best way to ensure she got a little taste of all the ingredients in each bite.

Flavor exploded in her mouth as she savored the amazing creation. Her father nibbled on a few bites as he jotted down some notes in his book. She polished off her plate while he was still writing.

"Any suggestions?" he asked her.

This was a normal question in their household. How could the dessert be improved? He wouldn't be insulted by anything she came up with. As a matter of fact, he'd be impressed if she could make it even better. She desperately wanted to come up with something, but she loved it.

After a few seconds she laughed, her stomach a bit bloated, she'd stuffed so much down. "I really want to come up with some powerful words of wisdom like 'More cinnamon, less nutmeg.' But seriously, Father, I can't imagine tweaking this recipe even a little bit," she finally said. "I wouldn't mind taking the leftovers home, though, so I can work on that later tonight," she added with a big grin.

Her father might've normally lectured her about always striving to be better, but her blatant excuse to get the dessert actually made him laugh.

"That's such a good way to get the dessert I think I shall let you have it," he said. "But you do have a task. I want you to find some way you could improve upon it. If you can't, then I guess you won't get to be my taste tester anymore."

That was a real threat. She'd hate to never get to sit there with him while he made his creations and be the first person to take a bite. That would be the ultimate punishment.

"I guess I have no choice but to figure something out, then," she said. "Are you going to give me the recipe?"

He shook his head. "You know that would be cheating," he told her. Then he heard students in the hallway. "It looks like your class is here. You'd better go relieve your mother."

"Yes," she said, her smile falling away. It wasn't that she didn't love her mother. She very much did. It was just that her mother very rarely loosened up like her father just had. She never did when it was all of them together.

Yes, her father wanted perfection, but her mother wouldn't accept anything less than that. Which meant she didn't have time to joke or play. Chloe was a bit jealous of the dynamics of the Anderson family. They were so different than her own. Brandon didn't truly realize how lucky of a man he was.

He'd lost his mother, which was beyond horrible. And he'd lost his father when he was young, which had been a blessing since the man was so terrible. But he'd inherited a family unlike anything she'd ever seen before.

The Andersons were beyond wealthy, but they were also filled with love and happiness. They were the family everyone wanted to be a part of. They made mistakes and weren't belittled because of it. They were encouraged to forge their own paths. She wasn't sure who she would've turned out to be with a family like theirs. Would she still have been a chef? Would she have been married with children? Would she have ever been happy being mediocre?

She didn't know, because she hadn't been raised in a home like that. She'd been raised with love, of course, but she'd been raised with drive and ambition. Could a person fight against that?

If she'd been brought up in a different home, would her competitive nature have been squelched? It was an interesting theory. It was something she hadn't really thought about—not before meeting Brandon and all of the Andersons.

They were obviously filled with just as much, if not more, drive as her parents—as her, as well—but they did have a loving, wild, almost crazy family. Would they be rulers of the entire world if they were as strict as her parents? She wondered if research had been done on that.

Maybe somewhere out there twins had been separated at birth. One given to a set of easygoing sleep-on-Sundays-all-day-long parents, and one given to a type A, go-go-go set of parents. And then the babies were followed, watched, observed, day and night. Maybe it was a *Truman Show* type of experience.

Even if someone had done something like that, they'd never admit to it, so there wouldn't be a way of showing studies. It would be unethical— unlawful in most places. She wasn't quite sure why her mind worked the way it did or why she thought of things like this. Maybe because she was always trying to achieve more. And most people did that by constantly thinking.

She kissed her father goodbye and made her way to her assigned classroom. She was going to put away her thoughts and enjoy her day. If it was a good group of students, it would be fun. If it wasn't, then she could tell herself at least she might learn something new she could use in her restaurant.

If she was positive about each moment in her life, then she'd have no regrets when looking back—just plenty of wins and a lot of learning experiences.

CHAPTER FOUR

Brandon sat on his back deck, his thoughts on Chloe. Of course, that seemed to be where his thoughts were every second of the day. It was now interfering with his work. He wondered if he was truly as into this girl as he felt he was or if the thought of having to chase her was what made him chase her that much harder.

He didn't normally chase women—not even when he was younger and didn't have much to his name. It had taken him time to make a name for himself. And he wasn't talking about the Anderson fortune. He'd built a successful career long before he'd found out he was one of *those* Andersons.

He had gone to trade school, gotten his electrical license, and owned his own business by the time he was thirty-two. He'd worked hard at building trust with clients, and they'd gladly followed him when he'd branched out on his own. Now with the veterans center under his belt, he felt as if the sky was the limit. Not because it was with the infamous Anderson collection of projects, but because the world's eyes were going to be on it and see that everything had been done right and fast. He didn't slack because of who he was. That only made him push that much harder.

He heard his brother approaching before he saw him. This wasn't unusual. He'd always been close to his siblings. There was no need for knocking on the door when it was always open to those he loved and trusted.

With four siblings, sometimes that door never had a chance to fully shut. He wasn't complaining. He couldn't imagine what a quiet life would be like. Probably pretty dang boring. Brandon didn't allow himself to get bored.

"What are you sitting here smiling all goofily about?" Noah asked as he took a seat next to Brandon.

"I'm just feeling good today," Brandon told him. Noah popped the cap off the soda he'd grabbed. "You must be working." Otherwise, he'd most likely have grabbed a beer.

"Yeah. We've had delays and any number of other things going wrong, and I've been back to the drawing board over and over again. I have to keep my mind sharp, or Sarah takes too much pleasure in showing me up," he said with a laugh.

Noah and Sarah were the head architects for the veterans center, and it was their only project together. They loved each other immensely and said they didn't want to risk fighting over work. They'd done enough of that while designing the facility. "One and done together" was their motto for a happy marriage. Brandon thought that might be a smart rule to follow.

That was *if* he could even get Chloe to work on this *one* project with him. He sure hoped so, because right now he wasn't feeling too optimistic about that. He'd been confident, but she was great at avoiding both him and Joseph, which wasn't easy in a town the size of Cranston.

"I hate all the delays," Brandon said. "It's taking too long to get this up and running for all of those who really can use it right now."

"I agree. But that's why I love doing it with Joseph, too. At the end of this, it's going to be the gold standard of facilities others will need to follow. So the first one has to be just right. The rest will go more smoothly," Noah said. "But enough talk about work and delays. How are things going with Chloe?"

Brandon sighed. He almost lost his smile, but he kept it in place. There was no way he was giving any of his siblings room to mock him.

"She's being difficult—won't talk to me."

"Is that why you're slacking on the kitchen?" Noah asked.

"There's no kitchen yet, so it's not up to me. But I don't want anyone else to do it. I want her, and so does Joseph, so we're being patient."

"She's worth waiting on. I had a nice chat with her the other day," Noah said.

That wiped the smile off Brandon's face.

"What do you mean you talked to her?" It seemed she was talking to everyone *but* him. He hadn't done anything wrong. He didn't get it.

"I'm easy to talk to. Lots of people like to do it," Noah said with a chuckle. "But since I *am* married to one of Chloe's two best friends, I see her often. She's a pleasure to have over."

"Ugh. She isn't as much of a pleasure around me. I somehow got on her bad side, and I haven't figured out how to change her image of me."

"What did you do?" Noah asked. It was a perfectly reasonable question, but Brandon wasn't sure how to answer it. He didn't want to kiss and tell when it came to Chloe, but he also needed some help, and that meant he'd have to give something.

"We had some time the night of your wedding," he said. He figured that wasn't telling too much.

"What kind of time did you have?" Noah pushed.

"I don't want to get into details. But I just know I want more time with her." It wasn't often that Brandon was serious. But the rare times he was, his siblings usually listened. That was the nice thing. They could joke around a hell of a lot, but when it came down to it, they were there for each other when it counted most.

"If this is more than lust, then you need to show her."

"How will I know it's more than that if I don't get the chance to find out?" Brandon honestly asked.

Noah was quiet for several moments as he thought about the question.

"I'm not an expert in the area of dating. You know that Sarah and I went through our own personal hell, but in the end it all worked out. I just know that when I stopped playing games and let her know how I truly felt, she responded to it."

"I don't know exactly how I feel. I haven't been playing with her, but I have been cautious. You can't blame me for that when she keeps me at a nice distance."

"Is she worth pursuing?" Noah asked.

"Yeah, she's totally worth it," Brandon said without hesitation.

"I'd think so from what I know about her. But at the end of the day, it would be you and her and your own compatibility. She might be perfect, and you might be close to perfect, but maybe you aren't a perfect couple," Noah pointed out.

"I haven't even thought about that. I can't imagine we could be any-thing less than spectacular if our one night together is any indication."

"I thought you weren't going to kiss and tell," Noah pointed out.

"I didn't," Brandon said with a grin. "But what's the point in trying to hide the amazing chemistry between the two of us?"

"We all know she's beautiful, smart, and talented. But is she the one?"

"I'd like to find out," Brandon told him.

"You've tended to lean toward the Barbie-type girls for a long time. I believe this might be the one, 'cause she has you tied up in knots, and she's nothing like the typical girls you've had on your arm before."

"Hey! I'm not a playboy. I don't treat women with disrespect," Brandon said, somewhat offended.

"I didn't say you do. But you haven't exactly brought a woman home for Christmas," Noah pointed out again.

"Maybe this is the year I do just that," Brandon said.

"I hope so," Noah said, shocking him.

"Why is it so damn hard to admit I might want more?" Brandon finally said. He was frustrated and maybe speaking out more than he normally would've done before. He almost expected his brother to laugh. But Noah shocked him.

"Because I think this one matters. It's up to you to figure out what you want to do about it and what that means. I do know that it's useless to fight it, though."

"What's useless to fight?"

Brandon and Noah turned to see Crew approaching. He stopped at the cooler and grabbed a beer before joining them.

"No way am I telling *you* anything," Brandon said.

Crew was a psychologist, and unless Brandon wanted to pretend he was in a stuffy office and have his brother pick apart everything he was saying, he was keeping his mouth shut. They'd always teased Crew, saying he needed to loosen up. But it was somehow different now. His brother had loosened up. They just couldn't figure out why or what was happening. Crew had even bought an old ranch and was fixing it up. He was the last person on earth any of them would've thought would do that.

"Come on—you both know I'm the smartest one out of all of us. Maybe I can help," Crew said. He took a long slug of his beer, and Brandon was again surprised. It wasn't that Crew didn't drink; it was just that he didn't often do it during the day.

"What is wrong with you?" Brandon asked. For once he wasn't trying to deflect when it came to his brother. He was just trying to figure him out—and he couldn't. Something was seriously off. It took several moments for him to put his finger on it. "You haven't shaved."

He paused as he looked at his normally well-put-together brother. "And you're wearing a hoodie. How in the world did I not catch that immediately?"

"I'm with Brandon here—what in the world is going on?" Noah said.

"Maybe I'm making some changes," Crew said.

They gaped at him. It was nice for Brandon to not have the full extent of his brothers' attention on him, but this was truly odd behavior from Crew.

"I don't buy that for a second. You know what they say about leopards and their spots and all," Noah said.

"I'll tell you about it when I can," Crew said.

That shut both brothers up. Something was going on with Crew, and they immediately wanted to help him. But they had a code among each other that if one said they couldn't talk about something right then, then they had no choice but to respect it.

"It really sucks you're invoking the 'Can't talk about it now.' You realize we're going to be obsessing on this, right?" Brandon said.

"Yes, I know that. And I know you'll respect me," Crew said. Then he took another drink before focusing his laser eyes on Brandon. "Now tell me about your problems."

And that was the end of that.

They sat back in silence for a while. Then Brandon pretty much outlined to Crew what he'd been talking about with Noah. Crew listened without offering advice. There wasn't a time in history Brandon could remember that ever happening. They grew very quiet after that.

Something was going on with his brother that was big enough to make him forget about his problems, at least for the short term. He decided he'd give Chloe a few days to make up her mind if she'd talk to him or not. He'd told his sister-in-law that was exactly what he'd do. He just hoped he had the patience for it.

Brandon liked instant gratification. Always had and always would. But maybe the fact that he wasn't getting just that with Chloe was the reason he liked her so dang much. He guessed he was going to find out.

And maybe because he was going through hell, he could respect that his brother might be as well. Maybe it had to do with a woman. It might take a while, but eventually everything would come to a head. He'd see how all the pieces lined out when that did happen.

CHAPTER FIVE

Chloe turned for the hundredth time as she tried to get comfortable in her bed. She'd been around Brandon plenty of times before Sarah's wedding and after. She wasn't sure why this last time seeing him was affecting her so much. It made no sense to her.

Maybe it was because there was a big part of her that wanted to take on the Anderson project, and she knew that meant she'd be working side by side with Brandon. Maybe it was because she hadn't been out on a date in a very long time, and her body was needy and filled with an ache she had no doubt Brandon could cure in one night.

Whatever the reasoning, she couldn't stop thinking about Brandon or that night. It had been three months since then. The wedding had been perfect, with her and Brooke next to their best friend as she'd said her vows to a man they had no doubt their friend was deeply in love with.

Watching Brooke and Sarah so happy had made Chloe ache for something she'd never wanted before. It had made her wonder if she'd ever change, if she'd ever want a happily ever after. That was nonsense. She had her reasons, and they were valid and smart.

She hadn't been pleased with those types of thoughts the night of the wedding . . . so she'd drunk way too much that night. And of course

Brandon had been there. When he'd asked her to dance, she'd thought she'd say no. But instead she'd nodded at him. Yes, she'd been tipsy, but she'd also been fully aware of what she'd been doing. She had no doubt she'd had the wine to talk herself into doing what it was she'd wanted to do for months. A lot of people used alcohol as liquid courage. It allowed them to do what they wanted to do in the first place. And sometimes, that led to some really poor choices.

So she'd danced with Brandon. For one night she'd allowed herself to pretend she was on a date with a man who couldn't resist her. She'd pretended she wanted what every woman was told she wanted. She'd pretended it was a fairy tale, and she was the one getting a happy ending.

Chloe smiled as she shifted in her bed again. She had gotten many happy endings that night. They'd danced and laughed for an hour as she'd sobered up. Brandon had made her laugh more than any other man had ever done before.

He'd been funny and genuine, and she'd known this would be a one-night stand. It was what she'd convinced herself she wanted. When he'd offered to show her his room, she'd taken his hand and told him to lead the way.

The shock and satisfaction in his eyes had told her she'd made the right choice. He hadn't thought she'd be an easy conquest, which had made her feel better about herself. But he had taken her to his room, then sealed the decision in her mind when he'd asked her if she was sure it was what she wanted.

The first kiss had been pure magic. His lips had caressed hers in the most tempting way, coercing her to open her mouth to him. It hadn't taken much. Their clothes had melted away, and then he'd lifted her in his arms and carried her to the bed.

He'd stood over her as he'd gazed into her eyes before looking over her shaking body. Then he'd joined her on the bed, his hands and tongue tracing over every inch his eyes had devoured moments before.

The first orgasm had come with shocking speed, but the next few had built up, slowly and reverently. He'd touched and caressed her all night, letting her take turns doing the same to him.

They'd fallen asleep as the sun had begun rising. And when she'd woken close to noon, she'd had no regrets. She hadn't wanted to deal with a morning after, so she'd carefully untangled herself from him and thrown on her clothes from the night before.

She'd looked over his face one last time before sneaking away. In his sleep Brandon had looked as if he didn't have a single care in the world. He'd had a slight smile on his full lips, and his chest had gleamed in the slit of sun shining in through the cracked curtain. It hadn't been easy to leave.

He'd tried calling her that day and the next and next and next. She'd finally answered, telling him it had been a one-night stand and would never be more. But here they were three months later, and he still wasn't deterred.

Chloe gave up on sleep and rose from her bed. It was the middle of the night, and she knew the next day she was going to have to do something about this situation. She didn't want to be in a relationship, and if she didn't make that perfectly clear, the man wasn't going away.

Cranston was far too small a town to have this tension between the two of them. She was just going to have to be clear and concise and let him know she wasn't the type of girl to have flings, and she wasn't in any way interested in a relationship.

If he couldn't accept that, then she'd throw her hands up and ignore the man. It could be done. First she had to brave seeing him in person. She wasn't quite sure she could do it. She'd have to see if the morning light brought any inspiration.

She eventually went back to bed and finally fell asleep. But when she woke up in the morning, she groaned. Of course, Brandon easily slipped inside her head whenever she let down her guard.

And in her dreams they were absolutely fantastic together. If she thought magic could happen in the kitchen, it didn't even compare to the show that was made in the bedroom with Brandon Anderson.

CHAPTER SIX

What in the world was she doing? Seriously, she didn't understand what was going through her brain as she walked the long path from the broken gate to the huge front doors of the Diamond Hill place, which had sat empty for at least fifteen years.

Tugging on the belt that cinched her coat together like an armor suit, Chloe found her head a bit light—probably from lack of oxygen. She'd decided not to call Brandon—that a sneak attack was the best plan of action. Now that she was walking to the door in her heeled boots, she was thinking it might not have been the best plan after all.

The sounds of hammers hitting nails and people speaking as they attempted to gain back some control of the weed-infested yard could be heard all around her. But even with people scuttling about, she still felt alone, like her universe was closing in on her.

Chloe wanted to tuck tail and run. But she'd rather come to Brandon's place and face him away from her friends and customers than risk him showing up at the restaurant again or do this in front of his entire family. And she had no doubt he'd be around every corner if she wasn't careful. Brandon didn't often fall back on something he'd said he was going to do.

She'd only known the man about three years, and she'd learned that much about him in their limited interactions. When they'd first met, she'd felt sparks, but that hadn't meant anything. She'd felt sparks before. What shocked her was the fact that those sparks had ignited and had only grown stronger through the years. She couldn't seem to fight them. And that messed with her entire idea of sparks dimming after the initial getting-to-know-someone phase.

Of course, she could justify that by acknowledging that they hadn't been dating. Yes, she'd known him for years, but they had only bumped into each other or shared some family occasions together. They'd slept together only once as well. So of course there were still sparks.

But what completely refuted her claim of it all seeming perfect because people were on their best behavior was the fact that she'd never been on her best behavior when it came to him. And she knew for a fact he hadn't been on his.

He'd seen her with no makeup, seen her with flour all over her clothes and her hair a mess. He'd seen her practically at her worst, and yet he still pursued her. Everything she'd thought she knew about the magic of the beginnings of relationships was crashing around her. This wasn't good for her mental health.

That thought sent a pang through her that she was anything but happy about. She wasn't going to continue to barrage herself with these secret fantasies. She'd slept with the man . . . once. It was done and over with, and the sooner he accepted that, the better off all parties concerned would be.

Not paying attention to where she was going and staring up at the giant walls of his home that looked as if they could do with a good washing, Chloe's heel hit a crack in the sidewalk, sending her sprawling forward. She fell ungracefully, managing to take the brunt of the hit with her hands, which immediately began to ache. At least it took her mind off her ridiculous thoughts.

More embarrassed than in pain, she jumped back to her feet, tucked her shaking hands into her pockets, and looked around. It didn't appear as if anyone had witnessed her embarrassing fall, so at least she had that to be grateful for.

But on top of her anxiousness about coming to see Brandon, now her hands hurt, and she was beginning to feel the tinge of a headache coming on. She had about twenty minutes to get some medicine in her system before the ache became an unbearable splitting pain that took her vision away and made her want to throw up.

Since she'd be in and out of there in less than ten minutes, she could get through this just fine. The eight steps up to the rickety front porch were both treacherous and terrifying. Not because she was worried about falling through, which she was, but because she was that much closer to Brandon.

Lifting her hand to knock on the intimidating door, she didn't have the opportunity to touch the wood grain before it was being pulled back. And then he was there—standing two short feet in front of her.

Chloe looked up higher than she'd been expecting. Even with her taller heels, she felt inferior. It was a feeling she didn't appreciate. She also wasn't used to it. She was used to respect from all those around her. She'd earned that in her pursuit of perfection. There were many, many reasons she avoided this man.

"Chloe."

Frozen. Chloe was frozen to the spot, needing to retreat but unable to move so much as a pinkie, let alone get her legs to work. The deep drawl of his voice sent memories rushing through her of him saying her name as she'd looked deep into his eyes, of how he'd made her cry out multiple times. She couldn't even wish it hadn't happened, because it had been the best night of her life.

She'd thought she was a strong woman, but she realized she was at this man's mercy. It wasn't a feeling she relished. Had her parents taught her nothing? They'd be disappointed in her if they could see how weak this one man made her feel.

"Why are you hunting me down, Brandon?" she finally asked when she was sure her voice would work correctly. She might as well get to the point. She'd eaten up about two of the ten minutes she had until she needed to run away before her headache became unbearable. One word, and she was a mess. This meeting wasn't going as planned, not one little bit.

"How are you?" he asked, ignoring her question.

"I've been just fine," she told him. At the moment she wasn't, but that didn't matter. She'd be normal again as soon as she got him to leave her be—and she got some pills in her system to counter the headache. "Or I would be fine if you'd leave me alone. Seriously, you have to accept it was a one-night stand and it's over. I don't want it to be awkward when we're in a room together." If only she really felt this way. If only she didn't want him so much.

He smiled, then turned his head to the side. "Did you know that you're the first woman I've ever met who actually stops me cold at the sight of you? Yes, you're beautiful, and that's worth stopping for, but it's so much more than that," he said in awe. His praise fell so effortlessly off his tongue she wasn't sure what to say. No man had ever said anything like it to her before.

Sure, she'd been called beautiful and feisty and other compliments, along with some insults. But never had a man looked at her as if she hung the moon and stars and told her how she stopped him cold. She wanted to melt against him. Not a good idea.

Chloe took a second to compose herself and decided her moment of weakness was over. She wasn't going to allow this man to turn her brain to mush any longer. She was a strong, independent woman, not some fluttering teenager who quickly fell under a new boy's spell or carefully crafted words.

"I warned you our night together was a onetime deal. So I'll ask again, What are you doing bugging me at my work?" she said, more force to her voice. She was scared and had a headache taking over that was making her words sharper than they normally were.

"You know exactly what I want," he said conversationally. Though she did know what he was pushing for, his words made her think of something else. She hated that her mind didn't seem to get out of the gutter around him. Maybe it was her sending mixed messages. She wasn't sure. She did know she was damn confused.

A nervous laugh escaped her tight throat, and her slight hysteria finally elicited a response from him as he raised an eyebrow. They were both still standing in his doorway, and she wasn't sure where they went from there.

"I'm busy, Brandon. I have my restaurant I'm trying to make successful, my volunteer work, my time at my parents' cooking school. I don't have time for games, and I really don't have time for mind games."

That stopped him. His smile fell away.

"I don't want to play games with you, Chloe. Do you really hate me that much?" he asked. Her head was really beginning to hurt, and she wasn't sure why she was suddenly feeling like the bad guy here.

"It's not that I hate you, Brandon. I just . . ." She trailed off. She wasn't sure what to say. "I don't know what I want." She was shocked when those words came from her mouth.

"I don't know how to respond to that," he said after a minute. She was feeling worse and worse that she'd hurt his feelings.

"Brandon . . ." His name fell off with a sigh. She'd come to put her foot down, and suddenly she was feeling like the villain. What made that even worse was that she knew it wasn't what he was trying to make her feel.

"Why is this so complicated?" she finally asked.

His gaze was so intent as he looked at her. She couldn't have spoken at that moment at all. She was practically shaking as she stood before him. This hadn't gone as she'd planned at all. This was more of a mess than ever before.

"I've thought about our night together every single day since," he finally said, the words casual, as if he weren't shattering her into a million pieces. She didn't want to take the bait, but she couldn't help herself.

"You're confusing me." The pain in her head was growing, and she knew her night was ruined. Even taking her migraine pills wouldn't help at this point. She was in for a very long evening.

"I'm confused myself. I don't know what to do about it," he said with a shrug.

Her head was throbbing, and she seriously didn't know what to do about it. If she wasn't in pain, she knew she could be stronger, knew she could make better decisions, but right now she knew she needed to run. She didn't like running, but she didn't think she had a choice.

"Coming here was a mistake," she told him. "I'm leaving."

Her ten minutes were up. She knew the man could stop her, but she hoped he wouldn't. Even after a million pep talks, she still wasn't strong enough to face Brandon Anderson. She knew as she began making her way back down his uneven sidewalk that she never would be.

He said nothing as she left, but she never heard the door shut behind her. Most likely he was watching her walk away. She was sure not too many women turned him down. Maybe she'd start a trend. She could be proud of herself. She'd come and looked him in the eye, and she'd left with her head throbbing, but she was leaving.

Neither of them had agreed to anything, making this visit a giant waste of her time. She even wondered if there was a part of her that had wanted to see him today. Was she playing games . . . with him? With herself? She honestly wasn't sure.

After the burning in her head was settled, she might be able to feel proud of herself for trying to face the situation even with her thoughts completely muddled. But for now, all she felt was pain. She knew from experience the pain would dull. It would just take a very long time.

If she could get Brandon off her mind with some magic pills, she'd take them in a heartbeat. But she had a feeling getting rid of the migraine was going to be a whole lot easier than getting rid of one very determined Anderson.

CHAPTER SEVEN

It took nearly twelve hours for Chloe to get control of her headache. She'd had to turn off all the lights, take a double dose of medicine, and then lie in bed with complete silence as she prayed her head wouldn't turn inside out. But finally the pain was gone, and Chloe was too restless to stay inside the house even a minute longer.

After donning her warmest coat, she stepped outside, inhaling the fresh night air. It was nearing midnight, but it didn't matter. She lived in a place where the only crime reported was bored kids setting off bottle rockets in public restrooms. It irritated the heck out of the local sheriff but didn't scare people into hiding away behind ten locks and a shotgun.

Moving down her quiet neighborhood, Chloe focused on the Christmas decorations that were out, people choosing to leave their lights on all night for those who stayed up late. The holidays were approaching quickly, and her Christmas spirit had been zapped. Normally this was a time of year she loved—magic and possibilities were in the air. And she always came up with some fantastic Christmas creations. Her favorite cookies were produced this time of the year. She always drew a crowd to try out the treats.

But all of that was now being tainted by Brandon's insistence she team up with him. Just because her friends had married his brothers didn't mean they should jump on the bandwagon. She was afraid she was beginning to want a ride, though.

The smell of snow was in the air. She was surprised it hadn't already fallen, but the weatherman had promised it would be there for Christmas Eve. Maybe if she didn't see Brandon again, she'd once again see the beauty of it all. She had to be open and willing for that to happen.

Before she saw him or heard him, she *felt* him. Maybe she'd known the second she'd stepped outside he'd be there—maybe some deep, dark place inside her that was a glutton for punishment had known. But without a doubt she knew Brandon was walking up behind her. She didn't slow and certainly didn't turn, but soon he was at her side.

"I heard you had a fondness for midnight strolls," he said, his voice quiet, almost subdued, surprising her.

She thought about ignoring him, pretending he wasn't there as she finished her walk. But if she did that, he'd realize the power he held over her, and that wasn't acceptable.

"I've always been a creature of habit," she said, keeping her tone moderated. "If I don't walk, then I can't get my mind to shut off, and then I never get any sleep." She didn't know why she was adding that, but talking to him had been natural from the start when she wasn't on edge.

"You might like your routines, but I've seen how much you've progressed in life just in the few short years I've known you," he pointed out. "You're a woman who likes to be the best and is never happy settling. It's something I truly admire about you. It's something I've always felt myself."

She was shocked enough by his words that she turned and looked at him. He was wearing a pair of sweats; what appeared to be several sweatshirts, making him seem a bit chubby; and a wool hat. It was chilly out, but he might have gone slightly overboard.

"You've never seemed to be an overachiever to me," she said.

"That's good because I don't want people to know that," he admitted. "If they know how important it is to me, then they'll know I'm devastated when I fail. I hate empathy as much as I hate failing. Besides, when you grow up with four brothers, what's the point in trying to compete? I'd rather they think I don't have a care in the world. The best victories come about when others don't even know you're in the competition until they're watching you from behind."

She actually smiled at that thought. "I never would've thought of that," she finally said with a laugh. "Oh, how much easier my life would've been if everyone I know never had a clue of how much I like to win. I've always been the one to beat, making me in a constant competition," she told him.

"It's not very fun, is it?" he asked.

"No, not at all. My parents are perfect in every way. That's a lot to live up to."

He took in her words as they continued to walk. "My father was a monster, as you know, but my mom made up for it in spades by being strong but compassionate. She had an uphill battle raising us, but she never failed. That's a lot to live up to as well."

"I was wondering if how a person was raised affected how they behaved—if they were drawn toward a certain personality. I think it has some bearing, but I think we are just who we're meant to be," she said.

"I agree with that," he said. "Because my father was raised in an incredible family, and he was a monster, while my mother was raised in a terrible family that caused her to have to be with my father, but she was still an incredible person. I do think we can make choices that change who we are for the better or for the worse, but at the end of the day, we are who we're born to be—minus adding chemicals like drugs or alcoholism to the factor. That will completely change a person, even making them go crazy."

She was shocked at how much she was enjoying her conversation with Brandon. She found herself not wanting this walk to end. She wondered if there was a chance the two of them could just be friends. The constant state of arousal she was feeling told her that would be nearly impossible.

"It appears both of us have done a lot in life," she told him. "That might be our personalities or maybe the way we were raised. But we'll never know for sure."

Maybe she was feeling easier also because they were on neutral territory. They were walking, which always calmed her, not facing each other. It made talking to the man seem natural. When she'd faced him in his doorway, she'd nearly passed out. Now, her heart beat a little faster, but she didn't feel a panic attack or a headache coming on. That was progress she could be proud of.

"I've done a lot with my life, but there's so much more I want to accomplish," he said after they'd made it another block down the road and turned a corner. She was coming up on the more expensive homes, the ones with the decorations that always awed her, the street that led down to the Diamond Hill place. She was far too close to where Brandon was now calling home for her comfort—especially at night, when her defenses were down.

"Have you lived all your dreams? What more do you want to do?" she asked.

He let out a sigh. She didn't know what it meant. "I've definitely made some of my dreams come true," he told her. "I've messed others up." There was such intensity in those words she didn't know what to think. "But I'll never stop going after what I want."

"That's good," she said, not questioning him on what dreams he hadn't fulfilled. She was curious about it, but she was trying not to like him, and this conversation wasn't helping with that one little bit.

"What dreams do you have left?" he asked.

"My dreams have always been pretty straightforward and maybe not that exciting to some people," she said. "I wanted a restaurant of my own that was successful. So next, I want expansion. I like to be the best, and that's very difficult to do in the world of food. There are too many people out there like me, so I think I want to continue to make amazing places in cities like Cranston. It's not that I'm trying not to compete with the world's top chefs. It scares me, but I know I can go head to head with them. It's just that I think these smaller towns are where people actually care more about having a quality place. When you go somewhere like Seattle, you can find many, many fine-dining options. But I want that amazing place that people will drive an hour into the country to experience. To me that's success."

"I think that's amazing and very doable. And one person's goals are no less than another's. We make decisions about what feels right to us. It's how we feel about what we've accomplished that matters," he told her.

"I guess it could be wrapped up that simply with a nice little bow on top," Chloe said. Her parents certainly wouldn't agree with that. But she could think on her own and choose her own path because they'd raised her to do just that.

"I want to know you better, Chloe," he said, surprising her and warming her heart at the same time. She didn't want to feel that way. If she opened herself up, she was going to feel things she had no business feeling, especially when she didn't want a relationship.

"Don't go there, Brandon," she told him as she turned. Maybe an ending to this walk was in order. It would be better than fighting Brandon . . . and herself. She'd been starting to relax with him while they'd had this conversation. That had been foolish. She knew what he wanted.

She took a few steps, and Brandon reached for her, turning their bodies so she was forced to face him, his hands on her arms, holding her in place; his face too close; his eyes intense; and his mouth turned down in a small frown.

They were both breathing heavily as they stood in the shadow of a streetlight. She felt the rest of the world disappear as she stood in the same position she'd stood that night in his hotel room. But that night she'd leaned in against him, holding her face up so he could easily access her lips. Would his kiss feel just as good now as it had that night?

Quickly tearing her gaze away, she realized she wouldn't know, wouldn't allow herself to find out. That was a path that was too dangerous to even think about going down again.

"I can't stop thinking about our night together. I can't get you out of my head," he said, raising one hand and cupping her cheek. He wasn't going to make it easy for her to turn away. She might not have any respect for him if he did. Yep, she was a mess.

Though it was cold outside, his fingers were almost scorching hot as they rested against her skin. Chloe had no response as she was forced once again to look into this man's eyes.

Chloe saw the kiss coming—the kiss she'd just determined she wouldn't have with him. She told herself to turn away, to tug against his hold, to scream—to do anything other than stand there paralyzed.

But then his mouth was on hers, his lips pressing and pushing, his tongue touching and demanding entrance to her mouth. Chloe wanted to refuse, wanted to push him away, but his kiss took her back to that night she'd felt nothing but pleasure.

Those sparks of electricity she'd felt with him surged through her body and ignited something inside her she'd thought was long gone. He was solid and strong, and when she was in his arms, she felt safe. Even if in the back of her mind she knew it was wrong, she couldn't stop herself from reaching for him, from getting lost in the moment.

Her traitorous body gave in to Brandon, gave in to his touch. A moan escaped his throat, and his hand wrapped around her head and tugged on her hair. Her body was a traitor, because she didn't want to pull away from him.

Finally, she accepted that this had been inevitable from the moment she'd seen him a couple of days earlier. She'd have this kiss, and then she'd firmly say goodbye. It would be the kiss she'd never gotten to have, the one she knew would be her last. Maybe that was why she'd been so hung up on him—because she hadn't gotten any closure.

Chloe's fingers tugged against Brandon's thick hair as one of his arms held her tightly, pressing against her lower back and pulling her against him as he deepened the kiss, their touching growing greedier and more urgent.

Her name was a soft moan that traveled down her spine as he said it, and she felt heat in places she hadn't for too long. Just that quickly, she was lost in his arms, lost in him—maybe too lost to find herself again.

That thought sobered her up, and Chloe pulled back, breaking the powerful connection they'd been sharing. He released her, but the look in his eyes told her he was reluctant to do so. That made it so much harder for her to take another step back from him.

They gazed at each other for several moments as they both tried to regain their breathing. What had just happened? Chloe wasn't really sure. It had been so intense, just how it had been the night of the wedding.

Chloe knew she had to end whatever it was he thought he'd come to start. She had to do so with finality, and maybe then he'd understand that he couldn't just get a craving for her anytime he wanted and show up on her doorstep.

"You need to leave, Brandon. There's nothing between the two of us," she said.

He gazed at her, and his eyes narrowed. "That kiss calls you a liar," he told her, taking a step toward her.

She retreated more, not quickly, not like she was running, but just enough so he couldn't reach out to her. She couldn't handle his touch, especially with the new knowledge that it was just as good as it had been before.

"You and I never even started, so it's easy to be done," she said. She stopped retreating and put her chin up, her hands on her hips.

"I disagree. I wasn't sure how it would feel to kiss you again, but it's more than just passion that fills me when you're in my arms," he told her. She didn't know how to take his words.

"I walked away after the wedding for a reason. I don't want complications in my life," she said, hating the tears choking her voice. She was scared, but she didn't want him to realize that.

"People can change," he told her. "I know I'm not the same man I was even a year ago. If I truly believed there was nothing between us, I'd leave you alone. But what we share together is unusual, Chloe. Give it a chance, and see where it leads."

She shook her head. "I don't think that's a good idea at all."

"I won't give up unless I think it's hopeless," he told her.

This time Chloe did retreat several steps. She couldn't let him touch her anymore. She was too close to caving in to him.

"There's nothing to fight for. Please accept that," she said. "Now leave me alone."

Chloe turned and didn't care if he saw her fleeing. She ran back to her place, feeling his eyes on her the entire way. He didn't say another word, but she knew he was there. She went inside her house, locked the door, then slid down it, clutching her knees to her chest as she shook with frustration.

She felt him on the other side of her door, felt him there for a while before emptiness took his place. The connection between the two of them had been damn strong since the beginning, but instead of dimming, it seemed to be growing stronger.

Chloe needed this man to disappear from her life, but she was afraid it was already too late for that. She didn't know what she was going to do. Maybe Brooke's advice to flee the country wasn't such a bad idea after all.

CHAPTER EIGHT

Brandon had always lived life with a smile. He made a joke when the rest of the world was living in stress, and he smiled when others felt like crying. It wasn't because he was insensitive. It was just because he liked to look for the gold at the end of the rainbow instead of the rain that had caused the colors to fill the sky.

When it came to Chloe, he wasn't sure which direction he should go. She was telling him she didn't want this. Should he give up? Everything inside him said to fight for this woman. But why her?

Did he want her so badly because she was the girl who'd gotten away? He'd decided he wanted her in his life, but he hadn't realized how powerful the connection between the two of them would grow to be. It had started with an intensity that had shocked him, but instead of waning like it had with so many others, it had been growing stronger over time.

She didn't trust him, but he didn't think he'd given her any reason not to. Well, besides the fact that he wasn't backing off. But that wasn't exactly a trust issue. That was him going after what he wanted, which was something he'd done his entire life. It was in his blood, who he was. He didn't think it possible to be anyone else.

He wasn't the same guy he'd once been. He had ambitions and goals in life, and the more he thought about it, the more he wanted to include Chloe in that dream. He would definitely be the first guy to crack a joke and light off a firework that made his siblings jump, but he was also just as eager to win as the rest of them.

Was that what this was? Was it a game? He honestly didn't think so. He saw something in Chloe that drew him to her. They had much more in common than she was willing to admit. They also had differences that made it that much more exciting.

Brandon paced the huge mansion that he didn't understand why he'd purchased. Maybe it was the history of the place, and maybe it was because he always had enjoyed a good project, but whatever the reason, the home certainly wasn't comfortable at the moment. It was too drafty, and the internet was terrible. He hadn't been able to get any work done. But even if he could have, his mind wasn't allowing it. He had one person on his brain, and there was no room for anything else.

Moving through the house, he got a whiff of something delicious. Were those gingerbread cookies he smelled? No way. He picked up his pace and turned a corner, then barged his way into the kitchen.

Brandon couldn't help but smile when he found his sister-in-law Sarah in an apron as she took cookies off a pan and set them on wire racks. He watched her for several moments before walking up and leaning down, kissing her on the cheek.

"What brings you to my humble abode?" he asked with fondness. She was one of the few females in his life he was truly excited to see. His brother Noah had married well. He was glad to call her *sister*.

"Brooke and I have discovered if we don't feed the bachelor holdouts of this family, you'll wither away," Sarah said, placing the last cookie on the rack and then turning to face him.

"That is in fact true. Without you and Brooke cooking for me, I'd have to rely on the convenience store." He wanted one of the cookies desperately, but he'd learned quickly that he'd better not just grab one, or he might get his hand slapped.

"Or at Chloe's restaurant," she said with a brow up.

He shrugged. "Busted," he told her. He wasn't even going to try to hide the fact he wanted to spend time with her best friend. There was nothing he could hide from either of his sisters-in-law.

"Sit down, and don't get in my way, and I'll *think* about giving you some cookies and milk," she told him after a couple of seconds spent analyzing him.

His mouth watering, Brandon did exactly what she'd demanded, then smiled to himself. There weren't too many people in this world who could boss him around and get away with it. He had mad respect for his brother for choosing such a fantastic wife.

"How did you manage to get away from my brother for the afternoon?" he asked. "Not that I'm complaining at all."

"He's working at the center today, and I needed an excuse to grill you about my bestie," she said.

"I love your honesty," he said with a laugh. "But I'm still waiting on these cookies. You're killing me here. I'm practically withering away." He tried to look as innocent and hungry as possible.

"I also really wanted to check out this place, and I figured cookie making would be a good excuse to come in. It was a good thing I brought all my own supplies. I've learned with you bachelors that you don't have much more than meat, bread, and beer in the fridge," she said.

"You never need an excuse to stop by," he said, meaning it. "The door is always open."

"I love that about your family. It's something I've grown quite fond of. And since I love your brother so much, that means I love you, too. Of course, if you do hurt my best friend, I'll have to cut you several times, but it will still be done with love."

She said the words with a smile, so it took a moment for them to process in his brain. When they did, he laughed aloud. He also had no doubt what she was saying was true. He admired and loved the friendship between Sarah, Brooke, and Chloe. It was as tight a bond as he had with his brothers. And their love was born from friendship. They'd chosen one another. He had no doubt he would've chosen his brothers, though, even if they hadn't been siblings.

"You definitely entertain me," he said. "And trust me—I know you'd kill me."

"I do what I can," she said. She finally slid a plate of warm cookies and a large glass of ice-cold milk in front of him. "And I wouldn't kill you, just harm you. There's a difference."

He laughed again. "Well, that's a relief. I don't have to sleep with one eye open," he said as he eyed the cookies. "So what do you want to grill me about?" He was more than willing to answer anything she wanted after his first bite of a warm cookie. She was fantastic at making them. If there was any cooking skill at all he wanted, it was the ability to make mouthwatering cookies.

"I didn't fail to notice how you bought your house pretty dang close to Chloe's place," she said. She slid her next batch of cookies into the oven, then turned to give him her full attention. He shifted in his seat.

"Yeah, that would be hard to miss," he told her. It wouldn't help him to lie. Sarah would see right through him, even if most people couldn't. She was smarter than the average person.

"I should tell you to back off," she said. He cringed. He didn't want her to ask him to do that. He respected her and didn't want her upset with him, but he wasn't sure he could walk away from Chloe, not now, not until he knew what this was between them. Not when he felt they had a chance. "But I don't think I will."

Her words sent a zing of pleasure all the way through him. If her best friends were on his side, he really did have a shot with the girl. They did everything together, and they relied on one another. Maybe he could make both Sarah and Brooke his allies. He couldn't believe he hadn't thought of doing that much, much sooner. Ideas were spinning in his brain. He knew honesty would be best with Sarah.

"I really do feel something for her. I can't seem to stop myself from pursuing the woman," he admitted. He didn't want to be too cheesy or reveal too much, but maybe a little bit of soul bearing was what he needed to get her approval. He definitely wasn't going to admit he'd kissed Chloe the night before if her friend hadn't said anything about it yet.

"She might not feel the same way about you."

"Did she say something to you?" he asked. He found himself holding his breath. He hadn't wanted to ask that question. He feared the answer.

"She hasn't talked a lot about you," she said. He flinched.

"Ouch," he said. Sarah smiled. "But I think she likes me," he added while giving her his cockiest smile.

Sarah gave him a quizzical look. "How do you know that?"

"I can see it in her eyes. She's guarded, but she likes me, and I like her, and that should be all that matters in the end. The rest we will work on."

"If the world operated that simply, we wouldn't have wars," Sarah told him.

"Not everyone's as smart as I am," he said with a cocky lifting of his lips.

Sarah laughed as she joined him. He snatched a cookie off the plate and took a bite before grabbing some milk and washing it down. He got up and refilled the milk and grabbed a few more cookies before sitting again.

"Not everyone's as foolish as you, either. If you aren't careful, you'll mess this up."

"I don't think so. I think being careful is what has us at a standstill. I think if the two of us go full force ahead, we'll make a lot more progress." It would certainly be more satisfying than sleeping alone every night. And every other tactic hadn't worked so far, so a new way was the only way.

His sister-in-law looked at him critically for several moments before she smiled and patted his arm. He'd have paid half his bank account to know what she was thinking when she got that twinkle in her eyes.

"I wouldn't mind having my best friend be my sister-in-law as a Christmas present," she finally said. "I think, as a matter of fact, that I'm going to head on over and have lunch." He'd gained an ally. He wanted to get up and do a dance, he was so happy about it.

The timer on the oven went off, and Sarah left him sitting there alone as she pulled the last pan from the oven and turned it off.

"She might hide from you like she did me when I went in there a few days ago," he warned.

"Chloe is one of two of my best friends. We never hide from each other," Sarah insisted. Then she took off her apron and walked back over to him. "Don't mess this up, or I'll have your brother pound you. And then when you're weak, I'll kick you while you're down." She said it with such an innocent smile he couldn't help but laugh. If only the world knew how tough Sarah truly was.

"I could easily take my brother," he said with a smile. There was no way he was going to say he could take her, because he knew he couldn't. There was no chance of winning a battle you refused to fight.

"Isn't that cute? That's exactly what he says about you," she said with a laugh before she leaned in and gave him a kiss on the cheek. "I think you *are* worthy, Brandon. And I also think you shouldn't give up."

He wasn't sure she could've said anything that would've shocked him more. But he was more than happy to have her full-blown approval. That would make a huge difference in how Chloe would react to him. *One bestie down; one to go,* he thought a bit too smugly.

"I love you, sis," he said, meaning it.

"I love you, too. Now I'm leaving before this magical moment fades," Sarah said. She bounced away.

Brandon sat in his kitchen for a very long time. He wasn't sure what he was going to do next, but he wondered how long he was going to be able to hold out before seeing Chloe again. He had a feeling it would be sooner rather than later.

He finished off a pan of cookies and didn't realize what a mistake that was until he stood, his stomach bloated and cramping. Maybe it wasn't wise for anyone to bake in his house. He'd get fat and lazy in no time.

Before he was going to do anything else that day, he'd have to lie down. But as he did, he couldn't help but smile. His cookie binge was 100 percent worth it. He'd gained a new ally on his side and had the best lunch he'd ever eaten. So far his day was a win. Next, he'd have to win the girl. It could be done.

Chapter Nine

Chloe was mystified. She liked to continuously be doing something and always have her mind turning, but right now she felt stuck. She couldn't even begin to figure out Brandon. She wasn't sure how to respond to him now after their walk.

The man had always seemed like the class clown from the first day she'd met him. She never would've guessed he was anything like her—motivated, competitive, and eager to win without hurting anyone in the process. He was so much deeper than she'd imagined he would be. And that wasn't helping her not like him.

He was like a dang spider, slowly weaving a web that was drawing her in. The more he spun his web, the more she wanted to see how it would be completed.

She wasn't sure what to do to stop it or even if she could stop it at this point. She sat at her favorite place on a pier overlooking the lake and mountains surrounding her small town of Cranston, and she was a hot mess.

As long as her thoughts were filled with Brandon, she wasn't concentrating on her restaurant, and she couldn't concentrate on the veterans project that she was being drawn into. Was that because she wanted to help the community? Or was it because she wanted an excuse to be near Brandon without feeling she was caving? She couldn't honestly answer the thought. The fact that she couldn't frustrated her.

She finally rose from her position and walked the short distance to town to her favorite coffee shop. Since it was the middle of the day, she decided to grab a treat and sit in the park. She wasn't in the mood to visit anybody. She wasn't sure she could fake a smile at the moment.

As a business owner in a small town, she couldn't allow herself to be less than perfect when she was out and about. If she scared off her customers, her place of business would go down in flames. That would end all of her dreams.

Beyond that, her parents had so instilled perfection in her it was the only way she knew. She'd be more mortified to run into her parents looking like a mess than any of her customers. She might put a lot of it on herself, but it was hard to change your ways after so many years. She wasn't sure she liked being this way. It made life so much more complicated. She would love to be easygoing like so many others she knew.

She sat on a bench and sighed with pleasure as she sipped on her peppermint tea. One great thing about the holidays was the yummy drinks that came with it. She might not like them as much if she could get them year round. The calories she consumed during the holidays certainly wouldn't like her over time. She absolutely hated working out, so she had to be a bit careful in her eating. She might have a great metabolism now, but studies she'd read proved that the older a person got, the more the body broke down. Someday her love of food was going to catch up to her in a less-than-positive way.

"What are you doing out here all alone?"

The booming voice that could only belong to one man about made her lose her cup. She jumped in her seat and was grateful when only a small amount splashed from the lid.

Turning, she found Joseph Anderson, along with Lucian Forbes.

Lucian Forbes was one of Joseph's oldest friends, and if the rumors were true, the two of them had been up to no good not that long ago, and suddenly all of Lucian's children were happily married. The rumors of Joseph's matchmaking were unconfirmed, as he'd never admitted what he was doing, but it seemed all of his friends with unruly children suddenly had exactly what they'd wanted—a lot of grandkids running around and in-laws they were proud to call family.

She should run—fast.

She was also completely tongue tied for a moment. Joseph and Lucian had that effect on people. Except she didn't usually allow the men to daunt her. That wasn't what they were currently trying to do, but their mere presence made the average person intimidated.

"Hi, Mr. Forbes, Mr. Anderson," she said after too long a pause. "I'm just enjoying some sunshine," she said as the sun was swept behind the looming gray clouds overhead.

"Now, Chloe, we've told you formalities are for the boardroom many times before," Lucian said with a smile.

"It's very difficult for me to address business tycoons by their first name," Chloe said with a smile.

Joseph scoffed. "You know how to stroke an old man's ego since you're a business magnate yourself," he told her.

She laughed, the sound real, and she suddenly felt wonderful. "For you to even sort of compare my small restaurant with your empire is downright funny," she said in between giggles. "But I'll take it, anyway. It's not every day a girl gets such a compliment."

"Well, we're hungry," Joseph said. "Come and join us."

He said it politely, as if it was nothing more than a friendly invitation, but Chloe wasn't fooled at all. Joseph had an agenda. There was a part of her that wanted to insert her independence and tell him she was busy, but she was very aware that not too many people turned Joseph down. She wasn't going to, either—not on something simple like a lunch invitation.

"I could grab a bite," she said as she stood. Her blueberry scone had done nothing more than whet her appetite.

"It appears they let anyone wander these streets nowadays."

Chloe froze as a new voice entered their conversation. She didn't have to look to see who it was, but she looked, anyway. Didn't the man ever work? It was almost noon on a Tuesday. She'd think he'd be knee deep in wires right about now.

"Brandon, it's good to see you, boy," Joseph said as Brandon approached.

"Hello, Joseph," Brandon said. "It's great to see you again, Lucian," he added as he shook both men's hands.

"You're just in time to join us for lunch," Lucian said. "I want to hear everything that's been happening with the veterans facility, and Joseph's planning on filling me in. I'd like to hear what the next steps are and what you've gotten done."

"I'd love to join," Brandon said with a smile that sent tingles traveling down Chloe's tummy and straight to her core.

"Do you ever work?" Chloe asked, instantly realizing how rude her words would sound to Brandon's uncle. But it was too late to take them back now.

Brandon didn't look offended in the least. He laughed as he winked at her.

"I've learned that it's all about working smarter, not harder. I have a successful business with men and women I trust to do their jobs, which gives me the time to meet and greet with people to bring in more business." Then he leaned over, as if he was telling a secret to only her, but his loud whisper could be heard across the entire park, and he knew it.

"Besides, do you realize the amount of money Joseph and Lucian have at their disposal? I could work for only the two of them till the day I die and still not finish all their projects."

Chloe would've totally thought he was speaking the truth in those words even a few days earlier. But he'd opened up to her recently, and she now knew he had as strong a work ethic as she did. But she knew he was so used to cracking that type of joke he might not even realize he was saying it until it was out of his mouth.

It was interesting. Very interesting. She wanted to delve in and learn more. She might've done just that if they didn't have an audience. But the sound of Joseph and Lucian both laughing at Brandon's words brought her back to reality.

"Very tactful, son," Joseph said.

"I like this one," Lucian added as he patted Brandon on the back. "And there is always work for those who earn it."

"I *am* the most charming out of my brothers," he assured them. "And you've seen my work. I'm the best."

"Apparently the most humble, too," Chloe said with a smirk.

"Humility is a virtue," Brandon told her.

"Let's walk," Joseph said as he led the group away from the park. Brandon stayed by her side, their arms nearly brushing. She wasn't sure if he was doing it to make her uncomfortable or if it was just that the man didn't know the first thing about a personal bubble. She'd guess it was a little bit of both.

"We'd go to your place, Chloe, but then you might try to run off and work instead of having a nice relaxing meal. I'm in the mood for street tacos, anyway."

"That sounds great," she said. "I could go for a bowl of guacamole, extra spicy. It's my favorite, and no matter how much I try, I can't make it as good as Maria."

The town was small, and it didn't take them long to reach the small Mexican cantina. It only held ten tables, but it was quaint, the staff was friendly, and the service was fast. Chloe ate there at least once a week. When a person was a chef, they tended to not want to prepare their own meals, and she couldn't beat Maria's tacos, not on her best day.

"Chloe, you've brought guests," Maria said with a smile as they walked in the door.

"Of course I did. You make the best food in town," Chloe said as she hugged the woman.

Maria laughed. "Let's say it's a tie for the best food in town," Maria said as she handed them each a one-page menu and led them to a corner table. Of course, Chloe knew the secret menu items as well as what was listed on the one Maria had handed over.

Maria took their drink order, and Chloe put in for appetizers right away. The smells coming out of the kitchen were making her stomach growl. "We want nachos with a double serving of your famous guac and an order of poppers," she said.

"Extra spice?" Maria asked.

"Of course," Chloe said.

The three men said that sounded good. She was so used to placing orders there she hadn't even thought of asking Joseph or Lucian if everything was fine. She squirmed a bit in her seat. It wasn't often that one forgot they were hanging out with billionaires and simply took over.

"I think I could eat an entire cow right now. I didn't realize I was so hungry until we walked in here," Chloe said with a laugh, feeling slightly uncomfortable at realizing what she'd done.

"I haven't been here for a few weeks. What a fool I've been," Brandon said. "And you ordered my favorite appetizers."

"At least you have good taste in food," Chloe said, letting her ordering dilemma go while also letting down her guard as she smiled. He beamed at her, taking her breath away. She was happy when Maria came back, setting down their drinks and a large container of chips and salsa.

"What thoughts have you put into the veterans project?" Joseph asked bluntly. It wasn't as if she hadn't been prepared for the interrogation, but instead of it irritating her as she'd thought it would, it made her smile.

"I've been thinking on it," Chloe admitted.

That earned her a huge smile from both Joseph and Brandon. She shouldn't give either man the victory, but the words were out.

"That's what I love to hear," Joseph told her. "We're behind schedule now, and I don't like making good men and women wait on us."

"Nothing like a little shaming to get what you want, huh?" she asked as she gazed into Joseph's steely-blue gaze. Maybe it was just these two billionaires who didn't intimidate her. Then again, maybe it was the way she'd been raised. Her mother and father had been the most intimidating people she'd ever known, and she'd survived growing up with them.

"I don't mind using different methods to get exactly what I want," Joseph said unapologetically. "It's how I've done so well in the business world. Just because I'm officially retired doesn't mean I'm going to stop now."

"Isn't that exactly what retirement means?" she asked.

Joseph laughed. "Maybe to the weak. But I'm not the type of man who is going to sit around and wait to die. Did you realize that most successful people who retire don't live long when they do nothing after? They need to be stimulated. I might've turned over the reins of the Anderson empire to my son Lucas, but that just frees up my time to work on other projects that have been on hold for too long."

Chloe had a feeling that would be her later in life. She didn't think there'd ever come a day when she'd be ready to hang up her apron. Maybe she wouldn't always run a restaurant, but she was sure she'd always be doing one project or another.

She sighed while pulling pieces of paper from her purse and setting them on the table as their waitress dropped off nachos and poppers. Everyone glanced at the papers as they grabbed food.

"This is a plan I sketched. I haven't been in the building in a long time, so it's very basic, but you'll have to assume the facility is going to be full more often than not, so you need a lot of counter and cupboard space. There's nothing I like less than a small kitchen," she said.

"That's why I wanted you for the job. My nephew gave us a great area to begin with, but we need a true chef to lay it all out," Joseph said.

"Okay, Joseph, you've effectively broken me down. I'll do this job on one condition, and *one* condition only," she said, her shoulders back, her expression firm.

He smiled at her, as if he loved nothing more than a good challenge. She waited for him to say anything that would tell her he was truly listening to her. It could've been a minute or an hour that the two of them sat there in a standoff. Neither Brandon nor Lucian interrupted the face-off. Finally, Joseph smiled.

"What is your condition?" he asked.

She felt victorious she hadn't squirmed beneath his stare. Brandon and Lucian remained suspiciously quiet, as if they were at a show, wondering if this was the plot twist they'd all been waiting for. Maybe they were enjoying this power match. It wasn't often a person had one with Joseph and came out the victor.

She took a sip of her iced tea and leaned back. "The matchmaking stops. I'll do this project and do it better than anyone else could even think of doing it, but I'm not interested in a relationship . . . with anyone." Her gaze briefly darted toward Brandon, who didn't appear offended. He seemed more curious than anything else.

Joseph's grin grew. "I never said anything about matchmaking. I simply have a job I need completed," he told her, looking far too innocent. She wondered how long it had taken him to perfect that look.

"Good. Then we're on the same page. Shall we shake on it?"

Joseph looked as if he wanted to say something more, but instead he picked up his bottle of beer and took a sip and eyed her, as if he was just now realizing he'd underestimated her. She felt pretty dang proud of that fact. A lot of people had underestimated her, and it hadn't gone well for them.

She held out her palm and shook the man's hand. That was as good as a contract in Joseph's opinion, and she was very well aware of that. She had no doubt the actual contract would make it to her restaurant within an hour of her returning, though. He liked to have no loose ends.

"What comes next?" Joseph asked.

She got a slightly evil glint in her eyes as she turned toward Brandon, who didn't look quite so easy, as he could clearly see something brewing in her eyes.

"Brandon and I are going on a field trip. To make sure we have the best facility, we need to see what's wrong at other places. We're heading into the city tonight."

She had a challenge in her eyes, daring him to refuse her. He looked as if he wanted to for a few moments before squaring up his own shoulders and nodding.

"Sounds good to me," he said. "I love field trips."

"Great. I can't wait to hear all about it," Joseph said. "Now, let's stop talking business and enjoy this delicious lunch."

And that was exactly what they did. Chloe actually found herself chuckling a few times. Joseph and Lucian were a riot to be with when their attention wasn't focused on bringing a person down. She did notice that Brandon was oddly quiet, which was very different from his usual personality.

They parted ways after lunch, with the understanding that Brandon would come to her place at five o'clock. She'd see if he was still just as eager to work with her after all was said and done. She didn't plan on making this easy for him. If she was hired to do a job, then only the best would do.

CHAPTER TEN

Chloe was running late . . . really late.

She hurried down her walkway, looking through her purse to make sure she hadn't forgotten anything. That meant she wasn't paying the least attention to where she was going.

She nearly got thrown to the ground when she walked straight into a solid wall . . . of muscle. Brandon's arms snaked around her before she could bounce backward and ungracefully land on her behind. She wasn't sure if she was grateful or not at the feel of his arms around her suddenly needy body.

"I'm sorry," she said, her breath knocked out of her. She'd tried to block out the fact that the man was nothing but solid muscle in all the best places. Pressing against him in a bed was pure heaven, but running into him while walking too fast felt like hitting a brick wall.

"You can press against me anytime you want," he said, his smile taking the rest of her breath away. Chloe ignored the extra thump of her heart. This project was only just beginning, and if she wasn't careful, she'd never make it to the end.

"I'm running late. Sorry for making you wait, but it seems these days I can't make it anywhere on time," she told him, breaking the connection of their eyes as she looked down. "And I absolutely hate that. I'm a punctual person. I think it shows a complete lack of respect to be late. But I have piled too much on my plate right now, and I can't seem to make enough time for it."

She was rambling on, and she knew it, but she could barely force herself to stop. She was incredibly flustered at the moment, and being in Brandon's presence wasn't helping at all.

"I just got here, so we aren't late at all. Take a breath, and we'll be on our way." She wanted to snap at him for no reason. Maybe it was just because she hated that she felt like a breathless teenager instead of a responsible adult when in his presence.

"Anything less than fifteen minutes early is late in my book. You can never predict traffic or unexpected delays," she said as she kept digging in her purse, her fingers finally landing on what she'd been searching for.

"Found my lipstick," she said with triumph. She was already getting in a better mood. She didn't think he was going to enjoy his evening at all, not with how spoiled he was. She definitely had an evil streak to her.

"Are you going to tell me where we're going?" His smile had faded, and he was gazing at her suspiciously. She might have gotten a bit too perky all of a sudden.

"It's an adventure," she said, feeling smug.

"We'll do your project, then have dinner and put our heads together," he told her. There was just the smallest amount of something in his eyes that made her think he was almost . . . vulnerable. It was something she couldn't remember seeing before. It made her pause. If he was cocky and overbearing, she could easily keep her armor in place. If he was vulnerable, it would make her want to protect him. That was the last thing she needed.

"We aren't going to be having dinners together. We're working on a project. That's it," she reminded him.

He shrugged. "I like to eat while I work. That way I'm not wasting time. It's killing two birds with one stone. I'm sure you do it all the time. Besides, we're friends, aren't we?"

She paused as she considered his words. "We aren't *exactly* friends." She wasn't trying to be rude, but she counted very few people as her actual friends. A former one-night stand definitely didn't fit into that category.

"I care about you, so that makes you a friend. Maybe it could be more," he said, as if it didn't matter to him one way or the other. He was playing this in an entirely new way that was throwing her off. She wasn't sure what he was doing now. She didn't like for him to be unpredictable.

"There's no chance of it being more, but maybe we can have a sort of relationship," she finally said. But they'd been standing there too long, making them run late. "We seriously have to go, though, so we're going to have to table this conversation."

"After you," he said as he moved toward his car. She decided to be a bit more difficult as she looked at the nice vehicle.

"I think I'll drive," she said. "You don't know where we're going, and I'm terrible at giving directions." She walked away from him and moved toward her small car. She stopped and gazed at him as he slowly approached.

He looked at the small car and gave her a fearful glance. "I *really* think I should just drive," he said. "I'm parked on the curb, making it a quick exit."

"Nope. My plans tonight, my car," she said. She pulled open the driver's side door and slipped inside, feeling immense satisfaction when he crammed himself into the passenger seat. That was, until his body was pressed up against hers in the tiny car. Maybe this hadn't been such a great idea after all. She hated how stubborn she could be sometimes. It got her into situations like the one she was currently in. Maybe she could change his mind about coming along with her before they pulled out of the driveway.

"Having regrets?" she asked. "You can change your mind if you want, and I won't think any less of you." That was a lie. She'd think a lot less of him, but if it would get him out of her car, she'd be more than happy with his decision.

"Not at all," he said, leaning just a bit closer to her and making her clench her teeth.

"Is this a game to you, Brandon?" she finally got the courage to ask. He looked at her, and she allowed the connection for a few moments before turning away.

"Why do you say that?" he asked.

"Because you touch me and make all these innuendos even when I tell you to stop. I don't know if you're so interested because I'm hard to get or what it is, but not knowing drives me slightly crazy."

"I haven't stopped thinking about you since the moment we met," he told her, sounding as if he was speaking the truth. "I've wanted to forget you and the power you have over me, but I've never been able to. So I keep on coming back for more. It's that simple. It's not a game at all. If I truly felt you didn't feel it, too, then I'd back the heck off, and this project would be so much easier for both of us. But as it is, we have to deal with it, and there's zero chance I'll stop flirting with you. Either deal with it or pull out of the project."

That was blunt. And she found herself respecting him for it. She could handle a man who said what he felt. It was a lot better than hiding behind innuendos and lies. She finally sighed. She'd been hard on him from the very beginning, and she didn't like being that person.

"We had our night. It was amazing and satisfactory. But it ended, and that's just how it goes sometimes. Now we live next to each other, but that doesn't mean it has to be awkward," she insisted. "I understand you flirt. It comes naturally, and I'm not going to lie and say there's zero attraction, but that doesn't mean we do something about it. It's not that simple."

"Don't you get tired of being alone? I know I do sometimes," he said. "Wouldn't you like to have someone by your side who understands who you really are and who'll keep you warm at night?"

Chloe felt tears in her eyes, and there was no way she was going to let them fall. Allowing him to come with her hadn't been the smartest idea she'd ever had. He simply affected her too much. She could only take him in small doses.

"I'd rather be alone than in a relationship where I feel lonely," she told him honestly.

"Have I ever ignored you when we're together?" he asked.

She paused. She couldn't lie. "No," she answered with truth. "But that's because we've never been in a relationship. You aren't the settling-down kind of man, and I'm too busy to give proper attention to a relationship."

"I don't know what I want this to be in the end. I just know I want something from you, and you won't give me a chance to find out what that is." She was thinking this was probably the most honest this man had ever been with any female in his life. She wasn't sure how she felt about that.

Those tears she was fighting were coming closer and closer to the surface, and she couldn't let them fall. If she gave into the weakness she was feeling, she was afraid the door would open, and he'd step through. If he did that, she might never have the strength to push him back out the door again.

"I've done the relationship thing, and it never works. I think being alone is worth exploring, worth taking a chance on," she said.

Chloe's heart was pounding as they pulled up to an operating veterans center in the city, where a dinner was taking place. She wanted to see how the facility was being run, so she'd volunteered to help. They had no idea she was working on the current project in Cranston. It helped that she'd volunteered before. Not as much as she'd like to, but enough that they always let her into the different community centers when she called and said she was free. She needed to run inside before she gave in to Brandon and what he was asking of her.

"We're here," she said in a tight voice.

"We need to finish this discussion," he insisted as he reached out and stopped her from opening the door.

"Please, Brandon. We need to get through this meal," she said. "If any of what you are saying is true, then you'll let go of me so I can do it with a clear head."

She was almost shocked when he instantly released her. She was afraid to even look at him as she opened her car door and stepped out. He walked around and stood by her side, this time without touching her, which she was grateful for.

"Let's go do some good while we find out the bad," he told her. "We have plenty of time to finish the discussion later."

Those words were like an omen, and she didn't bother replying as she made the walk around to the back of the center to enter through the kitchen.

The pastor from the church down the hill was there with a smile on his face as they entered.

"You made it, Chloe," he said before holding out his hand to Brandon. "And you've brought a friend. That's wonderful."

"I'm sorry I'm late, Pastor Bart. I got held up," she said.

"That's understandable," he replied graciously. "We're always glad to have you, as we know how busy you are."

"Brandon Anderson," Brandon said as he shook the pastor's hand.

"It's a pleasure to meet you, son," Pastor Bart said.

"You as well, sir," Brandon replied.

"Shawn will show you around so you can get started right away," Pastor Bart replied.

Chloe looked around the small facility with a bit of a broken heart. She was on a research mission, but she had wanted to find more good than she was finding. Maybe if they did this veterans project right in Cranston, other centers would follow suit and give more priority to all veterans. They certainly deserved it.

One good thing about their arrival was the fact that as soon as they'd walked in, the chatting had stopped since she and Brandon had gotten separated. He was put on serving duty, and she volunteered at the washing station. Because of the holidays, the church had come in and was giving out gifts to children of the veterans, and Chloe loved being there to watch the happiness on their faces. This was what the holidays were all about. She wasn't sure what Brandon would think of it all.

But as the night passed them by, she noticed how he went from looking uncomfortable to seeming almost awed by it all. After the meal had been served, he helped pass out gifts, spoke to the veterans, and smiled at their young kids.

By the time they were finished, Chloe wasn't sure what she was feeling, but the distance she was trying to keep between them was dissipating by the second. It was hard to stay away from him when she saw what a good man he was.

Even though the facilities needed to offer so much more, the men and women inside were grateful for anything they were given. Some of them were disabled, some suffering from horrific PTSD, and some were just there to be with other people who understood what they'd gone through. They all had stories to tell, and Brandon was more than willing to listen.

Beyond being willing, he appeared to truly enjoy talking to the men and women who'd served. He seemed to have a deep respect for what they'd done for their country. How could she keep distance from a man like that? She wasn't sure she could. Her fear had always been that the more you found out about a person, the more flaws you saw. She hadn't found flaws in him yet. What did that mean for everything she'd always believed?

When their night ended, he approached her, looking a bit sad, just as she felt, but also seeming more determined than ever to make things better for these people. He smiled down at her before they said goodbye to a few more people, then stepped outside the center. She was utterly exhausted. And Brandon hadn't acted as she'd expected him to.

"Let's have dinner," he said as they approached her car. Chloe knew she should say no, but she couldn't seem to voice the word.

Instead, she found herself nodding. Her heart nearly burst when Brandon looked as if he'd just won the lottery. She wasn't as strong as she'd thought she was. Maybe she was beginning to want to please this man. Maybe she was starting to want to put that light of happiness in his eyes. Maybe it was time to quit fighting what she'd wanted since the moment she'd met him.

She wasn't sure what it was, but she handed her keys to him to let him drive them back, and she climbed in the car, too tired and emotionally drained to do anything other than sit there and try to collect herself.

She was in a losing battle, and she normally didn't allow herself to get into this sort of situation. Any game she played with Brandon would end with her losing. But if they both got what they ultimately wanted, wouldn't that actually make them both victors?

It was too confusing to even try to comprehend. Instead, she leaned into her seat and closed her eyes. She was on a journey with Brandon whether she wanted to be there or not. She'd soon find out where they ended up.

Chapter Eleven

Chloe sat in Brandon's large kitchen, wondering how she'd gotten there and what she planned on doing about it. He was grabbing a dish from the refrigerator, and it made her smile to see him throw it in the microwave. He certainly wasn't trying to impress her with his culinary expertise. That would be difficult to do since she was quite the picky chef.

It was odd for her how comfortable she was in his house. It shouldn't be that easy. She should've put up more of a fight, but she didn't have the will for it. He'd been saying things to her no man had ever said before. She had a lot to fear, because she was falling for him. No matter how many ways and how many times she told herself she wasn't the type of woman to fall for a man, it was happening.

Maybe it was his sheer focus, his utter pursuit of her that was breaking her down. Whatever it was, she knew the chances of them not sleeping together again were slowing diminishing.

This was a no-win situation. And she was starting to not care.

"I see you haven't mastered the art of cooking now that you're a homeowner," she told him as he pulled out a bottle of wine and took the cork out before pouring her a generous glass. She sipped on it gratefully.

"You don't know that," he said with a wink. "I might just be trying to get the meal over with so we can settle down in the den, where it isn't quite so . . . bright."

"You're awfully confident in yourself," she pointed out.

"I want you to get to know the real me. I think there's a lot to like," he assured her. "And I can see you aren't trying so hard to fight it. I think it's because I'm so damn charming."

"Why don't you just feed me the meal you promised, and we won't worry about anything else?" she suggested.

"I can think of many activities that are a lot more satisfying than eating," he quickly replied.

Chloe's stomach twisted in a way that had nothing to do with food. Maybe it was true what people said—that there were soul mates. Many settled with an acceptable relationship and even found companionship in it, but maybe there was only one person who could ignite the spark inside your soul and make you shine and burn and feel like you were on top of the world.

Chloe was terrified to think that could be true. Because if it was, she had no doubt her person might just be Brandon Anderson. A shudder racked through her at the thought. This didn't fit into her plans—not one little bit.

Still, she was shocked by how tempted she was. She *needed* this man. Maybe it was because she could see how much he wanted her. Maybe it was because she could clearly remember their night together and how amazing it had been. After shaking her head, she took another sip of wine and tried to stay focused on their conversation.

"How long will you be satisfied living in this small town, Brandon?" she asked, taking the dish of pasta he'd placed in front of her.

She was surprised by how good the impromptu meal was. She had a sneaking suspicion he'd picked it up from the Italian place down the road and slipped it in his own dish, but she didn't need to call him out on it.

"I'm quite happy here," he said. He seemed relaxed as he ate and sipped his own glass of wine before refilling both their glasses. "My family is here, and I don't see myself going anywhere unless it's for a vacation."

"If we fell into some sort of relationship," she said with a pause, despising that word. He smiled as he waited for her to go on. "I mean, if we were to be together, and it didn't work out, it would just be awkward for us and everyone around us. There's no way to avoid each other in this town. It's one of the main reasons I don't do relationships."

Brandon seemed to think about her words as he looked at her, and Chloe was finding it difficult to eat her delicious meal with his gaze fully focused on her. But she also wanted to be as casual as him—as strong. It was easier said than done.

"I've spent a lot of years not caring about anyone other than me and maybe my family," he said, surprising her. "I don't want to shame them." She'd never dreamed she'd hear him say something like that. He didn't go on, and she pushed her plate aside, too confused to pretend she still had an appetite.

Him not wanting to shame his family was too close to home for her. She'd felt that same way her entire life. Her parents expected so much out of her that the smallest mistake made her feel as if she was a total failure. There was no way they could also have that in common.

"Explain," she finally told him as she picked up her glass and took another sip.

"You know my mom died, and I barely made it through it, but then I met this family I didn't know I had, and for a long time I told myself I was lied to and unappreciated. I thought even the heavens had it out for me. I loved and still love my brothers, but for a while I even pulled away from them, thinking my whole life had been a lie. Making this long story short, I played the victim. I think I woke up a couple of years ago, realizing that an attitude like that absolutely disgusted me. I was done feeling sorry for myself. It was time for me to start appreciating the good in my life and being thankful for all I have."

"You have a wonderful family," Chloe said quietly. She really wanted to reach for him, but she held herself back. "That's something to truly appreciate. They are so supportive and kind. Why would you think you'd disappoint them?" She couldn't imagine Joseph looking at any of his relatives with anything other than love.

As much as she loved her own parents, the worst pain they'd inflicted on her was by those disapproving glances they'd sent her way. She wanted them to be proud of her, and it cut her to the core when they weren't.

"I agree. They are always supportive. I think I was just angry at the world, so I pushed anyone who loved me away. My counselor told me it was because I thought if I let someone else into my heart like I did with my mother, then I risked them dying on me," he said with a frown before he forced a smile. "I think that's a load of crap, but I can see where he might have had a small point."

Chloe couldn't help but smile. "I can't believe you'd ever go see a therapist," she said.

"It was . . . um . . . sort of mandatory," he said as he shifted in his chair.

Now Chloe was truly fascinated. "I *really* want to know that story," she insisted.

He let out a small chuckle as he refilled their glasses again, emptying the bottle. He got up and opened another. She should tell him she'd had enough, but the story had just gotten good, and if she broke the mood, he might stop. She'd just have to try to sip her glass a little less often.

"Fine, I'll tell you the story, but we have to move to the den, where we can be a little more comfortable," he offered.

Chloe knew it wasn't the brightest idea to move to the den—most likely the den of iniquity. But she really did want to hear what he had to say, so she didn't argue when he grabbed the bottle and his glass and began moving through the house. She scooped up her own glass and followed.

The den was dimly lit, just as he'd wanted, a gas fireplace on high in the center of the back wall, a couch set up the perfect distance away.

He moved to it and set the bottle down, then beckoned her. She slowly walked over to him, moving to one end of the couch and hoping he'd stay on the other.

"I was in a pretty bad mood for a . . . let's just say an extended period of time," he said after a pause. She wondered what his idea of an extended period was. But she was silent. "A few complaints came in from my employees, and my lawyers told me if I didn't seek counseling, I was going to get my ass sued off of me. I told them to go to hell, proving their point, and then I reluctantly went. It wasn't too bad," he told her with a shrug.

"Did you get sued?" she asked. Her wine was depleting quickly, and she decided it would be safer if she set it on the coffee table, away from her fingers and lips.

Brandon smiled as he slipped across the couch, his leg brushing against hers, taking her breath away. This would be a good time to run and hide, but she was frozen to the spot.

"Nope. My attitude got better, and my office became more pleasant. Don't get me wrong—they still love when I'm away, but I've learned not to take bad moods out on everyone around me," he told her.

"That's progress," she said as she tried pulling away from him. There was nowhere for her to go. Chloe was trapped, and she wasn't sure if she minded.

By degrees, Brandon's expression altered. He set aside his wineglass and then reached up, his fingers slowly grazing her cheek and jaw. The heat trail he left behind had her forgetting to breathe.

"I've never felt about a person the way I feel about you," he said in a husky whisper.

Chloe didn't know what to say. He leaned closer, and she felt his lips brush against hers in tiny kisses. He didn't try to deepen the caress. It was more of a whispering of their lips, his hot breath brushing over her skin. She felt it all the way to her toes, and her core was heating to unbearable levels.

Her ability to think became dimmer by the second as his lips stroked hers, his tongue tracing her bottom lip, begging for entrance. One hand rested on her thigh, his thumb making beautifully enticing circles that were driving her a bit mad. The other hand was wound into her hair to hold her head in place.

But he didn't need to hold her there, because as she got lost in his embrace, she was taken back to the night of the wedding, and she just wanted one more taste of him, one more flutter in the pit of her stomach, one more flame of heat in her core. *Just one more,* she assured herself.

He kissed her jaw as he pulled her up to straddle his lap. She was putty in his hands as he moved his lips down her neck. She sighed, wondering if and when she'd be able to stop this from happening.

Maybe she'd known from the moment she'd accepted his invitation to come home with him that this would happen. Maybe she'd been in denial from the moment he'd shown up at her restaurant. But the more he kissed her neck, the more she wanted to stay the night.

"I can't seem to stop myself from wanting you," she admitted as a low moan escaped her tight throat.

He continued kissing her. "I want you, Chloe. I always want you," he said before sucking on her tender skin. Then he kissed his way up her jaw and finally kissed her the way she truly wanted: with heat and passion and a blinding loss of control.

His hands slipped easily beneath the back of her shirt and scorched their way up her back, making her arch against him, her breasts aching as she pushed into him. His kiss deepened even more, and together their moans filled the air around them.

It had been so long since she'd been with a man, and now that Brandon had lit the flame of her desire, she didn't see it going out again until she allowed him to quell the heat.

His hands circled around to her front, and soon he was cupping her aching breasts, making her cry out into his mouth as he pinched her nipples through her lacy bra.

He wrenched his lips away from her mouth. "I need to be inside you," he said, the words a mixture of a plea and a command.

She could walk away right now, and she had no doubt he'd let her go. Brandon wouldn't force himself on her. But she knew if she did just that, she'd ache all night and probably forever. Maybe this was what she needed to let him go.

"Then take me," she told him.

Brandon's eyes widened in delight, but only for a second before he spun the two of them around, laying her on the couch and covering her body with his. Just that quickly, his lips were back on hers, and she was wiggling beneath him in an ecstatic array of so much pleasure she wondered if she was going to combust. She wouldn't even care.

Somehow, with as little time as possible between kisses, Brandon managed to rip their clothes from their bodies, and then he was finally laid out above her, naked, hot, and hungry. She didn't want any more foreplay. She just wanted him inside her.

He must've had a condom in his pants, because she heard that unmistakable sound of foil ripping before he reached between their bodies and slipped it on. She was glad he'd thought of it, because she was delirious in her need for them to come together.

And then she couldn't think anymore. He surged forward, pushing deep inside her, and Chloe nearly lost consciousness at the pleasure of them being connected again.

"I need you so bad, baby. I'll take my time on the second round," he promised before his head descended again, and he mimicked the movements of his lower body with his tongue diving in and out of her mouth.

She felt the buildup of pleasure as he surged within her before pulling all the way out and pumping back inside over and over again. She lost all meaning of time as they connected, and she was lost in the only man she'd ever truly desired.

Her pleasure exploded through her as she threw back her head and cried out, the orgasm ripping through her, the gratification too intense for her to handle. Somewhere in the fog of her mind, she felt him surge deeper and faster inside her before he tensed, and she felt him pumping his own release.

Brandon collapsed on top of her, and Chloe raked her fingers up and down his slick back as she relished the weight of him. This was her favorite moment of sex, this moment when they were still one, basking in the pleasure of being together, fully sated. She wished she could hold on to it forever.

"That was amazing," he told her with a satisfied sigh.

"Ditto," she replied.

Several quiet moments passed before he shifted, then stood to dispose of the condom. At the loss of Brandon touching her, Chloe wondered if regret would set in. It didn't.

She knew beyond a doubt that this night would forever sit with her, and she knew that she was falling in love with the man. But she also knew she had to leave. There was no way for the two of them to simply slip into this role of boyfriend and girlfriend. It was far too complicated.

Chloe sat up and reached for her clothes. She had her bra and shirt on when he returned to the room, his eyes instantly narrowing.

"What are you doing?" he asked as he stalked toward her with purpose.

"I'm going home," she told him, making sure to keep emotion from her tone.

He dropped down to his knees, his arms caging her in against the couch. His eyes searched hers. She wasn't sure what he was trying to see, but she was still feeling satisfied. There wasn't sadness or panic—at least not yet. She wasn't sure if that would come later or not.

"We aren't finished," he told her. He leaned down and kissed her still-naked thighs, and unbelievably, Chloe felt heat spark again in her core. She pushed against his shoulder.

"I'm going home, Brandon. That was wonderful, and I can honestly say I haven't felt anything like it since . . . well, since the last time we made love. But I'm going home now," she finished strongly and then was relieved when he backed away.

He was stunning as he kneeled before her, completely comfortable in his nakedness. The man was gorgeous. Of course he was comfortable in nothing but his birthday suit.

"I don't want you to go," he told her, his lips set in a firm line.

"That's not your choice to make," she replied.

She stood and slipped on her panties and slacks, almost enjoying the heat in his eyes as he gazed up at her. Seeing him in front of her on his knees, his body hard and glistening, was almost enough to make her change her mind. That told her more than anything else that she needed to get the heck out of there.

"Why don't I come home with you, then?" he suggested as he stood and reached for his pants, sliding them on without bothering with underwear. Her knowing there was barely anything covering that most beautiful part of him made her core grow even more hot and wet. She shook her head.

"Nope. I'm leaving now," she said. Her clothes were in place, and she began the fairly long walk back to the kitchen, where she'd left her purse and keys.

Brandon didn't say anything else as he followed her, but she could feel his hot breath on the back of her neck. Her body had been reawakened, and even his breath was sending tingles all the way through her.

She grabbed her keys, and he stopped her from taking another step with nothing more than his hand on her arm. She schooled her expression before meeting his gaze.

"You've had a lot of wine," he pointed out.

"My last drink was well over an hour ago, and I feel fine. I'd never drive drunk," she said indignantly.

He assessed her, and then his shoulders drooped as he seemed to agree that she was perfectly capable of driving. If she'd had any more wine, she might not have wanted to leave.

Brandon walked her all the way outside, and even though it couldn't have been more than thirty degrees out, he moved onto his front porch, not even shaking as he stood there.

"Thanks for coming with me tonight," she said after stepping farther away from him.

"I was going to say that," he told her with a wicked gleam in his eyes.

That one little glance had her squirming on her feet. If she didn't want to end up in the man's bed or couch again, she knew beyond a doubt that she couldn't be alone with him. He was just too damn powerful for her to resist.

"This was great, Brandon," she said before firming her shoulders. "It was a great goodbye."

She turned to go again, and he called out her name. There was something so sexy and commanding in the one word that she couldn't help but turn back around and look at him.

"This isn't even close to finished," he told her with a smile she felt in all the wrong places.

Chloe knew she didn't have the strength or will to fight him any longer. She just turned on her heels and moved quickly to her car, feeling his eyes on her the entire way. She had no doubt that what he said might as well have been a prophecy. If Brandon wasn't finished with her yet, there was no way she wasn't going to get scorched some more.

Chloe should have felt a heck of a lot more upset by that fact than she did.

CHAPTER TWELVE

It was a week before Christmas, and the restaurant was filled to capacity with those picking up their bakery orders and others wanting a quick lunch while out doing last-minute shopping. The coffee machine had been running nonstop, and Chloe's feet felt as if they were about to fall off.

It was a normal holiday week for her at the restaurant, and she was grateful for the business, but that didn't mean she wasn't going to fully enjoy the annual spa day she and her friends took on December 27 to repair the damage to her body from a full week of nonstop work.

Brooke had come in to visit with her, and her friend could barely keep up as she trailed Chloe around the busy kitchen and dining room.

"You've been somewhat off since the second I stepped in here. I demand you tell me what's going on," Brooke said as she passed Chloe in the kitchen.

"I wanted to tell you everything, but we haven't had a single second of time," Chloe said, her order already up.

"You really need to hire more holiday help," Brooke told her.

"I know, but this is what pays for my expensive spa trip each year," Chloe reminded her friend.

"We wouldn't need to go for so long if you weren't torturing yourself," Brooke pointed out.

"That's pretty . . . um . . . logical," Chloe said with a laugh.

One of the bartenders called out Chloe's name, and she sighed with displeasure. Brooke glared at her.

"We're taking a smoke break in five minutes," Brooke said as she watched Chloe walk away.

"We don't smoke," Chloe pointed out.

Brooke rolled her eyes. "Exactly! We should be rewarded with a smoke break like the rest of them because we're healthier," she said before Chloe disappeared.

Chloe couldn't help but laugh, even though she hadn't felt like laughing much in the past twenty-four hours. She'd left Brandon's place the night before last, and she didn't regret doing it, but she'd opened a floodgate that was now coming in way too strongly for her to be able to close it again. Chloe was in trouble. Every time the bell on her door signaled a new arrival, she was looking up with bated breath, and today especially, that door was opening every minute or so.

Chloe was exhausted. She didn't even want to think about the disaster that was her restaurant. The floor was covered in crumbs, the walls most likely dotted with dirty fingerprints, and the tables were going to need a good scrubbing.

She'd hired a magician to wow the kids with Christmas magic, and the dang man had set off a confetti gun, making the children laugh and glittering her floor with an even bigger mess. She made a note to herself not to allow confetti guns ever again. Then she looked at the joy on the kids' faces, and she amended that. It'd be worth it if these memories stayed with them long into their lives.

The doorbell chimed again, and this time Chloe didn't look up, but she didn't need to. Brandon had walked in. She couldn't hear him, couldn't smell him, couldn't see him—she just *knew* without a doubt that he was there. And the joy that thought brought scared her to death.

Because she wanted to look so desperately, she purposely finished putting food on the Johnsons' table before wishing them a merry Christmas and then turning to make her way to the back of the place, where she could hide.

She didn't make it far.

"Impressive crowd," Brandon whispered in her ear, his breath making her already-overheated body go into the hot flash of a lifetime.

"It's like this every year. I'm going to be busy for hours," she told him. "If you're hungry, your best bet is to try to squeeze in at the front counter and hope to get someone's attention."

She said this all without turning. She was afraid the sight of him was going to be too much for her to take. Would she do something foolish like launch herself into his arms and kiss him right there in front of half the town?

"I bet you have a place in the back where it's a little more quiet, and I can get serviced properly," he told her in an erotic whisper that had her wanting to melt right there at his dang feet.

Chloe spun around to tell him he couldn't speak to her that way in her place of business, but her words were lost at the sight of him in a red sweater and tight jeans. The man was too good looking to be unleashed on the public like this.

Judging by the gleam in his eyes, she could tell he knew exactly what she was thinking, and she had the urge to kick him in one of his perfectly shaped shins just to show him he didn't affect her like he did. This tendency to want to resort to elementary school antics was enough to make her head spin even more.

"You're beautiful," he told her before bending down and lightly kissing her cheek.

Chloe couldn't be sure, but it seemed like there was a hush in the restaurant. She was too embarrassed to look up and find out if everyone's eyes were on her. Never before had a man kissed her there, and for Brandon to do so was an open invitation for the town to gossip.

"I guess our break's off the table," Brooke said as she gave Chloe a wink. "But that kiss just answered half the questions I had for you, anyway."

"Brooke," Brandon said before wrapping his arm around Chloe in a possessive hold she couldn't shake off.

"Brandon," her best friend said back. There was a suspicious light in Brooke's eyes, but Chloe was surprised to see respect there, too. Was Brooke turning to the dark side and accepting Brandon as hers? That wasn't good. Chloe needed Brooke to hate him so her friend could slap Chloe back into reality, even if he *was* Brooke's brother-in-law.

But before she could voice any of this, Brandon was pulling her away from the crowd, and Chloe found herself going through the back of the restaurant and straight into the small office she spent too much time in. The door was shut, and then she was alone with Brandon, something she'd promised herself the night before last she wouldn't do again.

"I need a real kiss," he told her.

He backed up to her desk and pulled her into his arms, not giving her any more warning than that before his head descended and he was kissing her breath *and* her senses away. It was several moments before he released her, and Chloe found her head spinning. She wanted to lean back into him so they could continue what he'd started.

"I've decided I can make you a very happy woman," he said as he sifted his fingers through her hair and smiled in a way that made her want to believe him.

"We can't do this, Brandon," she told him. But man did she really want to do just that. She wanted to fall into this make-believe world he was pulling her into, forget all about the reasons it was a bad idea, and just get lost in him over and over again.

"I think we can. I think you want to."

Chloe did want to. She wanted him. But this wasn't the time or the place for it.

There was a knock on the door, and Chloe let out a sigh of frustration and relief.

"This is one of our busiest weeks of the year for me. I can't hide out in here," she told him with reluctance.

"When do you get off?" he asked before leaning in and taking her bottom lip in his mouth, gently biting down, sending flames through her before releasing her mouth.

"I'm closing today at . . . uh . . . at two," she managed to stutter. "I have to change out the tables for a big party tomorrow. Someone rented the entire place."

"Good, I'll be back then to get some coffee and a pastry *and* to help you clean," he said.

Chloe was about to argue, but he didn't give her the chance. He kissed her hard one more time, and then he was opening the door, where two employees stood wide eyed as they gazed at the beast of a man.

Brandon wished them a merry Christmas, then slipped quietly away, and Chloe had no choice but to focus on her work. Even the look she received from Brooke as her best friend tapped her foot outside the door wasn't enough to shake her from her romance-induced semicoma.

Merry Christmas, she thought with a dreamy smile. She was in trouble . . . in big, big, *big* trouble.

CHAPTER THIRTEEN

Brandon was back at Chloe's restaurant at 1:40 p.m. He wasn't taking a chance of her closing earlier and slipping out the door. Never had he chased a woman like he'd been chasing Chloe, but right now he couldn't seem to stop himself.

Every moment he was with her, he just wanted more. Every minute he was without her, he was in a hurry to get back. They needed to work on their project together, but that was the last thing on his mind at the moment. For now, all he could think about was this woman and how much he wanted to be with her.

He slipped past the hostess with a wink, not unaware of the blush that brightened her cheeks. A woman's reaction to him had been something he'd never noticed before until it had been pointed out to him. He hadn't wanted to play with women; he'd just always enjoyed flirting. He'd loved multiple women, just hadn't wanted to be with one for any amount of time. Now, he was more cautious on how he spoke to them. They deserved his respect, as they weren't toys there for his amusement.

Also, the older he got, the more he realized time was a precious commodity. He didn't want to wake up one day and have regrets. He was beginning to think that meant he was going to want Chloe to be the last woman he was ever with.

When she slipped from the kitchen and found him sitting at the bar, he watched her face. She wasn't as good as she thought at hiding how she was feeling. A blush stole over her cheeks, brighter than that of the hostess, and a sweet smile filled her lips.

"You didn't need to come back. I really am busy, Brandon," she told him in a husky voice that had him wanting to drop to his knees.

"If we let life pass us by, then we'll have regrets," he said as the bartender slid a cup of steaming coffee in front of him along with a gooey cinnamon roll. His mouth watered almost as much for the pastry as it did for Chloe.

"I like my life. I'm not worried about it passing by," she assured him.

"As long as you etch out some time for me, then I'm all good," he said as he took a bite of his roll and sighed. "Heaven."

"That's because it's one of the rolls from my dad's secret vault that he doesn't share with the world. Enjoy it while you can," she told him with a laugh. "Now, back to the subject at hand. Let's just say I agree to go on some dates with you. What then?" she finished.

He wasn't sure how to answer. He hadn't been expecting her to say that. She'd pulled the rug out from under him. It was a good thing he recovered quickly.

"I'd say we'll have a blast," he said. He took another bite to keep himself from spouting out a bunch of other words that didn't need to be said.

"Is that all?" she pushed.

"What am I supposed to say?" he asked. That was probably a much safer bet.

"What happens when it ends? Are we going to be awkward around each other?" she pushed. She leaned on the other side of the counter from him, giving him a delicious view of her perfect cleavage that was making it hard for him to think. But he shook his head and repeated her words in his head before he opened his mouth.

"Why does it have to end?" he questioned.

"Are you proposing?" she asked, an impish look in her eyes.

Melody Anne

His gaze narrowed. "Are you trying to scare me away?" he asked, wondering if she was playing those games she'd said she hated. She'd accused him of doing just that, but it seemed she was the one holding the dice at the moment.

"I'm just asking logical questions," she said with an innocent shake of her head.

"We'll never know what's going to happen if we let this feeling slip away from us," he told her. He was surprised by how much he meant those words. He wanted to explore all he was feeling when it came to Chloe.

She tilted her head to the side, as if she was considering what he was saying. He liked that. Maybe this was the progress he so desperately wanted and needed. Before he could find out, the door chimed again, and he felt a chill travel down his spine. He turned around to find out why.

"Hello, Brandon."

He froze, unsure of what was happening.

"Alexandra?" he questioned. She smiled, her perfectly painted red lips turned up in a fake smile that had once turned him on, her blonde hair perfectly straightened, and her three-thousand-dollar shoes clicking on the tile floor.

"Hey, lover." She stopped in front of him and leaned in, placing a kiss on his stunned lips. He was so shocked he didn't have time to stop her.

"What are you doing here?" he asked. He hadn't seen her in over a year. They'd had an incredibly hot weekend, but he'd known it was a mistake from the second he'd woken up with her at his side.

In his younger and more carefree days, she'd been the perfect woman. She hadn't asked for much, and he had been able to walk away guilt-free. But after meeting Chloe, he'd discovered he wanted more than that. They'd parted, and he'd thought it would be the last he'd ever see of her.

"I just thought it was time you met your son," she said.

The room went utterly silent. Brandon stared at her in horror before turning to see the devastated look on Chloe's face. Before he could say a word to her, she was gone. His eyes narrowed as he turned back to face Alexandra. Fury washed through him.

"There isn't a chance I have a son with you," he said, his voice quiet but filled with rage. She didn't so much as blink as she gazed back at him mockingly.

"Do you not understand how babies are made?" she said as she pushed a piece of her hair behind her shoulders. She barely moved. The woman was a robot. How had he not seen that before? How had he ever been attracted to it? Maybe it was because he'd put himself through hell after losing his mom.

"I understand clearly how they're made, and we slept together once, and the condom didn't break," he said with steel in his voice.

Her eyes narrowed. "Accidents happen, Brandon. Do you want to meet your son? It's time you step up and take some responsibility," she said. That's when he noticed the panic and fear in her eyes. She covered it quickly, but it was there.

"Let's take a walk," he said. This was the last place he wanted to have this conversation with a former fling. He wasn't sure he'd be able to convince Chloe this was nothing more than a misunderstanding. That infuriated him more than anything else. He'd been making progress, and now this was going to take him right back to the starting line.

Alexandra followed him from the restaurant, and he kept several feet between them as they moved down the dreary street. It wasn't raining, but it smelled as if it was going to start at any moment.

They made it to the park, where no one seemed to be around. "Explain what's going on," he said.

She lost some of her composure. But he was fascinated as she pulled herself back together again. She hadn't had an easy time lately—that was for sure. Though he knew there was no chance he had a child with her, he had slept with her and owed her a few minutes of his time. Even if that meant he was going to have to do a lot of groveling with Chloe because of this.

"We have a child," she insisted. "He's two months old."

"I can do math, and it's been fourteen months since we were together, so unless you have the longest pregnancies ever, there's even less of a chance it's my son than before, and that was slim to none," he said.

Her shoulders slumped. Maybe she hadn't been expecting him to remember exactly when the two of them had been together. He might have been a bit of a dog, but he didn't forget when he'd been with a woman.

"No, it wasn't that long ago," she insisted.

"Tell me what's going on, Alexandra," he said, his anger draining. She was obviously in trouble.

She broke down, her cool exterior evaporating as she looked at him with helpless eyes. Tears streamed down her cheeks as she slid onto the bench they were standing by. She leaned her head into her hands and wept. He didn't want to touch this woman, but he was left with little choice. He sat next to her and put an arm around her shaking shoulders.

"I don't know what to do. My father has disowned me. My son doesn't have a father, and I'm all alone," she gasped.

"And you thought I could make it all better," he said. It wasn't a question.

"You were good to me, Brandon," she said as she regained her composure. "And we were good together. We can be again." She leaned into him, trying to connect their mouths.

He stopped her this time, placing a hand on her shoulder and holding her back. "I'm not interested, Alexandra. I'm with someone else now, and you know the two of us were never going to turn into a relationship, anyway. Go back to your father, and show him this side of you. Tell him you need him, and maybe he'll soften. We all make mistakes in life, but that doesn't have to define who we are or who we're going to be in the future. Ask him for help with your son."

"That's not how it works in my family," she told him with another sob.

"I'm sorry you're going through this. I really am. But you can't lie to me and tell me I have a child I don't have and expect me to be your white knight. You're stronger than you realize, and you'll be okay," he told her. "And sometimes you'd be surprised how a family reacts when you are completely vulnerable with them. I tried pushing my family away when I was hurting, and they didn't allow me to go away."

"You don't know my father."

"You're right. I don't know your father because I don't know you. I'm sorry for that. I'm sorry I took sex so callously before. I'm not the same guy I used to be. I'm also not the guy for you."

She was quiet as her tears stopped. "You are different," she said. "I wish it was because of me. One night with you wasn't nearly enough." The final words came out barely above a whisper.

"Go to your father. Tell him you're scared. Tell him you need help, and tell him what your plan is to help yourself. I know most people respect you if you have a plan," he assured her.

She didn't reply. She simply sat next to him and cried. It took another hour for him to get away. By the time he'd made it back to the restaurant, Chloe was long gone. He wasn't sure what she was thinking, and it might do him good to give her a night to calm down before he tried explaining himself.

That also might bite him in the butt. He'd soon find out. But right now he was drained. He'd been callous and hadn't once thought of the women he'd slept with before. That showed a flaw in his character he didn't respect or like. He couldn't change the past, but he could certainly be aware of how he acted in the present.

Sometimes it took a reality check to wake up. Sometimes it took looking in a mirror. And sometimes it took a blast from the past to make a person understand they didn't ever want to take steps backward. He was only interested in taking steps toward the future—a future he could look into and have respect for. A future that would make his family be proud of him and see him as a man and not a class clown.

Was this all because of Chloe? He didn't know for sure. He just knew he was a better person for knowing her. Maybe that was all it took to find the first stirrings of love. Maybe it really did begin with a whisper and not a bang.

CHAPTER FOURTEEN

A night of sleep hadn't stopped the irritation Chloe had been feeling since one of Brandon's exes had stumbled into *her* restaurant and demanded his attention. She hadn't believed the woman's story for a single second, but it did remind her of what a player the man had been his entire life.

Anger made a person make very poor choices. She was aware of that, even if she couldn't stop herself from acting on those impulses. They did say there was nothing like a woman scorned. However, if she was being logical, she'd know without a doubt she hadn't been scorned. He'd been with that woman long before her. They weren't in a relationship, anyway. He'd flirted. They'd slept together twice. They hadn't even been on a real date.

So she was beyond frustrated that she was giving a second thought to him being with anyone else. It was absurd. She could tell herself that all day and night, but it didn't matter. She was still irritated. Most likely it was because it was a reminder of why she'd veered away from relationships in the first place. They were messy, and they caused her to lose focus.

The woman's showing up had reminded her of why it was important not to get attached to the man. It had also made her petty enough to accept the date with an old friend when he'd called her that morning and invited her out. She had no desire to go with the man, but the timing had been impeccable on his part.

Currently the man she couldn't stop thinking about was sitting at a table in her restaurant. He'd tried to talk to her when he'd walked inside with his uncle Joseph, but he hadn't persisted when she'd given him her most aloof smile and walked away. His eyes had been glued to her for the past hour, though.

She wondered how well it would go when her date showed up, which would be in about ten minutes. She was wondering how foolish she'd been to have done that. She didn't want a fight breaking out.

But that was nonsense. Brandon wasn't going to stake some imaginary claim that didn't exist. She was just being foolish. But then again, the entire date was foolish. It was right before the holidays, and she didn't have time for it. But it was too late to back out now.

Jordan walked inside five minutes early, and Chloe felt her gut tense. She watched as he approached, an easy grin on his face. He was a good guy, making her feel even worse that she'd accepted a date with him because she'd felt . . . what had she felt? Was it jealousy? That was a new emotion she wasn't used to feeling.

"Good evening, beautiful. Are you ready?" Jordan asked as he stepped up and gave her a hug. It took all of Chloe's willpower not to turn in Brandon's direction. Maybe he wouldn't notice what was happening.

And maybe pigs truly would begin to fly.

"I'm almost ready. It's just been so busy here lately I lose track of time," she told him, giving him a halfhearted hug in return.

"I don't mind waiting on you," Jordan said. She truly did feel like a jerk. He was excited for their evening out, and she was already anticipating the date's end. It wasn't a good start to her day.

"Do you have big plans tonight, Chloe?"

She froze as Brandon made his presence known. She couldn't believe he would approach when she was with another guy. Did he have zero pride at all? There was no way she'd come up to him if the roles were reversed. As a matter of fact, she'd turned and run when his ex had shown up.

Both she and Jordan turned to face Brandon. Jordan's arm slipped behind her back comfortably, not seeming to feel the tension radiating from both Brandon and her.

"Hello, Brandon," she said through somewhat gritted teeth. "This is my friend Jordan Skye. Jordan, this is Brandon Anderson. We're working on the veterans center together," Chloe said, making reluctant introductions. Jordan didn't live in Cranston, so he was probably very unaware of anything that was going on in the town.

Jordan's eyes lit up at the introduction, though, and Chloe wanted to roll her eyes. Of course the Anderson name got a reaction from most people. It didn't mean she had to like it one little bit.

"It's a pleasure to meet you, Mr. Anderson. I've been following the news on the veterans facility. You guys are doing an amazing job. I wasn't aware Chloe was working on it." His words were full of wonder as he turned and faced her, looking impressed.

"I just signed on," she said with a shrug. "But I'm pleased to be a part of it."

Brandon ignored all talk of the project as he eyed her with suspicion. "What are you two up to tonight?" He wasn't backing off.

Jordan seemed completely unaware of the tension. It was something she'd always liked about the man. He was generally happy and worked hard and played even harder. She'd always been curious why she wasn't attracted to him.

"I'm taking this beautiful woman to a show and dinner," Jordan said as he squeezed her waist and smiled at Brandon. "She doesn't often say yes, so I have to move fast when it does happen." He chuckled, as if they were all sharing an inside joke.

Brandon wasn't smiling. He looked at Jordan for long enough the man began to look confused. Then Brandon turned and faced Chloe. "I thought you were swamped with the restaurant," he said.

"I do own the place, but that doesn't mean I need to be handcuffed to it," she said. She was shocked at how rude he was acting. She hadn't seen him behave that way before. It was odd. Jordan definitely couldn't ignore what was happening.

"Of course," Brandon finally said. "Have a great night." With that he turned and left, not going back to his table but walking out of the restaurant entirely. There was an awkward silence at his rude departure.

Finally Jordan spoke. "Is there something I'm missing here?" he asked. "I don't want to be stepping on anyone's toes." He didn't seem annoyed or jealous, simply curious at the rude behavior.

She shook off the strange meeting and smiled at Jordan. "There are no toes being stepped on. Brandon was talking with his uncle. Maybe it's work stress," she said with a bright smile. "But I'm sure that has nothing to do with us. He's just a very busy man."

"Sounds good," he said, his smile back in place. He'd taken her explanation easily enough.

She told him she'd be right back and ran to the back room, going as quickly as possible, afraid Brandon might return.

She splashed her face and threw some fresh makeup on, then ran a brush through her hair and quickly changed into a skirt and blouse. It wasn't ideal for a date, but it was the best she was going to do for the moment. She wanted to get out of there. She should've had him pick her up at home, but she'd been avoiding that. She wasn't sure why.

She was only gone about fifteen minutes, but she felt much better when she emerged to find Jordan sitting at the bar, sipping on a glass of wine.

"I'm sorry to keep you waiting," she told him.

His smile never faltered as he looked at her and then whistled. "You're worth waiting for," he assured her. The look of appreciation in his eyes actually made her feel better. She didn't feel too great at the moment. She hadn't been out on a real date in a long time. She wasn't sure if she even remembered what it was like.

Jordan lifted her hand and brushed his lips across her knuckles. She was disappointed when the gesture didn't send butterflies to the pit of her stomach. Maybe it was just because she was nervous about Brandon or was being peevish. Brandon always gave her butterflies, but maybe her traitorous body would wake up by the end of the evening. Not that anything more than a kiss was going to happen. It was far too soon after being with Brandon. That was just wrong, in her book.

"You are very handsome," she replied. He took her arm and led her outside, where he had a limo waiting. She stood there in shock. He was pulling out all the stops. She didn't know what to say. It was making her feel even worse about the evening. There was no possible way this was going anywhere, and she was wasting his time. It was wrong on many levels. Her parents had definitely taught her better than this.

"Your carriage awaits, my lady," he said with a flourish. The driver opened the back door, and she climbed inside, delighted to find champagne and strawberries. He poured her a glass, and they had a pleasant ride with meaningless small talk.

They drove into Seattle, where he took her to the theater. She was far too underdressed, making her slightly self-conscious, but she pushed that aside. She wasn't trying to impress anyone.

They continued their small talk on the way to their seats, and then she was grateful the show started. All of her thoughts were turned toward Brandon, no matter how much she wanted to focus on the man next to her. She tried feeling something for Jordan, but she just wasn't able to muster even an ounce of attraction.

It was too bad, because he was a handsome man with charm to spare. She was truly cheating him of a night out with a woman who'd see how amazing he was. She was feeling more and more guilty by the second.

But in her defense, how was she supposed to feel anything toward anyone else when she was thrown together with Brandon Anderson on an almost-daily basis? She was only human, after all.

They finished their show and managed polite conversation on the way to a beautiful candlelit dinner. Jordan reached for her hand often during the dinner, and she smiled and laughed and found herself having a good time. But even as they drove home, there wasn't a spark of romantic connection between them.

He reached her home and walked her to the door, stopping as she pulled out her keys and unlocked the handle. She turned toward him, unsure of what to do next.

"I've had the best night I've had in a very long time," Jordan told her.

"It really has been a great night," she said, meaning it. If Brandon hadn't been on her mind the entire time, it would've been perfect.

"I'd love to do it again," he said. She wondered if he wasn't seeing the distance she was trying to insert between them. It was obvious he wanted to kiss her good night, maybe even have more, but she was keeping her bag between them. She shifted, and he saw an opening.

Before she was able to utter another word, he clasped her in his arms and brought his lips to hers. She decided she needed to see if she could feel something other than friendship for this man, so she wrapped an arm around his neck and kissed him back.

Nothing.

She stopped trying and stood there stiffly as he tried getting a response from her. Finally, he pulled away. He took a step back and looked at her with disappointment. They remained there in an awkward silence for a few moments before she finally spoke.

"I'm sorry, Jordan. I had a really amazing evening with you, but I'm just so tired," she said, not sure if she wanted to end things completely. "Christmas week is always a lot for me. It should slow down soon." She hoped it was enough to soothe his bruised ego.

He looked thoughtful for a moment, then gave her his usual bright smile. "I understand fully. I'll leave you to rest." He then pulled out a couple of tickets from his pocket. "I was hoping to get you out one more time this week, though. There's an outdoor Christmas concert tomorrow. Will you come with me?" There was almost childlike hope in his eyes. She should tell him no, that it wasn't going to work, but he'd been so good to her that night, and she didn't want to disappoint him. Maybe she just needed one more outing to really feel something. Brandon couldn't have this big of a spell over her. It was absurd.

"That sounds like fun," she replied. "I'd love to come." She really didn't want to go, but she loved Christmas, and dating anyone besides Brandon might break the spell he had over her. That was the ideal ending to all of this. Besides, she might grow to like Jordan as more than just a friend. And if not, maybe their friendship would remain intact.

"You've made my night. I hope you have sweet dreams," he said. He turned and quickly walked down her path. Chloe had a feeling he'd done that so she wouldn't have time to change her mind. She was already thinking it was a bad idea. Chloe took a deep breath as she leaned against her door and watched him depart.

She was feeling slightly depressed but was unsure why. She'd had a great evening. Jordan had been excellent company, and she was disappointed to not feel *any* attraction toward him.

She'd turned to head inside when a voice stopped her.

"How did your night go?" Brandon asked, making her heart thunder and her feet leave the ground as she jumped about a foot in the air. It took several seconds for her to respond to the man, who stepped up on her porch.

"Do you like to lurk in dark corners just so you can give me a heart attack?" she asked, ignoring his question. It was none of his business how her evening had gone. Where she'd felt nothing with Jordan but an easy companionship, she felt a myriad of emotions simply standing there with Brandon.

"Do you like to avoid questions?" he replied with what seemed like a permanent scowl on his face. She wasn't used to seeing that. Of all the brothers, Brandon was the most likely to wear a smile twenty-four seven.

"I had a very nice evening. I'm tired, though, so I'll talk to you later," she said, dismissing him. She'd placed her hand on the doorknob and had gone to turn it when he spun her around. She looked at him in shock. Brandon was definitely a man who knew what he wanted, but he'd never acted like this before.

"Think about this tonight," he said seconds before his head descended. She had no time to react before his lips were pressed against hers.

Brandon wrapped his arms around her, pulling her body tightly against his. There was no hiding the arousal she felt pressed against her or the reaction of her response. Chloe's pulse beat out of control, and she could barely breathe. She raised her arms around his neck, clinging to him, while his hands roamed up and down her back.

She couldn't seem to get enough of his taste, scent, or touch. She was quickly forgetting why she shouldn't be kissing him and the fact that she'd just ended a date with another man.

"Invite me inside," he growled in her ear before he ran his skilled tongue down the curve of her neck, making her moan. All she had to do was say yes, and they could have a passion-filled night. She opened her mouth to utter the simple word as his hand slipped around her side and cupped her aching breast. He flicked his thumb over the sensitive bud, making her feel intense pleasure even through the layers of her clothes.

She cried out and felt a shudder ripple through his body as it pressed closer to hers. He pushed her up against her front door. He brought his lips back to hers, devouring her, reminding her she was a woman with needs. He moved his hand to the edge of her skirt, sliding it upward, touching her bare skin. She shook with the intensity of the pleasure.

She heard a car door shut somewhere close, and that small bit of noise helped bring her back to reality. What was she doing? She was practically making love to Brandon on her brightly lit front porch, where a neighbor could easily walk by.

"Brandon, we have to stop," she whispered. She could barely get the words past her desire-filled throat. She brought her hands down to his chest and pushed. He lifted his head, looking at her in confusion. His eyes, filled with desire, were almost her undoing. She wanted to keep going, which made it so much harder to stop.

He bent his head to take her lips once more, and she didn't know how she found the will to pull away. He let out a deep sigh and finally stepped back. He didn't say another word, just turned and left. Chloe let out her own sigh and stepped through her door. She leaned against it, and a shudder racked her body.

What was she doing? She wasn't this woman. She wasn't the type of person who went on a date with one man and made love to another on the same night. She wasn't that person who played games with men, and she wasn't a cheater. So what in the heck was she doing?

She wasn't sure, and she didn't know how to get out of the mess she'd put herself in. It was just a reminder that no person should ever make decisions when they were angry.

Chapter Fifteen

Chloe was sitting on her best friend Sarah's bed with her head in her hands. Brooke was in a chair, and Sarah was pulling dresses from the closet. Chloe was a mess, and thankfully her best friends weren't judging her too harshly.

"I think you need to wear this one," Sarah said as she pulled a gorgeous red calf-length dress from her closet.

"Whatever you think will work," Chloe said with little interest.

"That's the smartest thing you've said all evening," Sarah said.

"And not like you at all," Brooke added.

"I just don't have a bunch of dresses," Chloe said. "I have plenty of skirt suits and things appropriate to wear to the restaurant, but since I opened, I've had little interest in dating."

"Well, it's a good thing you have us to make you beautiful," Brooke said with a laugh. "Though, we're still trying to figure out what in the heck is going on. Why are you going on a date with Jordan when Brandon has obviously staked his claim?"

Chloe let out a frustrated sigh. "I don't belong to anyone," she informed her friends. "And though things have obviously happened between Brandon and I, that doesn't mean we're in a relationship."

"Do you feel something for Jordan?" asked Sarah as she sat next to Chloe.

Chloe wanted to lie, but she never would to her two best friends. She frowned. "No, I feel nothing more than friendship with him. But I want to feel more. I hate that I'm playing a game like so many men do. I hate to feel that I'm using this man. I don't want to. I truly want to feel for him what I've been feeling toward Brandon. It's so complicated. Maybe I've been too judgmental of other people. Maybe they are just as confused as I am and not playing games."

"I've been there," Brooke said. "But you can't force feelings." She rubbed her hand on Chloe's shoulder.

"But feelings can grow," Chloe said almost desperately.

Sarah laughed. "Yes, they can grow, but not when you're carrying a torch for someone else."

Chloe rolled her eyes. "I don't understand what my attraction toward Brandon is all about. He's not the type of man I ever go out with. This is becoming more and more of a mess each and every day."

"Yeah, but how boring would it be if everything was wrapped perfectly with a pretty red bow?" Brooke asked.

"I think we all fail to realize the blessings of boring. With boring we don't raise our blood pressure, have stress, get angry, cry, or get hurt," Chloe pointed out.

Brooke and Sarah shrugged before Brooke spoke. "That's all true. But with boring, we also don't laugh till our bellies hurt and love until our hearts burst. I'll take some pain any day of the week to have true and utter joy."

Chloe sighed once more. "You might have a point there," she reluctantly admitted.

"You better get ready. Isn't Jordan going to be here any minute?" Sarah asked.

Chloe looked at the clock, and her eyes widened. "Crap!" she said as she jumped from the bed and grabbed the dress before rushing to the bathroom. She was definitely running late, and after the stunt Brandon had pulled the night before, she didn't trust him to not pull something similar this night. She hadn't told him she was at Sarah's house, but it was also his brother's place, and she didn't think it would take much investigation on his part to figure it out.

After twenty minutes Chloe came running down the stairs. She was definitely late, and she wasn't normally one of those women who made a man wait on her. Now she'd done it to Jordan two days in a row.

She heard talking in the front foyer and came around the corner, slightly out of breath from her lightning-fast job of getting ready and coming to meet Jordan. She was less than thrilled when she came to a stop to find Brandon standing with Jordan, who looked slightly uncomfortable in the man's company.

"I'm so sorry to have kept you waiting again, Jordan," Chloe said as she walked up to the two men.

"It's always a pleasure to wait on a beautiful woman," Jordan said while taking her hand and bringing it to his lips. She noticed Brandon roll his eyes and quickly turn away. She couldn't believe how he was behaving. After their hot kiss the night before, maybe she could believe it a little bit.

"That was certainly the right thing to say," she said with a small laugh she had to force from her tight throat.

"So Jordan said the two of you are heading out to attend the annual Christmas concert. I might see you there," Brandon said. He looked as if he was trying to make polite conversation, but his words came out more as a threat. She glared at him, quickly wiping it away as Jordan turned toward her.

What in the heck was Brandon thinking? He couldn't show up where she was having a date. That was insane. He couldn't be that clueless.

"I'm sure it will be very crowded, and I wouldn't advise you getting mixed up in all the mess," Chloe said while looking straight into his eyes with a clear message that he wasn't wanted there. She was certainly trying to convey the message not to interrupt her date.

"We'll just have to see. Have a wonderful evening," he replied before walking off. She let out the breath she'd been holding, grateful he hadn't said more and that his brothers hadn't joined him to try to intimidate Jordan. The man might've given up at that point. He'd be well within his rights to do so.

"Are you ready to leave?" Jordan asked, obviously wanting to get away as much as she did at that moment. At least he wasn't a stupid man. It was obvious Brandon wasn't thrilled about the two of them dating. She just hoped Jordan didn't realize it was because the two of them had some weird connection between them.

"Yes, of course," Chloe answered. He placed his hand on her back and led her toward his waiting car. This time he had a silver BMW, gleaming in the setting sun. It was a beautiful vehicle that screamed money. He was obviously trying to impress her. He hadn't figured out yet that a man's wallet wasn't what made her all tingly inside. He helped her into the car, where she sank down into the luxurious seat. She decided to put some effort into her date this time and forget all about anyone with the last name of Anderson.

"I really enjoyed our night last night, but what in the world is going on between you and Brandon?" he asked. He seemed more curious than upset.

She wanted to lie to him, but she didn't appreciate when people lied to her, so she pushed off the cavalier answer she'd wanted to give and took in a long breath.

"I honestly don't know how to answer that. We're working on this project together, and he's definitely made his interest in me known, but I've told him it can't work. I'm not sure what he's doing right now."

The car was filled with silence for a few moments as Jordan took it all in. Then he sighed. She waited for him to say something, though she desperately wanted to fill the void with words. She was really uncomfortable at the moment.

"I knew this would one day happen," he finally said. She finally looked at him, and he was giving her a smile, but not the bright one he normally wore.

"What are you talking about?" she asked.

He chuckled. "I know you feel bad every time we're together, and it's my fault for pushing it. We're friends, Chloe, and we've never been more than that. I was just hoping it could become more. But I'm pushing it, too. Neither one of us feels the fireworks exploding when we kiss. We've managed to push ourselves into the friend zone," he said with a shrug.

"Now I feel really bad," she said. She didn't want to tell him he was inaccurate, though.

"Don't feel bad. It's been obvious for some time," he said. "But I knew some man would one day come along and make you go crazy. I think it's happened."

"No, Brandon isn't the one for me," she said a bit too loudly. He chuckled again.

"I guarantee he's going to show up tonight. That man is green with jealousy. He's let me know—in every way except for coming out and saying it—that you're his woman."

Chloe bristled. "I don't belong to anyone," she said with a narrowing of her eyes. "I'm independent and do just fine on my own."

"I wasn't trying to offend you. But the guy is head over heels. Maybe you can give him a little bit of a break," he said. "I am very aware of what it feels like to be rejected. It might not happen often, but it happens, and it hurts. Male pride is real."

"Are you trying to end our date?" she asked.

"Nope. We're going to this concert and will have a fantastic time . . . *and* make your man jealous. Who knows? Maybe some woman will be jealous of you," he said with a waggle of his brows that made her laugh. She was already cheering up immensely. Knowing there were no expectations of this evening ending romantically had lifted her mood considerably.

"Can we be friends forever?" she asked.

"Most definitely," he assured her as they pulled into the busy parking lot of the arena where the concert was happening.

"Good, because you are definitely a person who brings light into a dark room."

"I think that's the best compliment I've ever gotten," he said.

He stepped from the car and held open her door. As soon as she climbed out, he pulled her in for a bear hug. "I am still a man, though, so if you want to grope me or give me a scorching kiss to make him even more jealous, I'm your willing puppet," he assured her.

She smacked his hand as it moved toward her butt. "You're absolutely terrible," she said. "And I love it."

They laughed as they made their way toward the front of the crowd. Jordan had gotten them great tickets. Now that they had an understanding on the table, she was actually pretty glad to be there with him. She knew it would be a fun night.

The concert began, making talking impossible. It was a variety of country music artists putting on one heck of a show, singing some of her favorites and a bunch of crowd-pleasers. They had everyone singing and dancing along as they sipped on buttered rum and spiked eggnog.

They'd made it to intermission when she noticed Jordan wasn't looking so good. She walked with him to the bathrooms and waited awhile until he came out. He wasn't smiling any longer.

"Are you okay?" she asked. She hoped she wouldn't have to leave. She was having a remarkable time, more fun than she'd had in a long time. She needed it with all the stress of the past month.

"I'll be fine. Something I ate must be disagreeing with me," he said, then winked. "Or maybe it was one too many glasses of eggnog." They moved toward some unoccupied benches, and he sat with his head in his hands.

"We'd better get you home then," she told him, trying to hide her disappointment.

He looked up, then looked behind her and smiled. "Not a chance, Chloe. You've been having a fantastic time. I want you to finish the concert," he insisted.

"I'm not going to finish while you're feeling like this," she said. "I'm not that big of a jerk."

"Be a jerk," he said in a hushed whisper. "I think my replacement just walked in."

Chloe turned to find Brandon walking up to the two of them. She sent Brandon a withering stare. "What are you doing here?" she snapped.

He smiled, ignoring her question as he turned to Jordan. "Is everything okay, bud?" he asked, practically giddy.

"No. My stomach isn't doing so well," Jordan said.

"I'm sorry." She could see Brandon was torn. He'd been raised to not be gleeful in someone else's misery, but he was sensing that things were about to go his way. She really, *really* didn't want things to go Brandon's way.

"Chloe, I hate to leave you, but since you have a ride home, I'm going to have to cut this short," Jordan said.

"I'll go with you," Chloe quickly told him.

"I don't want you to miss out on the concert. You've been having a wonderful time. Please, stay," Jordan said. Chloe felt torn, but she really did want to stay at the concert. She looked back and forth between Brandon and Jordan. Ugh. "I'm not letting you go with me," he finished as he stood.

"Fine," she conceded. "But I'll walk you to the car to make sure you can drive."

"That's a deal," he said as he gave her a wink and wrapped an arm around her. "I could use the support." His hand slipped low on her hip, and she knew he was doing it to goad Brandon. She let him, not looking at the man who had probably lost that smug look on his face.

She didn't say anything to Brandon as she walked away. Maybe he'd get lost in the crowd, and she'd find another ride home. There were several people she knew attending the concert. If all else failed, she could take an Uber.

They reached Jordan's car, and he stood there for a moment with a smile. "Don't be too hard on the man. He's obviously obsessed," Jordan told her as he gave her a hug.

"I'm not into obsession," she said.

"I wouldn't mind someone being obsessed with me. It's not such a bad thing," he said.

"In your opinion," she countered. He laughed as he climbed into his car. She walked back as he drove away. She really was torn on what she should do when it came to Brandon. She was going to try to enjoy the end of the concert for the moment, though.

By the time she returned, she'd missed a few songs, but the artists were still going strong. Brandon found her in a heartbeat, leaving her no other choice but to stand with him unless she wanted to make a scene. She simply tried to tune him out. After a while she got lost in the fun of it all. She hadn't forgiven him, but she wasn't going to let it ruin her evening.

At least the noise of the crowd made it impossible to talk. It didn't keep Brandon from brushing against her every five seconds or singing along with the crowd. It also softened her resolve. It was hard to stay aloof with a man singing "Grandma Got Run Over by a Reindeer."

When it ended, he kept an arm around her as they exited the arena. They'd made it to his car before he turned to her and decided he was extending their night.

"Let's get hot chocolate and pie," Brandon said.

She wasn't going to admit it, but she truly didn't want the night to end, anyway. She was having an amazing time, even if she didn't want to say so. "Okay, I could use some more sugar," she said.

They drove to her favorite diner, which was far enough from the venue to not be crowded. There were only a few people inside. Most of them had had a bit too much to drink and were now looking for fried food and coffee before heading home.

"What was that date all about?" Brandon asked after they'd placed their order. She'd changed her mind from pie and ordered onion rings and mozzarella sticks. It was a perfect midnight snack.

"He's an old friend," she said, knowing she couldn't avoid this conversation.

"Do you always go out with multiple men?" he asked.

That had her glaring at him. Then the look fell away as her shoulders slumped. "No, I don't. I was mad about the woman showing up," she admitted.

"It's not my child," he said, throwing his hands in the air.

"I know that," she told him. "I know you aren't that guy. I don't know why it upset me. We aren't a couple and haven't ever been a couple. I don't want a boyfriend, and it makes absolutely no sense whatsoever why it bothered me at all," she said.

He gazed at her for so long she wondered if he was going to say anything at all. Finally, he laughed. Then the waitress placed their food down. He had two slices of pie and a large cup of coffee. She had her fried treats and a diet soda. The sugar-free soda made her feel better about her food choice.

"I'm glad I'm amusing you," she said after devouring her first mozzarella stick.

"You always make me feel plenty of emotions," Brandon said. "Maybe that's why I keep seeking you out."

"You make me feel a lot of emotions as well. I don't like it so much," she told him.

"Why does it bother you so much?" he asked.

"I don't know," she said. "It's just that I have a plan for life. I've always been a perfectionist, and there's nothing predictable about a relationship. I like dating when I have the time, but I don't ever want it to be a priority. I don't want to have the lows along with the highs. I don't want to fall in love. And it's just easier to focus on my work so I can have one thing in my life that's as close to perfect as I can make it."

He listened to her speech while he slowly ate his pie. When she was finished, she dipped an onion ring in some ranch and popped it into her mouth. She'd sobered up from her spiked eggnog, and she was filling up fast. She was also getting pretty tired. It really had been a longer-than-normal week.

He didn't push her when she told him she was tired. And then their evening came to a close, and soon Brandon was driving her home. She was hoping he'd stay in the car and let her walk to her own door, but she knew that wasn't going to happen. They were, however, silent as they approached. The second they were on her porch, all she could think about was how amazing the night before had been from the second he'd pulled her into his arms.

She didn't want to be presumptuous and think he was going to start kissing her again, but at the same time she wanted to make sure and stop him before he started, because she didn't think she'd have the willpower to stop him two nights in a row.

"Thank you for a wonderful evening," Brandon said, shocking her. She was afraid to even make eye contact with him. Her body was humming with desire, and she wanted nothing more than to fall into his arms.

"I appreciate you inviting me to join you when Jordan got sick," she said, still not looking up. She was counting the dirt clumps she saw on her front porch. He gently grasped her chin, and she fought to not panic.

He looked into her eyes and slowly bent his head forward. He lightly brushed his lips against hers, causing her heart to thunder. Then, before she knew it, he let go and backed away. He smiled down at her, then turned and left her leaning against the door.

She stood looking at the empty path in front of her house, but she couldn't seem to move. Her knees had turned to rubber, and her back felt as if it had no spine. Brandon had knocked her off of her feet with one gentle brush of his lips.

When she finally felt some confidence in her legs' ability to hold her up, she turned around and went inside.

She tossed and turned in bed all night, dreaming about her and Brandon doing so much more than simply kissing. Maybe she was done fighting the man. Maybe she was willing to admit she wanted to start taking some risks that had nothing to do with work and that just might get a little messy.

CHAPTER SIXTEEN

Chloe was dead on her feet at the end of a very long day. Only a few more days until she'd get some time off. When you owned a restaurant, there weren't a lot of days you could afford to leave the place—not in the beginning. She wanted it to run beautifully so she could truly make a name for herself.

She might have been slightly worried that Brandon hadn't called her in two days or shown up unannounced. Maybe her stunt with Jordan had turned him off. Maybe he'd only shown up at the concert to prove a point that she did want him, and now that he knew that, he was gone for good.

This was the exact reason she hadn't wanted to get involved with anybody. Instead of focusing on her work, she was obsessing about a man whom she'd continually pushed away for the past several months.

She was walking from the kitchen when she heard familiar laughter. She looked up to see Brandon . . . walking in with her mother on his arm. What in the world was going on? Was she seeing things?

Her mother laughed again. The sound was almost foreign to Chloe. Yes, she'd heard both of her parents laugh before, but not too often. Genevieve was laughing like a teenage girl, and Brandon was grinning. They both moved to her bar. She looked at the counter to make sure it was sparkling clean. She didn't want to give her mother any excuses to criticize her.

"Hello, Chloe," her mother said as she moved over and leaned in, giving Chloe a half hug and lightly kissing her on the cheek.

"Hello, Mother," Chloe said, not able to hide the confusion in her voice.

"I was walking up to the restaurant when I found this beautiful woman out front with no one to open the door for her," Brandon said as he held out a stool for her mother.

"Oh, Brandon, you are such a charmer," Genevieve said with another girlish giggle that had Chloe completely baffled.

"Ah, I just never like to leave a lady waiting," Brandon said with a slight bow. He waited for Genevieve to sit before he took the stool beside her. Chloe wasn't going to sit with them. Instead, she moved behind the counter and grabbed her mother's favorite bottle of wine. She didn't bother asking her if she wanted a glass, just poured it and handed it over.

"What has you out and about? I didn't know you were coming to Cranston," Chloe said.

"I was doing some shopping. Your father had meetings all day today, and I was lonely," Genevieve said as she pulled up her bag. "And I also wanted to give you a copy of your father's latest book. He just got the advanced copies."

Genevieve pulled out her father's newest cookbook, and Chloe grabbed it, excited to see the beautiful picture on the front cover. She'd worked with her dad on that particular recipe.

"I can't believe the copies are in already. This is his best book ever. He put so much time into it," Chloe said.

"This was also the first time he had a coauthor," her mother said.

Chloe was confused. Then she looked back down at the front cover. Her eyes filled with tears that she desperately tried to blink back. She took some deep breaths as she pulled herself together.

"I don't understand," she said.

"He wanted to surprise you," Genevieve said. "That recipe on the front is both of yours. He also included three of your cookie recipes in it." She pulled out an envelope. "Here's an advance. You get ten percent of the sales."

Chloe never would've expected something like this from either of her parents. They only gave credit where credit was due, and they'd never praised her for anything in her life that hadn't been done to perfection. But the front of the book—in small letters, but still there—said WITH CHLOE HITMAN. She was speechless.

"I didn't do enough to earn this," Chloe said. "I was just playing with Father in the kitchen."

"Your father pointed something out to me that I wasn't aware of. I didn't know quite how to process what he was saying to me, and so it took me a while to work through it," Genevieve said after several moments. She then reached across the counter and took Chloe's hand.

"I love you very much, and I've always wanted what's best for you. I haven't always been able to say the right things or do the right things. I see the world very black and white. So does your father, but not quite as badly as I do. You've worked incredibly hard to get where you are, and we are both incredibly proud of you," her mother said.

Chloe was fighting to keep tears back. "I know you just want me to be the best I can be," Chloe assured her. There were many times she'd wanted to scream at her parents that she was trying her best, but her mother saying these words to her made her feel bad.

"I'm not going to promise to change my ways, as I don't know if I can completely do that. But I'm going to try to not nitpick you so much and try to appreciate what a fine young woman you've become. It's very hard for an old woman to change her ways, but I think between the two of us, together we can navigate the waters."

Chloe smiled. "I think the two of us can do anything together if we put our minds to it."

"That's for sure. I raised you to believe in yourself and to never settle for second best. You've proven yourself more than capable of that over and over again," Genevieve told her.

A tear slipped down her cheek. "I'm sorry, Mother. It's been a long week," she said, trying to explain away her emotional state.

"Yes, the holidays take their toll on us, for sure." She squeezed Chloe's hand. "You earned this spot on this book. I want you to celebrate it and enjoy it. This definitely wasn't given to you because of who you are. If anything, it was more difficult for you to get there because we expect so much more from our daughter than we do anyone else."

"I'm glad you expect so much from me. I don't think I'd be who I am today if you and Father hadn't pushed me so much. Some people might think kids don't need that, but I think that's exactly what we all need. I'm glad I don't easily give up on things."

Brandon had sat there quietly the entire time they'd had this conversation. She was well aware of him sitting there, but she didn't mind. A part of her didn't want him to see her this vulnerable, but another part of her—a bigger part—trusted him to not take advantage of the situation.

Genevieve seemed to remember he was sitting there right then, as she turned toward him. "I'm sorry you had to witness our little moment," she said, seeming slightly embarrassed.

"I feel privileged to be a small part of it. I love Chloe's cooking, and what a beautiful moment to see." He then turned to Chloe. "You're officially an author."

Her eyes widened. "No, I'm not," she said, shaking her head. "My father is the one with a magic way of speaking. Look," she said as she opened the book. She'd seen some of his early drafts.

"What makes his books stand out in a sea of cookbooks is that he adds pictures of the process with little anecdotes of failures and humor in the kitchen. What's really funny about it is that he only really lets go when he's working on one of these books. He finds humor in the process."

She found a picture that brought more tears to her eyes when she came to one of her cookie recipes. There was a picture of her laughing, her eyes sparkling as her father tossed a spoonful of flour her way. She could practically see the tiny granules flying in the air through the picture. Her mother must've snapped it. She hadn't even been aware of a camera coming out. That had been a fun day.

There hadn't been a lot of time for fun and games while she'd been growing up. Her parents were overachievers, making her that way, too. Or maybe that truly was just her personality. That made those little moments that much more special. This cookbook would be her favorite book of all time.

She turned the book to the beginning and found the dedication. "To my beautiful wife, who has always supported my goals and my career, even when that took me from my family for eighteen-hour days, seven days a week. And to my daughter, who makes me realize it's not what I've learned in life—it's what I've been able to see, touch, and feel. I've found magic in the kitchen once more, and not just a formula that needs to be perfected. Without the balance both of you bring to my life, I wouldn't be the man I am today. I love you both more than I've ever been able to express."

Chloe felt another tear fall. "I guess I've learned a lot from your father, as he's learned from both of us. We're a family. I forget that sometimes. I'm so focused on what's before me that I forget that you and your father are the reason I do what I do," Genevieve said.

Chloe rushed to the other side of the counter and threw her arms around her mother. It was the first time she'd done that since she was a young child. They hugged often, but they were side hugs and quick embraces. They weren't those tender embraces that filled you with warmth.

"I love you, Mother," she said.

"I love you, Chloe."

They stood there for several moments before pulling apart. Chloe looked up to see Brandon beaming at them. Chloe couldn't remember ever feeling this happy in her life. She couldn't wait to see her father next. She'd give him just as big of a hug.

"Now, enough of all this emotional stuff. Would you and Brandon join me for dinner so I don't have to sit alone?" Genevieve asked. "I'm famished after shopping all day."

"I would love to join you," Chloe said. "Let me tell my manager so she can take over."

"It would be my honor," Brandon added.

Chloe got them a table, and it was the best meal she'd had in a very long time. She truly hoped this was a new phase in her life with her parents. And maybe, just maybe, it would be a new phase with Brandon as well.

CHAPTER SEVENTEEN

Chloe was sitting outside on her porch swing, perfectly content—well, somewhat content. She was reading a particularly erotic scene in her newest romance book that was making her slightly hot and bothered, but that was nothing new lately.

When a voice spoke, it made her jump, and her cheeks flushed as she guiltily looked up, as if the person would know exactly what she'd been reading and what that had led to in her mind. Brandon was standing before her. She'd been so immersed in her book she hadn't noticed him.

"Come take a walk with me to the veterans center. It's a beautiful day," Brandon said as he looked at her, then tried to see the book she was quick to cover. He seemed confused. She understood why.

"What did you say?" she asked, realizing he was waiting for her to speak.

"I asked if you'd like to go for a walk with me to the veterans center. We're truly behind schedule now," he repeated, glancing at her book again. She quickly tucked it inside her jacket. She wasn't going there.

She was having a really difficult time going from fantasy to reality, especially when her fantasy was now standing before her, looking better than ever in a pair of tight jeans, a molded sweatshirt, and running shoes. Of course, he could wear anything and look just as good. It was criminal how amazing he looked day and night—especially at night.

"That sounds like a great idea. Let me run inside and get a warm coat," she said. She jumped up and had no doubt she was fleeing from him to try to gain some of her lost composure back.

She took her time getting her UGG boots on and finding her warmest jacket that wasn't too bulky. She needed a good walk. Though she'd been on her feet all day at the restaurant, it wasn't the same as strolling outside. She got really sick of artificial lights all of the time.

When she'd made him stand around long enough, she finally made her way back downstairs and found him in her living room. She could've made him wait on the porch, but she was tired of being rude to this man who was going out of his way to accommodate her.

"Sorry I took so long. I had a hard time finding my boots," Chloe said as she moved to stand beside him.

"You took hardly any time at all," he told her. "Most women I know hate to do anything last minute because they need hours to put on makeup and do their hair."

"I'm not sure if I should be offended by that statement. Are you saying I don't care about my appearance?" she asked, only half teasing. She was a woman, after all, and didn't want to look as if she'd just woken up when she was exiting the house.

He held up both hands. "I was totally giving you a compliment, because you're naturally beautiful, and it would be a shame if you tried to cover anything up with a bunch of silly paint," he told her.

Though she didn't want it to feel good, the compliment made her glow inside. She couldn't stop the beaming smile she sent him. "I guess I can't complain about words like that," she said, then giggled.

Her hand flew over her mouth when the sound escaped. She was acting like a nervous teenager on her first date. Brandon put an arm around her and gave her one quick kiss before releasing her just as quickly.

"You're adorable," he said. She didn't know how to reply to that, so she just walked toward her front entrance.

They stepped through the door into the cool afternoon air. There was a bit of snow falling, but not enough to keep them inside. It couldn't be a more perfect winter day for a brisk walk.

"It's so beautiful this time of year. Every time I look out the windows or step through the front door, I'm reminded of a winter wonderland. It's like it snows here just to make a perfect Christmas," Chloe told him.

"I've lived all over the place, and coming here feels like home. My family was originally from the Seattle area, then we moved away. I love it here, though, and never want to settle anywhere else."

"I've done my share of travel, and I have to agree with you. This place does feel like home."

They'd made it about a half mile when she slipped, the ground slick from the snow and low temperature.

Brandon was quickly there to catch her fall. Then he took her arm and ran it through his so he could help steady her. She didn't pull away from him. She liked being this close.

They walked in silence, enjoying the quiet around them. There weren't too many people out and about as they left the small town. It was only about a mile and a half away from her house, but in this cold that might end up being quite the distance. Still, as they moved along, Chloe gasped in pleasure as they passed a herd of deer only a few feet from them. The animals looked up but didn't run for cover. She stopped and admired how regal they appeared as they gazed back at Chloe and Brandon, trying to determine if they were a threat.

"We should've brought some hay in our pockets. Maybe they would've come over and taken it from you," Brandon told her. "Next time we'll remember."

"That would be amazing," Chloe said, wanting to run back and get the hay right then. Brandon tugged her along, and she reluctantly walked away from the animals. It was too cold outside to be out for long. "I know a lot about your family since my two best friends are married to your brothers. But is there anything you can tell me I don't know?" she asked after a while. She loved learning about family history. Everyone had a unique story, even if they didn't think so.

"Hmm, you should know it all. My mother died a few years ago, and that's when my brothers and I discovered we had an entire family we hadn't known we had," Brandon said.

"That had to have been a huge shock," she said. "I can't even imagine if that happened to me."

"I wasn't in love with it at first, but it all worked out really well in the end, so it isn't as if I can complain about it. My mother didn't do it out of spite. My father was a horrible man, and my mom felt a lot of shame because of it," he said.

"Everyone has skeletons in their closet, but you seem to have more than most," she said. "Maybe that's the way it is in all wealthy families. They want the world to see perfection, but money can't solve all problems. It can buy pretty things, and it can also cause jealousy and conniving. So many people out there want what they don't earn. They don't look inside their own home first to fix problems, but look at the outside world and make unfair comparisons."

"I agree with that," he said. "But I think there are more good people in this world than bad."

"Yes, I believe that as well. I just get frustrated sometimes. We all want the American dream, but so few try to actually achieve it. On those days I've worked eighteen hours and my feet have blisters and I still have a few to go, I want to kill someone when they see my new car and say it must be nice."

He laughed. "I've been there. We lived in a tiny house growing up. We knew from the time we were young that if we wanted to have anything in life, we'd have to do it ourselves. Our mom taught us that hard work was the only way we'd survive. I watched her work hard every day of her life."

"Now, you don't ever have to worry about that again," she told him.

He laughed. "Maybe if I was a spoiled brat. But I love my work. Without it, I wouldn't have the same drive and purpose. Sure, there's security in having a hefty sum of money in the bank, but that doesn't mean I want to do nothing more than jet around the world. I want there to be meaning to my life. I did my playboy days, and that's empty. I want to show something for my life. I want a legacy. I don't need my name in lights. I just want to have made a difference."

She paused for a moment. "Which is why you and your brothers were so eager to work on the center." It was a statement.

"Yes, we all served, and to give back is pretty much amazing. I want to know I helped. And when I have children, I want them to know I did all I could, and my hope is they'll follow in the great footsteps of the men and women before them. Many people don't realize how much Joseph gives back. Yes, the man is a multibillionaire, but he does so much for his community. No, he doesn't give it all away, but he gives the opportunity for anyone who wants to succeed to have a chance at doing that."

"I guess that goes back to the saying of 'Give a man a fish, and he eats for a day, but teach a man to fish, and he eats for life,'" she said.

"Yeah, exactly. I'm all for giving to those who truly need it. I love this project. I love what it means to so many who have already given their all. I will give everything I have to someone worthy."

"What makes you the judge of who is worthy and who isn't?" she asked.

He looked at her with a smile. "That's a great question, and one I've never thought about before. I don't know the answer. What makes someone more needy than the next? We're going to have this amazing center for veterans, but we obviously can't help every single person who comes through the doors. Do we turn away a sick mother asking for help because she's not a veteran? Do we put a cap on who we help and who we don't? I have no idea what that answer is."

Chloe looked at him with new respect. "I love that you're thinking about it. Because I honestly don't know the answer, either. I'm not sure any of us do. But I do know I don't want to do nothing. So that leaves me trying to figure it out. Maybe if more people try to do the same, all of the world's problems will get solved, instead of us all just complaining and talking about it nonstop."

"At least we are talking about it," he told her. "If we didn't care at all, we wouldn't discuss it, and we wouldn't try to solve anything. We'd just worry about ourselves."

"That's a good point, but I do remember my younger days when I went to church, and one thing stood out to me. It was a saying an old Sunday school teacher said to me. She said that faith without works is dead."

"What does that mean?" he asked.

"I guess the simple explanation is to say that we can tell ourselves and our neighbors all day long that we want to make a difference, that we want to help others, but without action it doesn't mean a lot. Now, saying that, I don't think we help anyone by simply handing things over, but I do think we make a difference by doing something like building the veterans center. This facility will help so many who deserve it. I also love that Joseph has set up so many programs and brought in so many community members so the people who will be staying here will also be doing work, will also be giving back. It gives them a sense of pride and some more skills for the next steps in their lives."

"This is obviously something you've thought about a lot," he said.

"Yeah, when I can't sleep at night, my mind is constantly turning. I can't watch the news in the evening anymore, because that leads to too many YouTube clips, and then I feel hopeless as I try to figure out who I am. Why do I feel the way I feel? Why can I turn my back on one person and not another? It makes me judge myself harshly as I try to figure out the world."

"I think that's a good thing, though," Brandon told her. "I think when we believe we can't do any wrong and our own opinion is more important than the person's next to us, then we aren't growing. I can have a different opinion than my brother and still love him. I can have a different opinion than you, and you could possibly change my mind. I don't want to be so closed minded I won't listen. I've changed my mind many times before."

"I don't think I'd ever have thought that about you. Since I've known you, you haven't seemed a man to be easily swayed."

He laughed. "I'm not easily swayed. I just said I could change my mind if you give me a reason to."

That was definitely something for her to think about. Brandon wasn't in any way the man she'd thought he was. It was truly easy to judge a book by the cover, but it was foolish as well. There was a lot inside that made it a manuscript. She could write an entire book about Brandon and his family. And even then, she'd be shocked by the twists and turns the book took.

They arrived at the center, and Chloe gasped. It had been a while since she'd been out there. "Oh, Brandon, this is so beautiful. I can't believe how much they've gotten done."

"Everyone has worked really hard. I'm pretty impressed with my brothers."

"And you," she pointed out. "I see a lot of lights going."

The main lodge was grand, standing about three stories high with huge windows and doors. It was majestic, but they'd also managed to make it appear inviting. It was this massive center that looked like a cottage in the woods. She was beyond impressed with the architectural design by her best friend Sarah and Brandon's brother Noah.

"Yes, we've been right behind Noah every step of the way, getting everything wired. We want this fully functional within a year. We want this to truly be the standard for veterans care from here on out."

"I hope so. I think there's been a change in recent years where people realize these men and women who serve and get hurt or go through emotional trauma need and deserve help for giving us the privilege of freedom. Some countries don't allow citizens to live a life of freedom. It always amazes me when I see people out protesting soldiers, when the only reason they can protest is because of those soldiers. Can you imagine how scary a world it would be without protection?"

"I don't have to imagine it. When I was in the military, I spent time in countries where you absolutely didn't turn your back on anyone. I was also horrified at seeing women with their heads down being openly beaten. There were no rights for the average citizen. It was sickening." He paused as he entered a code so they could walk inside the empty lodge. "And I don't think most people protest the soldiers; they usually protest the wars," he said.

"I don't like war," she told him.

He shook his head. "No one likes war. There are those that think some are war hungry, but it isn't about that. It's about protecting our rights and trying to help oppressed people find a voice. But anyone can turn anything into what they want it to be with a few choice words on a news channel. As long as that's happening, these men and women will continue to get disrespect. Once a soldier, always a soldier. It's a brotherhood that we will always defend and respect. And those people that spit on us can do so because that's their right as free citizens. They wouldn't want to see a world without soldiers, though—that's for dang sure."

"Yeah, it always breaks my heart when I see disrespect for anyone who serves, such as soldiers, cops, firefighters, and others. I know there are bad apples in every profession, but I also know that the majority of people who serve do it because it's who they are. It's certainly not for the pay," she said with a roll of her eyes.

"I wish they'd get paid more, but on the other hand, I think more people would do it for the money instead of because it's a calling, so maybe that's why the money is so low," he said.

"That's a good point," she told him. "But maybe a little bit more money wouldn't be such a bad thing."

He nodded.

"I've always wondered that when it comes to preachers, too," she added. "If they're paid to do their job, what happens if they lose their faith? Do they keep doing it for the check, or do they quit?"

"Your mind really does wander," he said with a laugh. "I don't know a lot about preachers, as it's been a long time since I stepped inside a chapel, but I do know they aren't paid much. I don't think any of them would do it for the money."

She laughed with him. "I guess you make a good point."

They finally reached the huge space that was ready for the kitchen. Catalogs and tables were set up, just waiting for her to get her hands on them.

"Oh, we should've done this so much sooner," she said as she moved to a portable table and picked up an appliance book. Every model a chef would drool over was in the thick catalog. She was instantly absorbed.

"I think I'm going to lose you for a while," Brandon said.

"Most definitely," she told him.

It was a good thing, she decided an hour later. Their talk had grown a bit depressing as they'd arrived at the center. She loved being a chef because it was a job that was sometimes frustrating, but it was also amazing and generally made people happy. You couldn't please everyone. That was for dang sure, but most who walked out of her restaurant were very happy and incredibly full. She didn't do those tiny servings that sent a person to Taco Bell after they'd eaten at her place. She didn't like overpriced meals. It was absolutely ridiculous for someone to have to spend a hundred dollars on a slab of steak. Yes, she was a great chef, and yes, she wanted the best for her patrons. But she didn't need to gouge them to prove she was the best. A great meal could be affordable for a night out on the town.

She and Brandon spent two hours poring through the catalogs and circling what they needed. She had already spent some time online, so it wasn't hard to make her final decisions. She had the measurements of the kitchen, and she knew exactly how she could fit everything she needed.

"With multiple ovens, we can even have cooking classes as one more activity for the veterans. Do you know how many people don't know how to cook a simple meal?" she said, absolutely horrified at the thought.

Brandon squirmed in front of her, and she laughed. "I knew you didn't know how to cook. Where did you get our dinner from?" she demanded.

He laughed loudly as he leaned back in his chair. "I'll never admit to anything," he said, still laughing.

She decided to let him get away with his small deception. Everyone in life had to have their secrets. As long as it didn't hurt anyone, then there was nothing wrong with it. But she'd guess it was Bianca's in a heartbeat.

"We'd better get going. We have a half-hour walk home, and it appears as if the snow is falling down even faster now. We might turn into snowmen," he warned.

Chloe looked up from the books with reluctance. She didn't want to leave. Now that they were there, she was more excited than ever for the project. She hoped they could get the appliances quickly and get the counters installed. She wanted to be the first to test out this fantastic kitchen.

"Okay, but I want to come back tomorrow. Do you think we can rush order the appliances?"

Brandon laughed again. "I think there's nothing that can't be rushed when it's a Joseph Anderson project," he assured her.

"Good." She stood and slipped her warm boots and jacket back on. She loved her boots but absolutely couldn't wear them inside. She'd have sweat pouring down her entire body if she did. But they were great in the snow.

They moved outside, and she lifted up her face to feel the soft flakes of snow fall against her cheeks. She absolutely loved it.

"We need to get you home," he said again.

"I need just a few more minutes," she told him. "This will disappear as quickly as it starts, and I absolutely love it."

When she finally made eye contact with him, the heat in his eyes betrayed how cold it was outside. He was gazing at her, not seeming to be paying any attention to the snow at all. She felt her stomach instantly stir as he wrapped his arms around her.

There was zero protest from her as he leaned forward and his lips finally connected with hers. The second they were pressed together, something magical happened, and both of them lost all control. It was like that every single time. She wondered if it was because she'd been fighting it or because their connection was truly that strong.

His tongue was firm and wet against her lips. She darted hers out and tasted the salt and sugar of his mouth. He responded by pulling her more tightly against him as he traced the contours of her mouth. She was wishing the thick layers of clothing weren't between them, because she wanted to feel and taste his skin. She clung to his shoulders as he tugged on her lower back, bringing them as close together as their clothes would allow.

He moved his fingers through the silky strands of her hair while he deepened the kiss, slipping his tongue in and out of the warm recesses of her mouth, tasting her . . . making her lose all control over her own body. She was instantly ready for him to claim her and wished he'd started the kiss somewhere a whole lot warmer.

When he pulled back, she gave a little moan of protest. He chuckled, and she slowly opened her eyes. She didn't feel the cold anymore. Her body was on fire. But the longer they stood there gazing at each other, the more she realized where they were. The snow was falling, and they were getting covered.

"I have impeccable timing of where I kiss you," he said before bending and giving her one more quick kiss, then pulling back before they sank into one another again.

"Yes, you do," she said. Finally, she pulled back and looked at the route ahead of them. Their footprints from their walk there were almost covered. "I guess we should get going before we have to call for a ride."

"I can do that if you're cold," he told her.

"Nope. Not cold at all at the moment. A good walk is just what the doctor is ordering."

She moved away from him, and he took her hand before she started down the steps. She didn't stop him. She liked having her arm through the crook of his elbow or her fingers twined in between his. Maybe this was becoming a relationship. And maybe the two of them didn't need to label it. That sounded pretty dang good to her.

"I want a real date," he said when they were halfway home. She tripped a bit, but he kept her on her feet. They walked a few more steps before she said anything.

"What do you mean?" she finally said.

"Just what I said. I want a real date where I'm picking you up and you know it's a date."

His voice was stubborn, as if he expected her to protest. She found she didn't want to. She wasn't sure why not, but maybe the fight truly was going out of her.

"Okay," she said.

Now it was his turn for a misstep. That made her smile. She didn't add anything, and they went a few more steps before he said more.

"Then it's a date the day after tomorrow. This Friday."

"Okay, this Friday."

That was Christmas Eve Eve. She decided not to point that out. It didn't mean anything. If it wasn't Christmas Eve or Christmas Day, then it was just another day.

They arrived home, and she found herself highly disappointed when he didn't give her one more kiss. Maybe he knew if he did, they'd go inside again. That wasn't necessarily a bad thing, but then again, they were going on their first official date in two days. Maybe he wanted to wait until then.

She didn't stop smiling that night.

CHAPTER EIGHTEEN

Brooke and Sarah were grinning as Chloe shifted uncomfortably in her room. She was trying to play it cool, but they were her besties, and they were seeing right past her facade. She knew better, but she wasn't going down without a fight—a really good fight.

"You're going to spill your guts," Brooke said with an evil laugh.

"I need better friends," Chloe said with a chuckle.

"Well, you're stuck with us, so I don't see that happening anytime soon," Sarah said, not affected by those words. They all knew they were a joke. Friendships didn't get any better than theirs.

She'd learned young to be smart in her word choices with these two women. They all had. They loved each other fiercely, but that didn't mean they weren't going to push and push to get the information they wanted. Sometimes it was worse than getting a tooth pulled.

"You guys have been hanging around more than usual lately. But today, you storm in and demand I tell you a story. I've got none to tell," Chloe said. She didn't know what to say, anyway. It wasn't as if she knew what exactly was happening with Brandon. It was up and down and all over the place. In short, it was a hot mess.

"All I know is Brandon's smiling more than usual, and that's saying a lot since he always wears a smile. But it's different lately. He comes in and sees Finn, and he's all gooey and romantic. You've put him under a spell," Brooke said with a laugh.

"I can't control what kind of mood Brandon's in," Chloe said. She knew they were going to keep pushing, so she didn't know why she was fighting it so hard. Maybe because Brandon was their brother-in-law, and she was afraid of doing anything that might risk their friendship.

Maybe also because she'd told Brandon in no uncertain terms that nothing was going to happen between the two of them. She was failing on all counts.

Sarah looked around Chloe's room and grinned as she rose up and started sniffing around. Chloe wanted to stop her but didn't want to be suspicious, so she acted as if she didn't care. Sarah found the hidden bag in her closet.

"Why do you have a Victoria's Secret bag hidden in here with . . ." She paused as she reached inside and pulled out some lacy black lingerie. Chloe blushed in spite of herself as her friend gave her a knowing smile.

"We all shop there," Chloe said as she shifted on her feet.

"Yeah, when we want to do the badunkadunk," Brooke said with a laugh.

Chloe couldn't help it. She burst out laughing at the word they'd been using since they were kids to describe anything to do with sex.

"You two are terrible. Are your sex lives truly so boring that you have to be focused on mine?" she asked.

The words didn't offend her friends in the least. They both laughed. "I'll go into full-on detail of how amazing my sex life has been from the second I met Finn," Brooke said with a happy sigh.

"Oh, yes, I couldn't agree more. Noah makes me tingle even thinking about getting naked with him," Sarah agreed.

It must have been genetic, because Brandon was the best lover she'd ever had. She hadn't been able to even think about doing the act with anyone since him. He'd utterly ruined her. Sex hadn't been a need she'd felt had to be sated before him. It had been a natural progression in a relationship, but it hadn't been something she'd craved all too often.

Then she'd met Brandon. Now it was all she seemed to think about.

"Okay, I like Brandon. I like sex with Brandon. As a matter of fact, he makes it difficult to think of anything other than him. But this is temporary. This is hormones on overdrive," she said with a sigh.

She was putting on her makeup very carefully. She didn't want so much on that she looked as if she was trying too hard, but not so little that the shadows under her eyes were showing. It was even more difficult to get ready with two pairs of knowing eyes on her while she did it.

"Finally!" Brooke practically shouted. "Admitting the behavior is the first step to recovery."

"We're so proud of you for accepting the inevitable," Sarah piped in.

"There's nothing inevitable about being with Brandon. We're having some fun. When this all settles down, hopefully we can still be in the same room without it being awkward; otherwise it'll make family events uncomfortable for everyone."

"Maybe it will lead to more," Brooke pointed out.

"And it probably won't," Chloe told her. Then she grew serious. "I can't risk anything affecting what the three of us have together."

Her friends turned just as serious as they gazed at her. It was Sarah who spoke up first.

"Do you honestly think anything could ever affect what we have?" she asked. Chloe felt foolish, but there was a part of her that worried. She nodded slightly, and Sarah glared at her.

"I had the same doubts when I was falling for Noah. It's complicated. I know it is, but no man would ever come between us. Brandon might be our brother-in-law, but you're already our sister. If we had to hobble him, we'd do it," Sarah said.

That brought a smile back to Chloe's face. "I don't think there will need to be any hobbling," she assured her friends.

"Well, the offer is always on the table. I'm sure Finn and his other brothers would be slightly upset by it, but they'd also understand, because if Brandon did something terrible enough to need hobbling, they'd probably help. They love us, and therefore they love you. We'd never marry someone who didn't understand our friendship," Brooke assured her.

"You do have pretty fantastic husbands," Chloe admitted. "I always thought I'd dread the day we settled down, thinking that would make it impossible for us to have girls' time, but it hasn't affected us at all. If anything, you're both happier than I've ever seen you, and we get more time together as we mature."

"Then just tell us everything about him that makes you all tingly," Brooke demanded.

Chloe laughed again. "Fine. He's incredibly handsome, with the body of a Greek god." They sighed their agreement. An evil twinkle appeared in her eyes. "He's also a royal pain in the ass, too cocky for this small town, and the most stubborn human being I've ever met." She couldn't give them too much, or they'd start planning her wedding. She was in no way ready for that.

"Hmm, I think you're protesting a little too much. I think you say all those things to give yourself an out," Sarah said. "I remember doing that myself."

"Of course I want an out. I don't want to be in a relationship. That terrifies me."

"It's scary to let ourselves be that vulnerable," Brooke admitted. "But without pain, then we don't know how amazing joy really is."

"I thought the saying was something about being in pain meant you were still alive. I've always hated that saying," Chloe countered.

"Me too, but I see the benefit of it. Without some adversity in our lives, we can't appreciate the good," Sarah reminded her.

"I like him a lot. I truly do. But I've liked other men, too . . . or at least I would in the beginning. But after a few months those hormones calm down, and I go back to being my stubborn, independent self. With Brandon, I've felt things I've never felt before, but I know that in time, that will fade, and then it will all be a mess. I know wanting perfection is an impossible dream, but it's hard to change what I've been taught my entire life."

"You could settle for a boring man and have no drama, but then you wouldn't be lit on fire, either. I'd rather have burning passion and some drag-out fights than fall asleep every night at eight and wake up with a peck on the lips and a goodbye for the day. There should never be fighting on a daily basis in a relationship, but we should have passion and excitement. That's for dang sure," Brooke told her.

"Well, I've agreed to a real date with the man," Chloe finally admitted. She went to the closet and grabbed the pink and black bag. She'd given up. They'd figure it out, anyway. She had no idea where Brandon was planning on taking her, but this town sure as heck liked to gossip.

"We already know. We just wanted you to admit it," Brooke said.

"Of course you know. He told his brothers, didn't he?" Chloe said with another glare. "This was all just a game to get me to spill." She couldn't outwit these women, never had been able to do so.

"Yeah, we just like to help you come to the natural conclusions we've already come up with. I promise everything will be okay if you just go along with your gut," Sarah said.

"My gut is telling me to run fast and far. The man is too much alpha for me. This is probably going to go worse than I've been imagining."

"I don't think so. I think we're going to have another wedding soon. I do love a good party," Sarah said.

"Don't *even* start planning my wedding. I refuse to let a man put a ring on me. No way, no how."

"Want to make a bet about it?" Brooke asked.

Chloe almost said yes but then stopped herself. "There's no way I'm betting you guys, because then you'll do everything in your power to make it happen. I don't need you teaming up with Brandon to bring me down."

Brooke and Sarah laughed again, looking as if they were willing to sit there all day long and draw this out. There was no way she was letting that happen.

"I have an hour to finish getting ready, so you two need to scoot on out of here," she told them.

"We want to be here when he arrives," Sarah said with a pout.

"There's not a chance of that happening. I don't trust either one of you right now," Chloe told them.

"That hurts me deep inside," Brooke said with a big smile.

Chloe marched over to her bedroom door and held it open. "Begone with you. I promise to tell you about the date in as little detail as possible."

They rose. "You can fight us all you want, but you know we're going to drag the information out of you, so you might as well cave and just tell us everything right from the start," Sarah said.

"We'll see what happens," Chloe said.

She walked with her two besties to her front door to make sure they left. She loved spending time with them, but at this moment she needed to pull it together before her first official date with Brandon. Yes, they'd been out together, and yes, they'd slept together, but the two of them hadn't been on an actual date.

How strange was that?

She hugged her friends before firmly shutting the door behind them. She stood there and leaned on it for several moments. Maybe she should just cancel this entire evening. As soon as she had the thought, she pushed it away. That just wasn't going to happen.

She was too excited to see him. Instead, she marched up the stairs to finish getting ready. She was accepting the inevitable.

CHAPTER NINETEEN

How many outfit changes did a woman need to go through before she was truly satisfied with her look? For Chloe, apparently it was ten. And still, she wasn't fully satisfied with her choice.

She wanted to look nice, of course—she took pride in dressing well. But for this date she wanted to knock his socks off. It was strange for her to feel that way. She was trying to tell herself this wasn't going anywhere, but then she was worried about pleasing him. She wasn't even making sense to herself anymore.

She put on her favorite cream-colored Oscar de la Renta sleeveless wool crepe dress with a pencil skirt that had a slit high on her thigh. She had tried talking herself out of wearing the too-expensive dress, but it always made her feel like a million bucks. She added her metallic pointed pumps by Valentino Garavani, and her walk instantly changed.

It was the type of outfit that made you feel like an all-star when you walked in a room. She'd bought the outfit when she'd made her first real profit. If a person didn't reward themselves for doing well, what was the point in trying so hard?

With her sexy undergarments beneath and her hair and makeup complete, she was more than ready for her first official date with Brandon Anderson. Of course the man had more money than she'd ever dream of having, but that didn't make him better than her, and it didn't intimidate her at all.

Well, it might intimidate her slightly, according to her clothing choices, but money hadn't ever been that important to her. It was a necessary evil to survive in the world, but she took far more pride in earning her money than having it handed to her. Some of the girls she'd gone to school with had wanted to be nothing more than trophy wives. That was an utter nightmare to her.

She wanted to walk into her place of business and know it was hers, know it was successful because she'd made it that way. She was proud of all she'd done, and she planned on doing a heck of a lot more in her lifetime—man or no man.

She glanced in the mirror one last time. Her heart jumped when her doorbell rang. She took a calming breath before she moved purposely away from her full-length mirror. She'd checked herself two dozen times, and nothing was changing. She might have been slightly overdressed, but he was a guy and wouldn't have a clue about fashion or the thought she'd put into it. She could just say she'd thrown something together, not that she'd agonized over the decision for hours on end.

She had to blame her besties for her mania. If they hadn't gotten her all flustered as she'd been trying to get ready, she was sure she wouldn't be such a mess. Yes, it was much better to blame the two of them. That thought made her smile. They'd do the same to her if they had the opportunity.

She moved at a steady pace from her room and down the stairs toward her front door. She never had been one of those women to make a man wait on her. She could see the appeal of it, but it was tasteless to make someone wait just because you could. Sometimes life happened and there was no choice, but to do it on purpose was just downright rude.

She made it to her door and gave herself a couple of seconds to inhale some soothing deep breaths. She was truly acting like a girl on prom night. Brandon wasn't a blind date, and they weren't teenagers. They were both mature adults who'd interacted many times before. She needed to stop thinking of this night as having any significance at all. It was just another night in a long line of weeks and months and years to come.

Her utter fascination with Brandon Anderson was a mystery she'd given up on solving, but she could admit to herself she liked how he made her feel. She liked that he made her laugh and challenged her. She liked that he gave her butterflies in the pit of her stomach, she liked working with him, and she really liked being in his arms.

She was finally ready to open the door, so she smiled and undid her locks, then opened up, getting ready to get hit in the solar plexus at the sight of him. She wasn't disappointed.

He stood before her in a dark suit with a crisp white shirt beneath, the top two buttons undone. He was utterly breathtaking in his beauty. The man usually wore work jeans and a sweatshirt, but damn if he didn't clean up really nice. She was left speechless for several moments at the sight of him.

He just leaned there and smiled at her, and she desperately tried finding her voice. "I'll . . . uh . . . grab my coat and purse," she finally stuttered. She turned away, wanting to break the connection of their eyes. That was imperative if she wanted to keep her senses about her for the rest of the evening.

Apparently he had other plans entirely.

He stepped in after her, and as she turned back to face him before getting her coat on, his arms slid around her, and their faces were only inches apart. His smile faded as he gazed at her intensely.

"You're delicious," he said. Then before she could respond, he bent down and kissed her. It wasn't a *hello* kiss. It was a promise of passion and heat. She melted against him as she fell into his kiss, forgetting all about the fact they were supposed to leave the house. This was a good-enough date for her, she decided.

Just as she'd made that decision, though, he released her. She was slightly unsteady on her feet and grateful for the arm he kept around her as he reached up and brushed a strand of hair out of her face that had released during their passionate embrace.

"We have to get out of here now before I can't let you out in public," he whispered as he leaned down and gave her one more sweet kiss that had her sighing.

"What?" she asked, her voice husky and weak. She was his puppet in this moment.

"You look absolutely stunning—not that you don't every single day, but tonight you're making me hard and hot, and I want nothing more than to take you to bed. But I also desperately want a first date with you," he said. "You've left me in a quandary. We'd better run from this place."

Some women might have taken offense at his words, but they filled her with pride. She'd taken a lot of time with her appearance, and she'd wanted him to be pleased by it. Judging by his reaction, she saw he clearly was. She felt as if she were walking on clouds as she pulled from him, slipped on her jacket, threw the strap of her purse on her shoulder, and moved toward her door.

She loved that he held it open for her, then made sure it was securely locked before wrapping an arm behind her back and leading her down her pathway to his awaiting truck.

She knew Brandon could afford any vehicle he wanted, and she really loved that what he drove was a fully loaded Ford F-350 truck. It was for work and play. While it might have all the comforts a truck could offer, a lot of men with his type of wealth would be driving some luxury European sports car. She wasn't a huge fan of cars. She felt too vulnerable in them on the freeway. She drove one because she wasn't on the road much, and they were good on fuel, but she always felt better in something big with a lot of metal on it.

He helped her up inside, then jogged around to the driver's side and jumped in. The truck was warm and cozy and smelled like him.

She felt completely comfortable. This wasn't such a bad way to start off their night.

Brandon didn't break the silence between them as they began moving down the road, and she couldn't take it. She was afraid she was going to lean against the console between them and attack him if she didn't get her mind off of that kiss and sex with him.

"Where are we heading?" she asked.

"There's a place about thirty minutes away I really enjoy. Plus, it has the added benefit of probably not running into people we know," he told her. "I want you all to myself tonight. I don't want to make small talk with other people."

"That sounds good to me. I hate how gossip spreads faster than a swarm of bees in this town. It makes it hard to have any privacy," she told him.

"There are negatives and positives to a small town. The positives outweigh any of the bad, though. It's good to know your neighbors and to be there for one another when the going gets tough."

"You really don't have to worry about things being tough anymore," she said.

"You don't have to worry too much yourself. You have a successful business," he pointed out.

She laughed. "Are you a little touchy about the money situation?"

He sighed. She was wondering if talking was what they should be doing, because the more she got to know him, the more she liked him. That was a very dangerous road to go down.

He started to speak, then stopped and clenched his jaw. She reached out and touched his arm, feeling like that was what he needed right then. She wasn't sure why. He was facing forward, and she was more than aware of his chiseled jaw and high cheekbones. He'd been very lucky in the genetic lottery.

"I grew up very poor. But that didn't take away from an incredible childhood. Once my monster of a father passed away, all we had was love in our house. I wish so much you could've met my mother. She was the most amazing woman you'd ever get to know. She had strength and kindness in every bone of her body. The things she put up with over the years to keep her children safe were horrible. But she tried keeping it away from all of us. I have nothing but respect for her." He paused, but she knew he wasn't finished.

"There were times in my life I hated being poor, times I complained about it. But as I got older, I realized it was shaping me. Nothing was handed to me. Everything I wanted, I had to work dang hard for. That's something I truly appreciate now. When my brothers and I first found out we were one of those Andersons, at first I didn't want it. I knew it would cause major changes in my life—in all of our lives."

"Do you still feel that way?"

He finally turned and looked at her and smiled. "No. I always had an image in my head of what truly rich people were like. I mean, they're portrayed in the movies as utter snobs, and there's so much negative you see on social media with stars going crazy. I'd never met anyone to change my mind. That was until I met my uncle Joseph."

"Yeah, he's not what you'd expect," she said.

"No, not at all. He lives big, and he definitely likes his toys, but I watch as he gives billions of dollars away without any fanfare. Did you know he hasn't taken a single donation for this center?"

She blinked at him. "No, I didn't know that."

"Lots of money has poured in to help with it, as people love what he's doing, but he's forwarded all of that money into other veterans projects so they can get more help. He's footed this entire expense. And let me tell you—nothing about it has been done second rate."

"The appliances alone were a couple hundred thousand," she said with a gulp. Realizing one person was paying for it all made her shudder a bit. Maybe she should have been a bit more conservative on what she'd ordered. She couldn't have regrets, though, because she knew the joy the center was going to bring. And the kitchen was the heart of any home.

"He loves to give, and he's taught me a lot in the few short years I've known him. Yes, I have a lot of money in my bank account now, but it doesn't change my values or who I am. It just makes me want to be like him, to live up to this name he's made. I don't ever want to live off of a name. I want to do it on my own. I want to be like him."

"I can't believe I tried so hard to pass up working on this project. I'm even more grateful now to be a part of it," she told him.

"Me too. There was zero hesitation on my part. Not only do I get to work with my brothers and you and your besties and so many other people, but I get to be a part of something that I'm hoping will be the first in a long line of centers. I've done well in my career, and I'm set for life financially. I'm still young enough to make a difference in this world. I hope I can do it."

"I'm glad I'm helping you do that, even if it's just a small part," she said.

They stopped at a light, and he looked at her, the heat so intense it had her shifting in her seat as she had to fight not to lean into him.

"You being here and doing this with me is exactly the motivation I need. You've made a real impact in my life, Chloe." His words were spoken smoothly and reached her deep in her core. She believed him.

"You're putting a lot of pressure on me," she said, unsure why she was starting to panic.

"I know. I can't seem to stop myself. I've never felt about a woman the way I feel about you."

She could barely breathe. "What does that mean?"

"I don't know yet. I'm trying to figure it out. I think we both are. But at least we're being honest about it now. That's a start," he told her.

His gaze raked over her face before dropping to her cleavage and then down to her thigh, where the slit was showing more than it was covering. She was wondering if she was a genius or a fool for wearing the dress.

He'd opened his mouth to speak again when a car honked at them, breaking the intense connection between them. He grinned as he faced forward and put his foot on the gas. "Saved by the honk," he said with a chuckle.

She was trying to control her breathing as she squeezed her thighs together. She wondered when this intensity was going to dim. She wasn't sure she could take it if it never did. She couldn't concentrate when she was feeling this way. Maybe the two of them just needed to sneak off somewhere they could remain naked for a week straight. That would have to curb her appetite.

As he drove, he reached over and took her hand, clasping her fingers and running his thumb against the top of her hand. It wasn't doing anything to alleviate the tingles spreading out through her body.

Chloe was trying to remind herself she liked her life neat and tidy in a cozy little box. She went to work, hung out with friends and family, and went about her daily routine. Brandon had come in like a wrecking ball and had smashed her sweet little routine into a million pieces. She wasn't sure she'd ever go back to the way it had been before.

She attempted to pull her hand free, but he wasn't having any of that, so she gave up. She liked the warmth of his touch, and she'd already decided she was going to go with the flow this night. She wouldn't be wearing what she was if she didn't have plans for them to end up naked, anyway. So it confused her why she continued fighting with herself over the situation.

When he pulled up to a small restaurant that seemed to be in the middle of nowhere, she realized she'd been taking small little breaths. She was a bundle of nerves. There was a time in her life she'd liked that feeling on a date. This time it was just making her a mess.

Brandon jumped down from the truck, and she put some gloss on her lips as he opened her door. She took in a breath and tried to calm her nerves as he helped her down.

"I like that shimmer on your very kissable lips," he told her. It made her smile.

He slipped an arm around her waist, his fingers gently caressing her hip as he led her inside the small dimly lit restaurant. There wasn't a hostess and weren't many people inside. That could be a good or bad thing. They didn't have to interact with people, but maybe it was empty because the food was terrible. She wasn't sure she'd taste anything, anyway, so it really didn't matter.

He held out his arm, and she sat down at an intimate table in the corner, candlelight burning in the center, the aroma that of spring flowers. For a tiny place in the middle of nowhere, it was really very charming.

"Brandon, it's wonderful to see you again," a young waitress said with a smile. "And I see you've brought a woman this time," she added with a wink.

Chloe wasn't sure why the waitress's words pleased her so much, but they did. She liked that he hadn't brought a slew of women to this place. That meant it was theirs. It shouldn't matter to her, as this might be a first and last date, but for some reason it really did matter.

"It's good to see you, Jen. How's school going?"

"Blah. School bites," she said with a grin. "But I graduate in five months, and then my real adventures begin," she said.

"Don't grow up too quickly. You'll soon be wanting to turn back time," he told her.

She rolled her eyes. "That's what my dad says all the time. I think you guys are all just old and set in your ways," she assured him.

Brandon laughed. "I'm not that old, little girl," he said as he puffed out his chest. This made both Jen and Chloe laugh.

"I'm Jen," she said as she looked at Chloe. "I hope you can manage this guy. He can be a pain. Every time he comes in here, he asks about homework and boys. He's become an honorary uncle."

"That doesn't sound like such a bad thing," Chloe said with a real smile. She liked the kid. She was a sweet girl.

"Well, when you work at your mother's restaurant and have half a town of relatives, it makes it hard to get into trouble," Jen said. "Add my honorary family members, and I'll never get to do anything fun." Though she was saying it like a complaint, Chloe could see real affection in the girl's eyes as she talked about all the meddlers in her life.

"I'd love to have a messy, meddling family surrounding me," Chloe told her.

Jen leaned down and spoke in a mock whisper. "I love it, too, but I can't let them know that." This made all of them laugh again. "Okay, I'd better work before the boss comes running. What would you guys like to drink?"

Brandon ordered a nice white wine, which was her favorite, and appetizers. She wasn't paying much attention. She was trying to look at her menu as Jen moved away, but her mind was spinning. Brandon surprised her often, and tonight was just another example of that. He really was a good man. Was she really going to walk away from him and not give it even a little chance? She was beginning to hope she wouldn't do that.

There was a small piano in the back corner of the room, and as their apps were set before them, someone sat down at it and began playing Christmas music, reminding her that the holiday was two days away. It was easy to forget when you weren't surrounded by family or children. There were times she wouldn't have celebrated it at all if it hadn't been for her friends. Her parents were wonderful. She loved them a lot, but they weren't that messy, emotional family she'd thought would be so great to have one day. But it was better than having horrible, abusive parents. She needed to be grateful for what she did have.

"Do you think those in the world that don't have family or relationships bother celebrating Christmas?" she asked as she put a stuffed mushroom on her plate and took a bite.

One taste, and she knew the restaurant wasn't lacking for business because of the food quality. It was delicious. But even as they sat there, the door opened several times, and the tables filled up. Maybe they'd just gotten there really early.

"I can't imagine not celebrating. Even all the years I've been single, I have. When I was in the military, we celebrated, too. But I guess there are some people who don't care," he said with a shrug. "That's pretty dang depressing to think about."

"If you really think about it, it's just another day. And the weeks leading up to it are usually stressful for a lot of people. You have gifts to buy and don't want to forget anyone. You have decorations to put up only to take down again, and there never seems to be enough time to get it all done," she told him.

He laughed. "I guess I've been pretty spoiled in that sense. My mother always did all the decorating when I was young. Then when I did get my own place, I didn't bother, because I knew I was going home for the holidays. As for buying presents, I haven't really done a lot of that, either. If I see something cool throughout the year for a sibling, I'll grab it and put it away until the holidays, but I don't go out looking for a gift," he said with a shrug.

"I love buying gifts, but I don't have a lot of people to get them for. I do know lots of people who have twenty or more gifts they have to get. Not only does that hurt the wallet, but then there's the stress of getting what people like."

"If they don't like it, then tough. It's a gift and should be appreciated no matter what it is," he said.

"What's the best gift you've ever received?"

He leaned back as he thought about it. "I don't know," he said after a bit.

"My best gift ever was a coffee cup," she said.

He laughed. "A coffee cup?" he questioned. "That seems like kind of a lame gift. We all have a hundred of them in our cupboard, even if we are a confirmed bachelor."

She laughed. "First of all, a coffee cup is never a lame gift, no matter what it is. I love quotes, so I love funny and deep messages on my cups. I drink at least three a day, so I can have lots of mugs to smile at as I drink," she said. "But I'm getting off subject. This wasn't just any cup—it was a special one."

"Oh, please tell me what made this coffee cup so special," he insisted.

"I take my time drinking coffee. Sometimes I will drink a cup in ten minutes, but sometimes it'll take me a couple of hours. I just like having it there and sipping on it once in a while," she said.

"Okay, strange, but to each their own," he said.

She laughed. "So because I take so long, I normally have to reheat it several times before I finish a cup. So Brooke noticed that I do this all the time, and one day she showed up with a 'just because' gift and set it on my table. I opened it, and it was a teal YETI cup. She'd noticed I always heated my coffee, so she got me one of those cups that keeps your drink hot or cold for hours. It's the gifts that show a person really knows you that matter the most," she finished.

He smiled. "Okay, I guess I concede that a coffee cup is a pretty great gift," he told her as he reached across the table and squeezed her hand. She smiled back at him, in awe of how easy it was to talk to him, to share and be intimate.

"I love this place. I'm glad we came here," she said, not wanting to sit there in silence. It was too intimate.

"Yeah, I've been coming here for years. I usually come with one of my siblings, but I've had many lunches here, too, in the middle of a workday."

"I thought for sure we'd end up in some ritzy place in downtown Seattle," she said with a wrinkle of her nose.

"Not my style," he told her. "And not yours, either. I know you more than you realize," he assured her.

That sent a shiver down her spine she didn't want to feel. She couldn't help it when she was with this man, though.

"I might like it," she said.

He laughed. "You'd be stubborn enough to go to a place like that just to prove me wrong. Maybe I'll have to take the challenge and take you to one—maybe on your fifth or sixth date."

She couldn't wipe the smile from her face. "Do you really think you'll get me out on a fifth or sixth date? I'm not sure there will be a second." The sting of her words weren't so bad when she was grinning at him.

They hadn't even received their main course yet, and the two of them had finished an entire bottle of wine while talking. Jen dropped off another, and though Chloe knew she probably shouldn't have more, she accepted a refill. It was really good wine. And white did have a lower alcohol percentage than red, she assured herself.

"I don't think I'm going to let you get away," he said after a bit. There was a teasing note in his voice but a seriousness in his eyes that took her breath away. "Besides, I'm pretty irresistible," he added. "You'll beg me to date you."

"I'm sure you have many women begging you for dates," she said, not sure how she felt about that scenario. "You're handsome, which you already know; have a pouty mouth you use to full advantage; and the most flirtatious eyes I've ever seen. You know your appeal. You and your brothers all know your magnetism."

Brandon gaped at her for a bit before he laughed loud and mirthfully. She sat there unable to stop her own smile. His joy was infectious.

"I'm not exactly arrogant, but I know I don't look as if I've been hit by a train," he admitted. "But your beauty outshines me any day of the week," he told her. His eyes drifted over her face and lower. She felt as if he were caressing her. The dress wouldn't hide much, so she shifted as she felt her nipples harden and ache for his touch. The man had power even when he wasn't touching her.

"I forgot to add you're a smooth talker," she said, her voice slightly husky.

"It's not smooth when it's true," he said.

Luckily Jen brought their food over right at that moment. Chloe was more than happy to have the conversation interrupted. She'd begun almost joking, but there was truth in her words. Most jokes had a bit of truth in them. Not all, but most. And when she was as high strung as she was at the moment, she needed something to save her.

Their meal was delicious, and their talk was lighthearted as they ate, drank, and chatted about easy things. It was probably the nicest night she'd had in a long time. The woman playing the piano was setting the mood for the place that was now packed, and Chloe was glad she'd come out with Brandon.

It wasn't going to be good for her mental health being in this intimate setting with him, but maybe her spirit needed it. She was a woman, and there were desires only a man could fill. Maybe there were things in her life only Brandon could fill. That was a scary and humbling thought.

Jen came back and cleared their plates, and Brandon whispered something in the girl's ear. She grinned big before slipping away.

"What was that all about?" she asked.

He just smiled as he stood up and held out a hand.

"What are you doing?" she said more insistently.

"Trust me," he said.

She realized as he held out his hand and beckoned her with his eyes that she did trust him. She wasn't sure why, as she'd always believed trust was something that had to be earned over time, but she did trust this man. He hadn't done anything to her to prove she shouldn't.

She didn't say anything else as she gave him her hand and let him pull her to her feet. He moved the two of them over toward the piano just as the music changed to an intimate love song. The woman began singing in a low melodic voice that was made for lovers.

Brandon cradled her close, and she laid her head against his chest, the rest of the world falling away as he smoothly turned her in the small space.

"I guess you had Jen put in a request," she said with a sigh.

Brandon let go of her hand and cradled both of his behind her back. She lifted hers and put them behind his neck, allowing her fingers to rub against his hot skin and up into his hair.

They were quiet for the first song and kept dancing along to the next. A few other patrons joined in, each couple in their own little world. Chloe was so content at the moment she didn't understand why she'd been fighting Brandon as long as she had. Maybe it had been stubbornness and maybe self-preservation. Whatever it was, she'd lost the battle—at least for now.

"For such a class clown, you have some very smooth dance moves, Brandon," she told him in a whisper against his neck that made a shudder pass through his body, which made her feel feminine and powerful.

"I enjoy the feel of you in my arms, your sweet curves pressing against me. Dancing is a prelude to sex, you know, and obviously we've never had any trouble in that department."

As soon as the words were out of his mouth, she was wishing they were alone, where they could strip away their clothes and finish this dance horizontally. He leaned in and pressed a soft kiss to her mouth. She sighed in bliss.

He pressed harder against her lower back as he wiggled his hips, and she felt his hard arousal pushing into her. The ache she'd been feeling the entire night went into the danger zone. She wanted this man so much she couldn't function without him inside her.

His hands slid over the back of her dress, dipping dangerously low as their swaying slowed. Their eyes were locked together, and they were speaking a lot of words without a single sound being uttered.

He leaned down again, this time his tongue softly dancing over her bottom lip before he connected their mouths again. Her moan was swallowed by him as she pressed closer, needing him, needing her ache sated.

When he pulled back, she was a puddle at his feet. She knew she was only still standing because he was holding her up. Without his strength, she wasn't sure she'd make it out of the restaurant.

"I need you, Brandon. Take me home," she said. This time it was his eyes that widened. They'd both known where this night would end, but the fact that she was being so wanton was obviously a turn-on for him. Good. She wanted him as hot and bothered as she was.

"I'm going to take you right here on this dance floor if we don't leave now," he said, his voice choked and filled with need. She smiled as she licked her lip and ground her hips against his one more time. He groaned.

"You little minx," he whispered before leaning down and kissing her hard and fast. She smiled in pure satisfaction.

"Let's go," she said.

He pulled away from her and took her hand. They moved quickly back to their table, where their check was waiting. He glanced at it, then pulled out his wallet and grabbed a wad of cash. He slipped it inside, then moved swiftly to the door without bothering with any goodbyes.

They practically ran to his truck, where he kissed her the way she'd wanted to be kissed all night, with her back pressed against the metal door. She moaned her displeasure when he pulled away, and he looked pained.

"Let me get you home before I take you in the back seat," he growled. She smiled at him, thinking it wasn't such a bad idea to climb in the back. She wasn't sure she'd make it all the way home. It was thirty minutes. That was a long time when your body was on fire.

Brandon didn't give her the choice, though, just opened the door and practically shoved her up inside. She got a wicked smile on her lips as he entered the driver's side. Then she climbed over the console and straddled him.

Chapter Twenty

Brandon didn't even try to stop Chloe as she landed in his lap. Her dress was hiked up over her hips, leaving his most favorite place on her body hidden by only a tiny scrap of silk. She ground her hips down and pressed against his painful arousal as she clasped his face in her hands.

Her head descended, and she kissed him with all the fevered passion they were both feeling. He was about to undo his pants and take her right there, not giving a damn who walked by the two of them.

When she pulled back and buried her head in his neck, her lips tickling his skin, he shuddered again. "I'm barely keeping it together here, Chloe," he warned her as his hand slid between their bodies, and he cupped one of her luscious breasts. She wasn't wearing a bra, and that made him want to tear away her dress and have a taste.

He was seriously regretting his choice of restaurants. It was a great location, but it was also a half hour from his house. He wasn't sure he'd make the long drive.

"I don't want you to hold it together," she told him.

"There are people all around us," he warned. But he was losing this battle with her. She could do whatever she wanted to do.

"We're in the back corner. It's dark." She paused, and he held his breath. "And I'm wet and want you inside me."

That was it. He lost it. After reaching down, he tugged on the silk strap of her panties, and they ripped away. She was undoing his pants at the same time. He wanted her dress torn away, but in the chance someone did walk by, he didn't want her exposed, so he left it in place.

He sprung free from his pants, grateful he was wearing suit pants instead of jeans. They were softer and easier to pull away. Placing his hands on her hips, he lifted her up, then settled her back down onto his throbbing erection.

"Holy hell!" he growled. "You're so damn wet!" He almost lost it as he buried himself within her.

"I've been turned on all night," she said with a moan as she sucked on his neck and groaned at the pleasure of them being connected.

She began to move, slowly swirling her hips as she lifted up and down and did a little circle thing that was making his head spin. She leaned lower and bit his shoulder, muffling a scream.

"I'm losing it," he said as he held her close.

"Yes! Let go," she demanded. She whirled her hips again, then cried out against his shoulder as her insides clutched him over and over again.

He steadied her hips and thrust up into her a couple more times, then threw his head back with a groan as he released deep inside her. They sat there together shuddering as they shook in pleasure.

"That was just to get us home," he said, his voice gruff and his body only partially sated.

"I agree. I want so much more."

She climbed from him, and he instantly felt empty. She reached into the glove box for a napkin and cleaned up as best she could inside the truck as he pulled up his pants, not bothering to button them. They were coming off again the second they walked in the door of his house. He planned on making her come again and again, all night and the next day.

After turning on the truck, he slammed his foot into the gas pedal, determined to make it home in half the time it had taken them to get to the restaurant. He made the mistake of looking over at her when they came to a stoplight, and she had such a look of lust on her face he felt himself hardening all over again.

Their eyes met, and she licked her lips, making him groan. She leaned over the divide between them and ran her tongue along his ear before whispering, "I want more."

"What is going on with this traffic?" he thundered as he tried getting around some vehicles.

She sat back in her seat and giggled. "It is the day before Christmas Eve," she told him.

"Which means they should be home wrapping, not clogging up the streets." He was losing it and was sure someday he'd see the humor in it, but at the moment he just wanted her home. They'd never go out to eat again—just stay in, where he could get her to his bed as fast as humanly possible.

"I wonder how many other people are on the road right now, their bodies hurting as they try to find the nearest bed," she said as she wiggled on the seat next to him. "I'm hurting, I want you so bad."

"If anyone near us was this achy, they sure as heck wouldn't be standing still in the middle of the road," he disagreed.

"Maybe they just did what we did," she suggested with a smile as she reached over and ran her finger from his chin, down his chest, and over his abs, then circled his pulsing flesh. He jumped.

"We might be finding a dark alley if you don't stop doing that," he threatened.

"Promises, promises," she said with a wicked laugh. She squeezed him for a moment before sitting back in her seat and moaning as she ran her hands up from her stomach and over her luscious breasts.

He was losing it—and fast. If they hadn't had their time at the parking lot, he might've come in his pants. She turned him on that much.

They made it out onto a long stretch of road, and the traffic magically parted. Thankfully she stopped trying to seduce him before they ended up in a car crash. It was still the longest drive of his damn life.

When they reached Cranston, he turned a corner, practically on two wheels as he screeched to the front of Chloe's place. He'd been meaning to go to his, but hers was about a minute or two closer, and with the way he was feeling, that was an eternity.

He didn't even look at her as he jumped down from his truck and ran to her side of the vehicle. She had just gotten her seat belt undone when he wrenched the door open and pulled her out, taking her into his arms and kissing her hard.

She staggered back when he released her, and then he took her hand and led her up the walkway to her house. "Dig the keys out while we're moving," he told her.

Her fingers trembled as she searched in her thankfully small hand-bag. She was shaking too much to undo the lock, so he took the keys and did it himself, noting his own fingers had a tremble to them.

They practically broke through the door, and he barely had the foresight to lock it before he was pulling her in for another kiss.

"Bedroom," she gasped when he released her lips.

He grabbed her in his arms and ran up the stairs to her room. And then he calmed. He was where he needed to be, and he wasn't going to rush it this time. He gently set her down on her feet and took a step back. If he touched her dress, he was surely going to destroy it, and he didn't want to do that. He wanted to see her in it again.

"Let's take a quick shower together," she said. "We got a bit messy in the truck." She licked her lips again as she reached behind her to undo her dress. He turned her and helped her out with that, exposing her back as he unzipped the fitted gown. He loved the dress, but he loved her in nothing at all even more.

Her panties had been destroyed, so as the dress fell, she was left standing in front of him in nothing but the sexy heels she wore. He wanted to leave those on, but she stepped out of them as she reached for his jacket.

He shrugged out of it, then allowed her to undo the buttons on his shirt. She ran her nails down his bare chest and circled his quivering abs.

"You make me feel so damn much," he growled as she pulled down his pants and underwear in one move. They stood before each other totally naked before he lifted her again and moved to the bathroom.

Her shower was small, but he got the water going while she pinned up the rest of her hair. They stepped inside and quickly washed each other, only adding to their desire and need to come together again.

They'd barely dried off before he was carrying her back to her bed, where he laid her down and took a moment to admire how sexy she looked, her body glistening with water droplets, her thighs spreading as she beckoned him to her.

"I want you buried in me right now, Brandon, not just your eyes on me," she whispered, her voice filled with need.

He joined her on the bed as he cupped her cheek and looked into her eyes. He could gaze at her all night and not get his fill of this woman. There was no doubt whatsoever that he was utterly under her spell.

"I've never been so glad in my life to know a person," he said. "I've fallen very hard for you, Chloe."

Her eyes widened at his words, and he saw a sheen spring up in them before she blinked and looked away. She didn't take long before looking at him again. "I'm falling for you, too," she finally admitted as his fingers moved from her face and traced their way down her breasts and stomach. She shook beneath him.

He leaned down and kissed her, this time soft and slow, appreciating how their mouths molded together, as if they'd been made for each other. Then he kissed his way over the side of her mouth, across her cheek, and to the smooth column of her neck.

"You taste so good," he murmured before he kissed across her collarbone and in between her breasts. She sighed beneath him as her body turned to jelly at his touch. He knew the power he had over her, just as he knew she was very aware of the power she held over him.

When that power was held by someone you trusted, though, it wasn't a threat. It was a comfort. He couldn't get enough of her, and he planned on getting her to admit she couldn't get enough of him, either.

He took one of her perfect nipples into his mouth and sucked and nibbled until she was begging for mercy. Then he moved to the other side and gave the same attention to the other. She was squirming beneath him as he reached down, placing his fingers between her spread thighs and slipping them into her wet heat.

"Yes, Brandon, I want more," she begged. He pushed another finger inside her as he sucked on her nipple harder, making her back arch off the bed as she tightened around him. It was taking all his control to keep from plunging inside her body. They fit together like a glove, and he wanted more.

He moved his lips down her stomach and sucked while her fingers plunged into his hair and kept him tight against her body. He circled her belly button before moving lower and inhaling her sweet scent.

Then he spread her legs even farther apart and buried his face between her thighs, kissing her intimately in his favorite place. She screamed as his tongue circled her flesh, dipping in and out and circling her most sensitive area.

He sucked the ball of nerves into his mouth and flicked his tongue over it while grasping her hip and holding her steady. She cried out again as an orgasm washed over her.

While she was still shaking with her release, he climbed up her body and looked at her flushed face. Beautiful. She was absolutely beautiful.

He plunged inside her, and her eyes shot open as she squeezed him hard, her body still pulsing from her orgasm. He gritted his teeth as he began to move.

"Oh, Brandon, yes, yes, yes," she said, her words floating away as she grabbed his head and pulled him to her, their tongues crashing together, plunging in and out while their bodies did the same.

He moved slowly at first, drawing out the last orgasm before he began working on the next. Their moans mingled in the cool night air as their speed picked up. A sheen covered their bodies as they moved in perfect harmony together. He pushed in and pulled out over and over again, neither of them ever wanting it to end.

He thrust harder and harder, and she cried out as she let go again and tightened around him, her walls holding him, pulling him, bringing him so deep inside her they truly were one being.

He let go, buried deep. His mouth connected with hers as his release filled her. They collapsed together on the bed, their limbs tangled, their breathing ragged. It was a long time before he was able to move. A satisfied smile clung to her lips as she sighed. Her skin was flushed, and she looked like the angel she was.

"Thank you," he sighed as he pulled from her, and she groaned her displeasure at the separation.

"Oh, no, Brandon, thank you," she told him, her words barely audible.

"You can thank me again and again," he told her as he pulled her into the cradle of his arms and ran his hand up and down her back. She squirmed against him. He wasn't sure he'd ever get enough of her. No matter how many times they made love, he'd want more.

"I'm going to take a quick rest, and then I'm going to kiss and lick every inch of your body," he told her.

"Not if I do it to you first," she promised with a sigh.

He felt himself growing hard again.

They didn't sleep much that night.

CHAPTER
TWENTY-ONE

After waking up, Chloe lifted her arms and arched her back and groaned. She was sore—more sore than she'd ever been. There wasn't a place on her body that didn't feel the workout from the night before.

Though she ached, it was a good kind of ache. She and Brandon hadn't done much sleeping that night, but that didn't matter one little bit. She'd gladly give up all the sleep in the world to feel what he'd made her feel. She'd do it over and over again.

She could smell bacon, and her stomach rumbled. They'd gone to bed without dessert, and then they'd had a heck of a workout. She was hungrier than she'd been in a long time.

She didn't often go without enough food, not when cooking it was her life. However, she did often get home and not feel like cooking. Her staff would be horrified to know how many nights she'd had popcorn, chocolate-covered raisins, and wine for dinner.

Now, saying that, she was one heck of a great popcorn maker. There were no microwave sacks for her. She had an air popper, and she mixed in the perfect amount of butter and cheese seasoning to make your mouth water. If she wasn't on her feet so much during the day, she'd most likely weigh four hundred pounds. It would be worth it, too. There was nothing like buttery popcorn.

She was about to get up when she heard . . . singing. She sat up in bed and strained her ears. Luckily her home wasn't very big, so as Brandon moved about in her kitchen, his voice grew louder. She couldn't help but smile when he switched tunes and began singing "Frosty the Snowman."

The man was full of surprises, and it was just one more thing to like about him. He'd told her he didn't cook, yet he was currently in her kitchen making them something to eat while singing Christmas carols. She'd waited long enough to see him.

She climbed out of bed and threw on her satin robe, then quietly climbed down her stairs and leaned in the doorway to the kitchen. Brandon's back was to her, and she wore a big smile as she watched his shirtless back swaying as he flipped some hash browns. He was going all out, it appeared.

She stood there for at least a full minute before he turned, his beautiful eyes boring into hers. The smile he wore grew even wider, if that was possible, and she answered with one of her own.

He dropped the spatula and walked to her, throwing his arms around her and giving her a good-morning kiss that had her toes curling. When he finally pulled back, she was warm and tingly and thinking this was the only way to wake up.

"Good morning, beautiful. I was wondering if you were going to sleep all day," he said as he brushed her hair behind her ears before cupping her cheek. It was hard to turn away from him, but she did and looked at the clock over the stove.

"It's only seven thirty. I don't think that's sleeping the day away. Besides, we didn't get to sleep until at least three this morning," she pointed out.

"But you said you had to be at work by nine, so I was going to wake you in about five minutes."

Just as he spoke, her teakettle whistled, and her smile grew even more as she pulled away from his arms. "You're my hero," she muttered as she moved to it, where she found her favorite tea already waiting in a cup. He'd thought of everything this morning.

"I've been replaced by a cup of hot water," he said. "It's a sad day."

She poured the hot water and let the tea steep while she pulled out her honey and the creamer. She doctored her drink just the way she liked it before cupping it in both hands and inhaling.

"I do love a great cup of coffee, but tea in the morning is so much more soothing. Smell how wonderful this is," she said as she held it up to his nose.

"I have to admit it smells great," he told her.

With her cup in her hands, she moved to the breakfast bar and sat down, taking little sips while she watched him move back to the stove. It was difficult not to stare at how beautiful he was with his low-hanging sweats on . . . and nothing else. It didn't matter how much the two of them made love—she still wanted more.

It did take some restraint for her to not offer to help him as she watched him cook. But it truly was the thought that counted. Sure, she could make a gourmet breakfast, but he was cooking for her out of . . . she almost thought the word *love*. It was too soon for that. But he was doing it because he was *that* guy.

"Thank you for doing this," she said as he placed a plate in front of her. He'd made hash browns, over-medium eggs, bacon, and biscuits. She took a bite and was surprised how good it tasted. She'd always been a fan of diner food, and this was a perfect replica of a diner breakfast.

She grabbed her biscuit and slathered it in strawberry jelly and sighed. There was nothing better than a warm, buttery, jellied biscuit to start your day. Okay, making love to Brandon might've been slightly better than the biscuit, but if they started that again, she'd certainly be late for work, and she absolutely didn't have time for that on this day.

It was going to be busy from the second she walked in until she crawled out of there that night.

"I might get more into cooking if you give me private lessons," he told her as he sat next to her and began wolfing down his food. It appeared he'd worked up a bigger appetite than she had. Of course, he'd been doing a lot of thrusting. The thought made her giggle.

"What's so funny?" he asked.

"Nothing I'm willing to share," she told him. "And I might be able to arrange some cooking lessons."

He grinned at her, and before she was a quarter of the way through her plate, he was finished. He grabbed another biscuit and slathered it in goodness before eating it in two bites.

"I think I could eat everything in your fridge," he said with a chuckle. "I'm famished."

"We did get a workout," she told him. She ate about half of her food, then scooted the plate over to him. He didn't hesitate to finish it off for her.

"Yes, we did," he said, licking his lips. "The best workout ever. I plan on it happening again tonight," he warned.

Her stomach tingled. It was Christmas Eve. She should tell him tonight wasn't good. But she couldn't bring herself to do it.

"I have to do some cleaning when I close tonight, so it might not work out," she said instead.

"I'll come help you, and we'll get done twice as fast. Just tell me what time you close." He was buttering another biscuit. It was a good thing he'd made a double batch. She loved to make biscuits from scratch, but she also had a thing for the ones in a can and always kept them in her fridge. He'd found them.

She didn't hesitate to give him the time. She was enjoying herself too much to tell him not to come. Maybe something would come up, and if it did, she'd try not to be disappointed, but for now she was enjoying this too much to turn him down.

His phone rang, and he sighed as he looked at the caller ID. "I have to run. I promised my brother Noah I'd meet with him at the center. But I'll see you at four," he said. He answered the phone. "One second," he said. Then he pressed the mute button and grabbed her.

He gave her one heck of a kiss that nearly had her falling off her barstool before he let her go and ran from the room as he began speaking to Noah. She got up on wobbly legs and walked to her teakettle and refilled her cup.

She was moving slowly this morning, but that was okay. The night had been heaven, the morning just as good, and she had a feeling this night was going to be the best of all. Each moment with Brandon surprised and delighted her. She was really starting to get used to it.

CHAPTER TWENTY-TWO

Joseph sat at Chloe's bar and grinned while he sipped on a glass of her finest scotch and munched on some freshly baked blueberry scones. It was an odd combination, but the man would never be one to be placed in a category. That was for dang sure.

"You realize it's Christmas Eve, don't you?" Joseph asked her.

"Yes, I do. Why aren't you at home with your hordes of family members?" she asked.

"I had to do a little last-minute Christmas shopping," he said. "I was surprised to see you were open. I figured you'd be with that nephew of mine."

She smiled as she leaned over the counter and looked Joseph in the eyes. She was more comfortable with the man now, which shocked her. He certainly still intimidated her, but she now knew he was a good person no matter what his net worth was.

"You aren't matchmaking, are you, Joseph? I've been warned of your antics."

He spluttered and set his glass down as he gave her a firm look. She could see in that moment how he'd been such a fierce force to be reckoned with in the boardroom. She wouldn't admit she was intimidated, but she was.

"I'm offended," he said. "I'd never do anything against anyone's will."

She smiled. "But you might try to nudge people along?" she pushed.

He smiled as he lifted his drink again and took his time answering. "Let's just say that I sometimes see things others might miss," he conceded.

"And did you happen to see something between Brandon and myself?" She really wasn't sure where this brave new her was coming from. But she was feeling pretty good. She'd fought having anything personal to do with Brandon and had failed miserably, so she might as well go with it now.

"I'm pleading the Fifth," Joseph told her with a sly look in his eyes.

"Then I am, too," she assured him as she refilled his glass.

She was shocked when he laughed. "That's why I like you so much, Chloe. You're a spitfire, and I love it."

The praise was pretty amazing coming from a man like Joseph. "I can't sit here and chat all day. It is Christmas Eve, after all, and I have a lot to get done before I can leave."

He laughed. "I don't like holding people up."

"I don't think that bothers you one little bit," she told him.

"What are the two of you smiling about?" Sarah asked as she joined them, plopping into a chair next to Joseph. "I want a really, *really* strong mocha," she added. "It's been a killer day."

"We're smiling because it's Christmas Eve," Joseph told Sarah. "And why has it been a day?"

Chloe began making Sarah an eggnog mocha, her most popular order of the day, while Sarah sighed. "Noah has been secretive all week and leaving hints he wanted me out of the house, though not very good ones. I think he's making me something, and he's behind. Brooke wasn't feeling well, so I found her and did some shopping, but she's exhausted, and I still have a bunch of presents to wrap. Every year I think I'll be more organized, but it only seems to get worse as time goes on."

She thanked Chloe when her hot cup of coffee was set down in front of her.

"Maybe I should be grateful I've been here all day. It seems much less stressful and certainly calmer," Chloe said. "That *is*, when I'm not interrupted a dozen times." Her smile took away any sting to her words.

"You love us visiting, so don't try any guilt trips," Sarah said. "This is the best coffee I've ever had. Yummy."

"You should try some tea; it's healthier and calming," Chloe said as she sipped on her own cup. "And you look mighty jittery as it is. I'm a little worried about giving you more caffeine."

"I do love a good cup of tea with a ton of honey in it," Sarah said. "I'll have that next, with a blackberry scone."

"Coming right up," Chloe said.

Sarah and Joseph chatted while she made more drinks and grabbed pastries. With how many she'd been eating that day, she was going to be lucky if her pants buttoned by the end of the shift. And though she'd been on her feet for hours, her staff were incredible, and they were getting everything finished.

They had a very limited menu that day, as they used the week of Christmas to make to-go meals. It brought in a nice bonus flow of cash at the end of their year. Knowing the amount of work it took to prepare a full holiday meal, if she wasn't already a chef, she'd probably order it out like so many others were doing more and more each year.

The cost might've been a little high, but the savings on time made it totally affordable. She should've ordered the smallest package for herself to take home for Christmas, but by the time she was done cooking the stuff for a week straight, she was sick of looking at turkey and stuffing. She wasn't sure she could eat it again Christmas afternoon.

Now, the pastries were a whole different story. She could eat those day in and day out. She was really grateful for a fast metabolism. She'd probably die if she were forced to go on a keto diet. No bread, pasta, or potatoes was the cruelest form of torture, in her opinion.

Her bell chimed again, and she smiled as her mother walked in, looking beautiful in her red jacket and leather boots. She moved to the counter and sat beside Sarah.

"How are you, darling? I haven't seen you in forever," Genevieve said.

"Wonderful, Mrs. Hitman," Sarah said as she hopped off her stool and gave her a hug.

"That's fantastic," Genevieve said, then turned to her daughter. "I want your strongest, sweetest coffee. Merry Christmas."

"I thought you and Father were going to be on a plane today," Chloe said as she began making her mother a white mocha eggnog latte. It was extra sweet and extra decadent.

"Yes, yes, but there are delays as usual, so I wanted to swing by to see my only child before we head off to the sunshine." Chloe's parents had been heading to the Bahamas for Christmas since she'd gone off to college. They'd invited her every year, but she preferred to be in the cold for the holidays. She'd done one in the Bahamas and discovered it didn't feel like Christmas at all. She was so used to her parents being gone it didn't upset her at all.

"Why would you leave during Christmas?" Joseph asked.

"My husband and I get too restless without some sunshine. We definitely love this area, but we need to get away every few months, or we fear we'll wrinkle up and fade away," Genevieve said.

"I can't imagine being anywhere but here for Christmas," Joseph said. "But I do know many who like to get away."

"We try to talk Chloe into coming with us, but neither her father nor I have ever been big on the holidays, and Sarah and Brooke are as much family to her as her father and I, so we don't feel too guilty about it."

For the first time in her life, Chloe noticed that there did appear to be some guilt on her mother's face. This was the way it had always been, so she'd never questioned it. But maybe just because it had always been that way didn't mean it was the way she'd have to be. It also didn't mean she had to be upset with her mother or father. They loved her. She knew that. They just showed it in different ways than the Andersons did. Which way did she want to show love? Which did she feel was right? Had she been afraid to be in a relationship because she wasn't quite sure how a relationship was supposed to be?

These were all things she'd have to think long and hard about. But for this moment she just wanted her mother to have a beautiful Christmas, guilt-free.

"I know how much you love me, Mother. And I'm glad that you get to enjoy Christmas your way. I do have family I'm with every year, so there's no reason for you to feel guilt," Chloe said. She set her mother's coffee down, then walked over and gave her a hug.

"Thank you, Chloe," Genevieve said with a smile and what appeared to be a sheen of tears in her eyes. She turned away, and when she looked back, those tears were gone. Maybe Chloe had only imagined them.

Soon Joseph, Sarah, and her mother all left to get on with their days, and Chloe was sad to see them go. But then it allowed her to get back to work. Her staff were already moving one hundred miles per hour. Chloe really was thankful for all she had.

She wondered if she was getting a little bit more this holiday season—in the form of a six-foot-plus man with eyes and a body that made her fall into heaven.

Chapter Twenty-Three

Brandon almost didn't recognize himself as he strolled down the brightly decorated sidewalk, through the small town that would be his forever home, the town he and Chloe were making their own, where their families were, where their life would remain.

They hadn't slept much the night before, but he didn't care. He could live on sex alone, he'd decided. He'd loved having a nice breakfast with Chloe. He enjoyed a lot of things when it came to her.

Was it too soon for a marriage proposal? Yeah, probably. He'd scare the hell out of her if he pulled out a ring. That was the last thing he wanted to do.

Today was a busy day for her at work. It was almost all bakery items, but they were also doing a Christmas-dinner package, and a lot of people would be picking those up. She was closed on Christmas morning, of course.

Brandon whistled as he walked in and out of businesses, the owners cheerful as they got in their last-minute sales and handed out candy canes and Christmas wishes. There was a time he would've never thought such a simple, uneventful day could make him so happy. It was almost as if he'd slipped into an alternate universe. He used to feel a need for adventure. Now he was ready to settle down.

There was no work for his crew today, and he wasn't in a hurry, as he had hours to kill. He had a mission to find the perfect present for Chloe. He'd picked up a couple of items and was looking for that one thing to tie it all together. He needed it to be special, and he needed her to understand how he felt about her and that he knew her. He'd been more than clear that he wanted to be with her, but he was beginning to realize he wanted it to be forever.

Maybe it was the magic of the season—maybe it was his discovery that he was all-around happier with her in his life. Whatever it was, he wanted her by his side, and he had to make sure he proved himself worthy and stable, because she deserved that. She deserved the best, and she wasn't the type of woman to settle for anything less than that.

Brandon was far from perfect, but he'd been raised by a loving mother and with four siblings who had guided him through life, showing him what it meant to be a good man. He should buy them all thank-you gifts. It was odd how the love of a good woman could make a man a better person.

A smile permanently on his face, he stepped into another crowded shop and looked around. It was antiques. He didn't think there was anything in there he'd be looking for, but he wandered, anyway, and it wasn't long before he was stopped in his tracks. When you found the perfect gift, you just knew what you had.

Chloe had said her favorite gifts were the ones that showed a person knew her. Well, he was beginning to think he knew her quite well. Her passion was cooking—and, he hoped, lovemaking, now that the two of them had discovered the magic they could bring each other. But he'd watched as she'd designed the kitchen in the center, and he had a good idea of what would make her smile.

He gazed down at the case with his goofy smile in place. The shopkeeper stood behind the counter, and when he met her wise eyes, she was looking at him in a knowing manner that shook him even further. He'd always been an open book, but maybe it was becoming even easier to read him now.

"Can I have this gift wrapped, please?" Brandon asked, his voice slightly choked.

"This is why I love my store so much. There's magic in here when the right item is found," the woman said as she pulled the gift from the case and held it in her wrinkled hand.

"Yes, I believe I found exactly what I was looking for," Brandon told her. "Can you place these inside first?"

The woman took his items, then put his gift in a box and handed it to two high school kids sitting at a table, wrapping items. It took them about thirty minutes to get to his gift, and Brandon didn't let it out of his sight the entire time, too afraid of it being lost. He paid the shop owner and tucked his package away, then began walking to the restaurant.

It was closing time, and he wanted to be there to help. She was swamped, and he knew she wouldn't leave the cleanup to her crew to take care of on Christmas Eve. Brandon couldn't remember the last time he'd actually used cleaning supplies. He might be more of a hindrance to Chloe than a help, but wasn't it the thought that counted? He sure hoped so.

He entered through the front door as the last of Chloe's customers were gathering their items and wishing everyone a merry Christmas. The staff all looked exhausted, but they still wore smiles on their faces.

"Okay, crew, you did fantastic this year. There is no way this business would be even half as successful without all of you. There aren't words to express how grateful I am to you all," Chloe said as she spoke to the employees, who were all still smiling. "Now take your bonuses, grab your gifts, and get out of here to celebrate Christmas Eve with your families."

"We need to help clean up this mess," one young girl said as she looked around at the messy restaurant.

"Nope. Not today. Go home," Chloe said as she began passing out presents.

The rest of the crew didn't argue, and Brandon made his way to the counter and sat. Chloe smiled as she moved over to the coffee machine and began making a few shots.

"I need a triple," she said with a laugh. "What do you want, Brandon?"

"I can make it myself," he told her, feeling guilty having her do anything extra.

"There's no way I'm letting you handle my machine," she said with another laugh. She looked tired but happy. He could get used to seeing that expression every day for the rest of his life.

"I'll have an eggnog mocha, four shots," he told her. "And if all of the pastries haven't been cleared out, I wouldn't mind something to go with it," he added with a hopeful smile. He hadn't eaten since their breakfast together.

The doorbell rang, and Chloe groaned. "I forgot to lock it," she said in a bit of panic. Brandon didn't think she could refuse someone if they wanted a last-minute item. He sure as heck could, though. He'd turned to shoo them away, until he saw who it was.

"Please tell me you still have coffee," Brooke said with a sigh as she plopped down next to Brandon and dropped her bags to the floor. "I'm exhausted."

Brandon and Chloe laughed. "I'm sure it's been rough shopping all day," Chloe said with a smile and roll of her eyes.

"You wouldn't believe the mob out there. I thought shopping in our small town would be safer than Seattle. Boy was I wrong," Brooke said as Chloe continued making coffee. She knew what her bestie liked.

"You poor, poor thing," Chloe said.

"Why isn't your husband carrying bags for you?" Brandon asked.

Brooke laughed. "Because I needed to find him something. I've been terrible this year," Brooke told them.

"Well, get off your behind and go grab the tray of goodies I have stashed in the back," Chloe said.

Brooke didn't have to be told twice. She practically flew into the kitchen and came back with a large pile of sugary deliciousness. She set it on the counter, and Brandon's mouth watered at the sight. Chloe and Brooke took a stool on either side of him. Each of them snagged a doughnut and sighed in pleasure.

"There's nothing better than hot coffee and pastries," Chloe said with a sigh, a bit of sugar on the corner of her mouth. Brandon wanted to lick it off but barely managed to hold himself back, since they did have company now. He decided to focus on anything other than licking and kissing Chloe.

"You're very good to your crew," he told her.

"I couldn't run this business without them," Chloe said. She finished her doughnut and reached for another as she drank down large sips of coffee. "Most of the kids who work here are in their last couple years of high school. They're eager to earn a paycheck, and the customers love having them here."

"I've noticed teenagers in several of the businesses down the street," Brandon pointed out. "It's one of the things I love about this town."

"We do take care of each other here," Chloe said. "It's why I'm so in love with it."

"Yeah, I don't know why anyone would want to live in a city when they can have the closeness of a small community. Sometimes it's stifling, but most of the time it's safe and pleasant," Brooke added.

The three of them shared small talk while they drank their coffees and cleared off the platter filled with treats. Brandon found he was having a more perfect Christmas Eve than he could ever remember. It was because he was with the woman he loved, and he was no longer trying to protect himself from feeling those emotions of love and happiness.

"You really don't need to stick around for the cleaning. I'm only going to do what I have to tonight and then do a full top to bottom on the twenty-sixth," Chloe said as she stood and stretched.

"There's nowhere else I want to be," Brandon told her.

She looked over at him, and his heart beat a bit faster when he saw the one emotion in her eyes he hadn't realized he'd wanted to see so much. There was a look of love. Maybe, just maybe, they were getting closer to allowing themselves to feel the scary emotion.

She smiled at him, and Brooke laughed. "I'd offer to help, but since the two of you can't seem to stop making googly eyes at one another, I think you'd probably like me gone more than the help."

She finished off her third pastry, then grabbed her bags and said goodbye and headed to the door. Neither Chloe nor Brandon tried to stop her, and Brandon followed behind and locked it. He could hear her laughing as she moved down the street.

He turned and saw Chloe smiling at him.

Yep, this was about as perfect a day as he could have. And it was only halfway finished. He had tonight with this woman he wanted, and then maybe he'd have the rest of his life, too, if he was really lucky.

CHAPTER TWENTY-FOUR

There were so many advantages to living in a small town it would be hard for Chloe to name all of them. But at the moment one thing she appreciated was that her business wasn't too far from her home.

Though her feet ached and her back felt as if a sledgehammer had been pounding into it all day, she still liked the walk home so she could begin to let go of the stress of the day before she walked through her front door.

This walk was even more special because Brandon was by her side. He'd stayed at the restaurant for two hours straight, and she'd gotten so much more cleaned up than she'd expected. He'd been a huge help, and now she was bringing him home. For what? She didn't exactly know. But it was Christmas Eve, and the sun had gone down, the clouds were beginning to open, and small flakes of snow fell.

It was perfect, and for this moment she didn't want to feel sadness or worry. She wanted to take a walk with the man who was on her mind all the time and enjoy a beautiful holiday evening. Yes, her guard was coming down, but it was to be expected.

She'd just decided she was going to have to deal with the pain of it ending no matter what at this point, so she might as well appreciate the two of them together for now. She didn't want to be alone this holiday.

They didn't say much as they moved through the streets, the snow falling harder as they got closer to her home. She'd have to either lend him her car or give him a ride home later if the roads weren't too bad. That was something else she didn't want to think about.

They stepped up to her porch, and she pulled out her keys. He took them and unlocked the door, pushing it open so she could step inside first. It was such an antiquated gesture and still one she appreciated very much.

Though it was in the low thirties temperature-wise, Chloe felt warm and tingly on the inside. She shed her coat gratefully when the front door closed behind the two of them.

"Are you hungry?" she asked. They'd eaten a bunch of pastries and downed coffee, but that had been two hours earlier, before a ton of hard work. She was definitely feeling hungry. It was dinnertime, and she had a ham in the fridge she should throw in the oven for a special meal on this beautiful night. But she was exhausted as well.

"Let's just relax for a while. You've been on your feet all day," he said as he took her arm and led her to the living room. He pulled her to the couch and tucked her in close to his side as his fingers danced on her scalp, and she leaned against his chest, feeling at home.

"Don't you need to go to your parents' for the holiday?" she asked. She didn't want him to tell her he was leaving, but he had a wonderful family, and she was sure that was where he'd go. She wasn't his family, and it would be better for her to remember that. Of course, she'd been invited to hang out with Brooke and Sarah, but as their families grew, she'd felt like a third wheel at the holidays. They'd kick her butt for even thinking that thought, so she'd never dared to say it.

"I promised to be there tomorrow," he told her with a contented sigh.

"I hope the roads don't get too bad tonight," she said. "Where's your truck?"

He laughed. "It's still parked in front of your house. You're so done in you didn't see the huge thing."

"No, I totally missed it," she admitted. She wasn't sure if she was ever going to move from the spot she was in right at that moment.

"Well, my truck can get through pretty much anything, so we can get around town," he said. "We don't need to go anywhere tonight. This is too dang comfortable."

"I've always been freaked out driving in the snow. I don't think you'd have a problem with it in that beast of a vehicle."

Brandon chuckled before he lifted her, pulling her onto his lap and cupping her face as he looked into her eyes. She was so smitten with him.

"I plan on us having some fun winter adventures in that truck," he said, his voice growing husky. The exhaustion Chloe had been feeling quickly faded as desire took its place.

"I try not to make too many plans in advance," she said, forcing a smile to her lips. She didn't want to jinx what they were having right now.

"I have to think of the future," he said. "I've found that I'm growing a bit jealous of my siblings with their marriages and children. I'm beginning to realize the things I found important when I was younger aren't the same now. Making plans isn't a bad thing," he said, shocking her.

"I can't believe you're thinking of having kids," she said. Her womb jumped at the thought of kids with him. He wasn't saying he wanted them with her, but she couldn't help but imagine a beautiful little girl with his stunning eyes and intense gaze. What was wrong with her? She'd decided long ago she wasn't going to have the white picket fence and little ones running around.

It had to be the holidays—she tried convincing herself. There was nothing else it could be. It was that or the pure exhaustion of a very busy month.

"I've been thinking about a lot of things from the moment I met you," he told her as his fingers rubbed her cheek. Tears were fighting to escape her stinging eyes, but she pushed them away. This wasn't the time to fall apart, and this wasn't the night to think about what could be.

"You have to be careful saying things like that," she told him.

His hand slipped from her hair and ran down her back. Pleasure surged through her as she tried to focus on the conversation the two of them were having. But a great sex life wasn't one of their problems. She always went up in flames the moment he touched her.

"Why should I be careful? I'm saying what I feel," he told her, leaning closer and pressing a kiss to one corner of her mouth before moving across her lips and kissing the other side.

"Because I might forget we're not a couple," she said with more honesty than she cared to share.

"Let me see if I can make sure you forget," he said.

Brandon finally kissed her the way she wanted to be kissed, and Chloe realized she wanted to forget as much as he wanted her to. Wrapping her arms around Brandon, she held on tight while she kissed him back. This was three days in a row they'd been together, and she was moving dangerously into couple territory—and she didn't care.

Standing up with her in his arms, Brandon confidently moved through the house, never taking his lips from hers. She wanted exactly that. She was tired but not too tired to make love to him again.

He set her down in front of the bed, and the look in his eyes made her feel so beautiful and desired. She was shaking before him as he reached up and slowly began undoing the buttons on her shirt. When the blouse was open and his fingers lightly brushed her skin, she shook beneath his touch.

She reached beneath his shirt and ran her hands up the solid muscles of his stomach and chest, sighing at how good it felt to touch him. It didn't matter that they'd made love only a few hours earlier—it felt like it had been a month. That was how strong the need to touch him was. He stepped back a couple of inches and pulled the shirt over his head, tossing it into the dark recesses of her room.

They were still wearing too many clothes. But she also couldn't help but appreciate the beauty of touching and looking at one another. The rest of their clothes melted away, and he pulled her into his arms. She relished the heat radiating off him and the thickness of his arousal pressing against her stomach. She needed to lie down with him, feel the weight of his body atop hers.

"Bed," she murmured when he released her lips.

He smiled before kissing her again and then moved them and pushed back, both of them tumbling onto the top of the covers. They didn't need them. They were heating up each other's bodies just fine.

Chloe tugged against Brandon, not wanting an inch of air to separate them. She wanted it to be slow and beautiful, but with him so close, the urgency of her body began taking over. Her hands reached around him, her nails digging into the flesh of his back as she kissed him with hunger.

Brandon flipped them over, and she pushed her hips up. Yes. This was what she wanted. She felt the shake of his chest as she opened her eyes and saw him smiling. There was heat in his eyes, but there was something else there that almost terrified her. Could it be love?

"I want to taste you," he said before moving his lips down her jaw and kissing her throat in a delicious path to her trembling breasts.

Chloe gripped his shoulders as he slid down her body. His mouth latched onto her nipple, and she arched, the heat in her core becoming unbearable as desire ran through her.

Brandon lavished attention on her breasts before kissing his way down her stomach. He pushed open her thighs, and she felt his hot breath against her aching core. He opened her up and licked until she was begging for mercy.

She pleaded with him to take her, but he seemed to know when she was about to sink into dark bliss, and he moved places, drawing out her pleasure in an unending span of time.

"I need you, Brandon, please," she begged him, her voice shaking, her body wrecked.

Brandon climbed back up her body, and his eyes were wild with a passion that excited her even more. She wrapped her arms and legs around him as he positioned himself at her entrance.

"This will never end," he said.

Chloe wanted to argue, but he pushed forward, and the only sound that came from her lips was a cry of passion. He made love to her for hours and made her come many times before he pushed off her.

Chloe was barely even conscious when he shifted their bodies and tucked her into his arms beneath the covers. It was Christmas Eve. She allowed herself to take the gift he was giving her.

CHAPTER TWENTY-FIVE

Brandon woke up in the early dawn of Christmas morning and reached for Chloe. When he found nothing but her scent and empty air, he felt a surge of unease wash through him. She'd run away again. He'd thought they'd gotten past that.

But as he sat up in the comfortable bed, he caught the scent of fresh coffee and cinnamon and found his heartbeat slowing. She hadn't gone anywhere. She was preparing them a meal. He got up and took the world's shortest shower before throwing on his pants and nothing else. He was in too much of a hurry to find Chloe.

Stepping into her kitchen, he found her in a fluffy purple robe, pulling muffins from the oven. He walked over and pulled her into his arms the moment her hands were free.

"I missed you in bed this morning," he said before nuzzling her neck and inhaling her sweet scent. Each moment with her was a great one.

"You're in a good mood this morning," she said as she melted against him. It felt easy and right, as if they'd done this every day for years instead of days. He was kicking himself for the time they'd already wasted in the past couple of years. They could've been in a routine like this for a while. *But the timing had to be right,* he assured himself.

Far too soon, Chloe pulled from him, and the emptiness he felt as she let go was a new experience. Brandon was too stunned by the feeling to reach for her again. What was wrong with him? He'd never been this needy before. He didn't appreciate it one little bit. He moved over to the coffeepot and made himself a cup before snatching a muffin and going to the breakfast bar to sit.

"It's incredibly distracting to finish cooking when all of that beautiful body is in my kitchen . . . uncovered," Chloe said as she gazed at his chest. Pride filled him, and he felt himself puffing out a little. Damn, he liked how he was feeling.

"You can touch all you want, darling," he told her with a wink as he finished his muffin, then looked longingly at the pan, which was just out of reach.

Chloe laughed as she set the pan close to him, and he quickly reached in and grabbed another. "These are delicious."

"I've always liked to cook, from the time I was young. Of course, that was inevitable with parents that both worked in the food industry. That might have changed some kids from ever going into the same line of work. But I think it truly began for me because I noticed that people were always happy when they were in the kitchen. No matter what is happening in life, family and friends tend to gather in the kitchen over a cup of coffee, tea, and food. There's always food at any event—a wedding, birthday party, graduation, and even a funeral. I guess that's why I decided to have my own restaurant instead of joining with my dad. I wanted it to be unique and be my own," she said with a laugh.

"That's something I've never really thought about before, but you're absolutely right. No matter what's going on, food is normally involved, especially during the holidays."

He took his third muffin, and she laughed. "It's such a normal morning that it doesn't really feel like Christmas," she said.

"Why don't you have a tree?" he asked her. He couldn't believe he hadn't noticed sooner. Maybe because he'd been more interested in getting her to date him than worrying about the holidays.

"It's just me here. I usually spend it with Brooke and Sarah, so I haven't bothered with a messy tree in a long while," she told him.

"That breaks my heart. Next year we'll have a tree."

Her eyes widened at his words, and he could see she was beginning to panic. He wasn't going to give her time to do that. He got up and wrapped her in his arms, only giving her a second before he kissed her the way he'd wanted to from the moment he'd woken.

When he pulled back, she no longer looked panicked. She seemed very satisfied and dreamy. That was exactly how he liked her appearing. It made him smile. He could definitely be happy sweeping her off her feet over and over again.

"Merry Christmas, Chloe. I'm glad to be here with you," he said. The gift he'd gotten her was hidden in his truck. He'd have to slip something on unless he wanted the neighbors talking when he went out there to get it.

"Merry Christmas, Brandon," she replied. She seemed almost dreamy as she gazed at him. He loved big family Christmases and was looking forward to spending it with his brothers and their spouses . . . and with Chloe. There was no way he was letting her stay in her undecorated house on this magical day.

"I think it's time for your gift," he said, no longer able to wait. He was always eager to give a gift when he bought one. Probably because he didn't do it too often. He truly didn't like to give a gift just to give one.

"You didn't need to get me anything," she said, panic in her eyes again. He was guessing she hadn't gotten him something, and that was okay with him. She was the only gift he needed.

"Of course I did," he argued before he disappeared from the room. He decided to risk the neighbors talking and grabbed his truck keys to unlock the door. It was cold outside, and his bare feet were numb by the time he returned with the snowflake-paper-wrapped package.

"I didn't get anything for you," she said as she reluctantly accepted the box. She twisted it in her hands as she shifted on her feet.

"Yes, you did," he said. She looked at him with confusion. "You gave me you," he told her.

Tears brightened her eyes before she broke the connection of their gaze and looked down at the box. Finally she sat next to him as she carefully began undoing the wrapping. When she pulled the lid off the package, she looked at him with tears in her eyes.

It was an antique wooden tea box with a phoenix burned into it.

"Wow, Brandon. This is stunning," she said, her voice barely above a whisper as she turned it over in her hands. The date on the bottom said 1892. It was a true treasure. He was so glad he'd found it.

"I was looking for the perfect gift, and I found this in the antique shop down the road. I remember everything from our night of my brother's wedding and how you talked about always feeling the need to rise and be better," he said. "Nothing quite symbolizes that like a phoenix rising from the ashes. And of course, your love of tea made this the perfect gift." He pulled the antique case from the box and set it down on the counter.

"There were always so many expectations of me growing up. I had two perfect parents, and they always expected more from me. I realize now that I expected just as much of myself and others. I think with age, they are realizing we're perfect just as we are. I'm trying to realize that as well. I don't want to be so uptight I'm unwilling to change. I want to keep on rising, but because I want to, not because I have anything to prove," she said, tears streaming down her face.

"We can break free together," he told her, meaning every word.

He opened the lid to the box, and inside on a bed of tea bags was an infinity necklace embedded with diamonds. Chloe gasped as she looked at it. Then her face whipped around as she gazed at him.

"This is too much," she said, her words barely audible. "Especially when I didn't get you anything. I feel bad."

"Do you like the gift?" he asked.

"I absolutely love it," she assured him.

"Then it gives me pleasure. Please just take the next step with me to try this, to give it a go. We're obviously drawn to each other, so why don't we be true to ourselves?"

She gave him a watery smile as she nodded. "I think I'd like that," she said.

His heart burst it felt so full. "This is the best Christmas I've ever had," he said as he took the necklace from her and placed it around her neck. She lifted her hand and caressed the sparkling gift.

"Me too," she said. "Thank you for doing this for me. Thank you for your patience and understanding and for not giving up on me even while I've been a royal pain in the butt."

He laughed as he stood up and pulled her into his arms. He didn't want to leave the house, but it was Christmas, and he loved his family.

"Are you ready to be bombarded when we show up together at my family's house?" he asked.

Her eyes widened. "Oh no, I think I'll sit this one out," she said.

"Not a chance, Chloe. I'm not going into that lion's den without you," he assured her.

Finally, she laughed. "Fine. But only because I'm sure Brooke and Sarah would come drag me out if I didn't show up, anyway, and then be mad at you."

"Do you think they already know we're together?" he asked.

"I guarantee they know it." The oven went off, and Chloe walked back into the kitchen. She took the egg bake from the oven, and then he couldn't take not having her in his arms any longer.

She let out a whoosh of air when he spun her around and lifted her to the counter. It took them a couple of hours before they managed to make it out of the house together.

CHAPTER
TWENTY-SIX

Chloe was having second thoughts as she stood beside Brandon's monster-size truck and gazed at the huge Anderson mansion. When he'd said family dinner, she'd been assuming he meant Finn's or Noah's house. She could handle that. Even walking in with him, she could handle it because her best friends would be there.

This was an entirely different thing altogether. She glared at Brandon again as she crossed her arms and refused to move forward. If he'd told her he was coming to Joseph's house, she would've gladly refused. He'd known that, the snake.

She was used to mostly ignoring the holidays. It was easy, besides her besties pressuring her. There'd be no way of ignoring Christmas in this house, and she'd be surrounded by incredibly rich people who loved each other. She was the only outsider.

What in the world was Brandon trying to do to her? She was going to kill him when she could safely yell at him without a million Andersons overhearing.

"I'm not going in there, Brandon. Give me my purse so I can call a cab," she demanded. He hadn't quit smiling since they'd arrived five minutes before, and she'd been scowling at him.

Didn't the man get ruffled? It was insane how calm he remained while she stared daggers at him. It was downright ridiculous. It was very difficult to have a one-sided fight.

"I'm serious, Brandon. No way, no how am I entering the Anderson mansion on Christmas." She was putting her foot down. But she wanted to leave before anyone was aware the two of them were there. She had no doubt that if they were spotted, there'd be no chance of her leaving. She was tempted to start walking down the snowy driveway that stretched a mile. But it was cold, and she wasn't an idiot. She wasn't wearing the right coat or shoes for that.

"You already agreed to come with me, Chloe," he told her for the third time. His stupid grin hadn't dropped at all.

"That was before I realized it was here," she pointed out, hushing her voice when she realized it was growing louder by the second. She looked toward the massive front doors, but they hadn't budged. Maybe there were Christmas miracles after all.

"I can't just come to Joseph Anderson's house uninvited—on Christmas afternoon." She had to calm herself again. He was either playing dumb, or he was that dang rude to make her sweat. Either way she didn't like him much at this moment.

That was a shock after their amazing morning of lovemaking. She'd more than liked him an hour ago as he'd been making her cry out in pleasure. But that was then, she reminded herself. At this moment he was enemy number one.

Brandon made the mistake of winking at her, and she felt her fingers clench into fists. Her eyes must've narrowed, too, because he took a step back and held his hands up in surrender.

"I'm sorry—seriously, I am—but you know Joseph and know that he loves to have visitors. He's also matchmaker number one, and he adores you, so it'll be the best Christmas present I can possibly get him, bringing you to the house today."

She knew he was right, but that didn't make this situation any easier. She barely understood what was happening between her and Brandon, and she certainly didn't want to try and answer any questions about the two of them. That would be far too difficult. She was stuck right now and didn't know what to do.

Her fear of commitment because things just never lasted seemed to be unfounded. She'd known Brandon for three years now, and instead of him proving her right—proving that the longer you knew a man, the more flaws you'd find—he'd proven the opposite. The more she'd gotten to know him, the more respect she had for him.

She might not have liked everything he did, and she certainly didn't appreciate the feelings he was bringing out in her, but he also continued surprising her with his thoughtful gifts and the respect and love he showed for those around him. The more she was with him, the more she wanted to be. Wasn't it supposed to be the opposite? Was her entire world being flipped upside down?

"Fine. I don't think you're going to be a gentleman and let me leave, but just know I'll remember this for a very long time to come, Brandon Anderson," she threatened. She took a step away, and he reached for her. She shot his hand a glare and swore she heard him chuckle.

She spun to tell him what she thought about that, and her feet slipped—of course, at the perfect moment. Brandon caught her, and no matter how mad she was at the man, she tingled at being pressed close against him. He must've seen it in her eyes, because his head began descending, but then they heard a booming voice that froze Chloe in place.

"Are you two going to stand out here freezing all day, or are you coming in the house?"

Chloe's cheeks flushed more than they already had as she turned to find Joseph standing in the giant doorway leading inside his enormous mansion. She found herself completely tongue tied as she turned back to look at Brandon, who wasn't in the least embarrassed to be caught how they were.

"Hello, Uncle," he said before looking back at her. "Guess we're going in now."

"Is that smugness I hear in your voice?" she whispered.

"Maybe a little," he admitted.

"Ugh. Let me go," she told him.

"Are you sure you can walk now? I know I have a way of making your legs turn to jelly," he told her with an infuriating smile.

"It's good your ego's firmly in place," she said. She couldn't fight the smile trying to break through, though. One of the things she loved about Brandon was his utter confidence. It was hard not to be drawn to it.

"Are you ignoring me?" Joseph called out when they still took too long.

Chloe had momentarily forgotten he was there. She'd be burned at the stake before telling Joseph that. He wasn't a man to be ignored or forgotten, not ever.

"I'm trying to," Brandon called out with a waggle of his brows. Chloe couldn't even look at Joseph after those words.

She was shocked when she heard Joseph roar with laughter. "You have plenty of time to be alone with Chloe. But this is Christmas, and it's *my* time right now," Joseph insisted.

Brandon finally released Chloe, but not for long. He slipped his hand behind her back and led her to the huge staircase as they made their way up to where Joseph waited on them.

"Don't you have a houseful of people to pick on?" Brandon asked. Only when they'd made it to the door did Brandon release her so he could give his uncle a hug.

"I love having a houseful, but that doesn't mean my heart doesn't ache for the ones who aren't here," Joseph said.

She believed he meant those words. Family was everything to Joseph and Katherine. Chloe didn't think his family could ever grow big enough to make him fully happy. He wanted babies and more babies each and every year. His home was certainly big enough to house them all.

"Well, thank you for inviting me. I knew you wouldn't mind if I brought a guest," Brandon said, a bit out of breath from the bear hug Joseph had just given him.

"Chloe isn't a guest; she's a part of the family now," Joseph insisted, making her heart beat faster at the kind words.

"Thank you for your graciousness, Joseph. It means a lot," she told him. Living a lifetime with limited family had made her unsure how to react when she was welcomed in so warmly. Maybe that was why she avoided the holidays as much as she did.

"Ah, come here, sweetheart," Joseph said, and before she could blink, he'd grabbed her up in the best hug she'd ever received. She could truly understand why this man was loved so much. He really was *that* good of a man.

"Let's get into the kitchen ASAP. We're only waiting on a couple more people. If they don't hurry, we might just eat without them," Joseph threatened.

He led them down the long wide hallway, and Chloe could hear the voices long before she saw anyone. It really was intimidating to be in the monstrous home. But she was trying to act as if this was any other day with normal people. Joseph and his family would never be described that way, not in this lifetime.

She was suddenly terrified to go into that room and wanted just a few moments to compose herself. She looked at Joseph and tried to keep a neutral expression on her face.

"Can I use the bathroom before I go in?" she asked.

"Of course, darling," he told her. "The dining room is straight down this hall. Just follow the voices. The bathroom is two more doors down on the left," he finished.

She thanked him and didn't even look at Brandon as she took off for the bathroom, then stepped inside and shut the door. She leaned on the door and took a deep breath. So much was happening in such a short period of time. She was going to have to fight hard to not have a panic attack.

She'd been through much more trying times in her life. She'd make it through a crazy, chaotic, amazing family dinner with the Anderson family. Her besties were out there. She'd be just fine, she assured herself.

She walked to the sink and turned on the cold water. She was allowed just a bit more time before facing the crowd.

CHAPTER TWENTY-SEVEN

Joseph immediately went over and stood with his brothers, George and Richard, as he watched Brandon approach his siblings. If Joseph had been a betting man instead of a business mogul, he would've been just as successful in life. He had no doubt about it.

"Do you see Brandon over there? He's happier than I've seen him since he lost his poor mama," Joseph said. It wasn't easy for him to talk in a hushed voice, but he could do it when it was absolutely necessary.

"Yes, I see a lot of happiness with all our new nephews," George said as he sipped on his eggnog. "It's another beautiful Christmas, and I love how much our family keeps on growing."

"I can barely keep up anymore," Richard said. "Since I lived most of my life not knowing I was taken at birth and had two brothers, this is a wonderful chaos to be thrust into—but still overwhelming at times. I went from having no siblings to having two, and now there are so many nieces and nephews and grandkids I'm woefully outnumbered." He said this with a huge smile on his face.

"It's a good thing our story has been written for the world to know about. We've had a lot of twists and turns along the way. I can say with confidence, though, that there aren't too many people out there as blessed as this family has been. I say a thank-you prayer every night. I don't want God to ever think I take him for granted or don't appreciate all I've been given," Joseph said.

"I agree. We've certainly had our losses in this life, but we've had so many blessings as well," George said. When George lost his wife at a young age, he'd been angry for a while, but time really had helped him heal, and he got to see her face in those of his children every time he was with them. She was certainly looking down on them from up above.

"I wish we could stop time and have this forever," Richard said.

"Well, I don't know about you, but I know I'm not going to think too much about the future. I'm very happy with the right now," Joseph said.

"Are there any updates on Brandon and Chloe? I was hoping for an engagement announcement by now. Those two sure have been taking their time," George said.

"I agree. I wonder if we need to push them a little more," Joseph said.

"If you push too hard, they might fight back," Richard pointed out. He was the more reasonable of the three siblings.

"That's nonsense. A love like theirs can't be stopped," Joseph assured the group.

"Yes, they do seem pretty perfect for each other," Richard said.

"She's such a sweet girl, but she has enough sass to put up with an Anderson," George told them.

"It does take a strong woman to tame an Anderson man," Joseph said as he gazed across the room at his beautiful wife. She looked up from her seat, where she was holding one of her grandnieces, and gave him a loving smile. "She still takes my breath away even after all these years."

"You're an example for us all," George said. "A love that strong can't be argued with. I don't know why any of the kids try when you match them up."

Joseph hushed his brother. "Now, don't be saying that too loud. If they think their relationships aren't fully their idea, they'll get all upset with us."

"It won't last," Richard said. "They are too happy with the women they love."

"And the men," George pointed out as he looked at his daughter and her husband. "These kids have made us mighty proud. We really are lucky how well they all turned out. Statistics show that's nearly impossible."

"Yes, they've had their ups and downs in life, but they are all hard workers and faithful and strong. We couldn't ask for better than that," Joseph said.

"Where did Chloe go?" George asked as he looked around the room. There were certainly a lot of people there, but not so many a person could get lost in the crowd.

"She needed a minute to compose herself. I have a feeling Brandon didn't tell her she was coming here for Christmas. I can admit this place can be slightly intimidating," Joseph said.

George and Richard laughed. "I guess we're all just used to it by now," Richard said. "But I can see why someone would be intimidated. This is a wild bunch to be thrown into."

"I'm having a really great time looking at Brandon over there. He's been watching the door from the moment he came into the room. It appears he doesn't like to be away from sweet little Chloe too long."

"Want to take bets on how long it takes for him to get her?" Richard asked.

Joseph laughed. "Right now," he said as Brandon said something, then walked purposely out of the room.

"That took him about five minutes," George said.

"Maybe seven," Joseph said as he held up his glass. His brothers followed suit. "Here's to another merry Christmas where we have friends and family and all the blessings we could ever ask for."

"Here, here," George and Richard said as they clinked their glasses against his. They all took a sip as Lucas, Joseph's oldest son, stepped up to them.

"What are the three of you up to now on this beautiful Christmas Day?" Lucas asked.

Joseph smiled big at his oldest son. He hoped it was an innocent expression, but even under torture he'd never give away his secrets, so it didn't matter too much.

"We were just talking about how blessed we are," Joseph told his son.

"Yes, each year our family keeps on growing," George added.

"And each addition brings joy," Richard chimed in.

Lucas laughed. "I'll take that answer, even though I have no doubt you're up to something, and I have a feeling it has to do with my newest cousins. Someday you will get payback," Lucas assured them.

"That's a terrible thing to say," Joseph told his son. "After all I do for this family . . ."

Lucas laughed, true merriment in his voice. Then he leaned in and hugged his dad and then his uncles. "Yes, you all keep this family together. You three are the glue, and we are grateful for you."

Joseph felt a stinging in his eyes as he looked at what a fine man his son had turned into. He was too choked up to say anything. There was always a first for everything. "I love you guys," Lucas finished before he left.

"Yes, Joseph, we are truly blessed," George said with a sigh.

"More than words could ever express," Joseph said.

They sat back and looked over the room, truly happier than anyone had a right to be. And it would just continue to get better and better over time. Joseph had no doubt about that. He loved big, and that love showed in each one of his family members.

CHAPTER TWENTY-EIGHT

Brandon looked around the crowded Anderson dinner table. The noise level was enough to wake up a city block. But that wasn't all he noticed. No. What he saw were smiles and laughter, people eating and visiting and celebrating Christmas with those they loved. It went beyond love, though.

Some would say love was almost mandatory. When you heard of a child saying they didn't love their parent or a parent not loving their child, you wondered what was wrong with them. But it went beyond even that. When children were very little and you said you were going to Nana and Papa's house, their faces would light up, and they would grab their coats and boots.

At what age did that change? At what age did they groan, saying they wanted to go hang out with their friends? Family stopped having as much meaning in this new world of technology. You were able to make your own family with anyone you pleased.

So to truly love your family and your friends was a gift. To forgive when needed and to be there for those in your life who needed you was something not as many people were willing to do now that civilization was more dependent on technology than on each other.

But it wasn't the case for the Andersons. Sure, technology had made their lives much easier. But as Brandon looked at this table filled with family he hadn't known he'd had a few years ago, he realized that even if they were sent back into the Dark Ages, they would stay together. And it wouldn't be out of obligation. It truly would be done with love.

"It's hard to imagine this is all real, isn't it?" Katherine said.

Brandon was pulled from his trance as he looked at this regal woman who was the real head of the house in the Anderson empire. Sure, Joseph was loud, and he was the business mogul, but Katherine was the true heart of the family.

"Yes, it's still a bit overwhelming for me at times," Brandon admitted.

Just then Chloe laughed, her voice carrying to him as she leaned against Sarah, the two of them beaming as they animatedly spoke of something. Brooke pushed Finn aside as she moved closer, not wanting to miss out on whatever her two best friends were discussing.

"I agree. My family has grown more and more each year. First my children married and gave Joseph and I grandchildren, and then my nieces and nephews have married. And as if we didn't have enough blessings, we discovered Joseph had a triplet stolen at birth who we've gotten to know and love, and then you and your brothers have been brought to us. I can't imagine asking for more. The holidays are a great time to celebrate how much we've been given."

"Do you ever blame my mother for not coming sooner?" Brandon asked.

Katherine reached out and patted his arm. "Your mother was placed in impossible circumstances. As I see the incredible boys she raised, all I feel for her is respect. I wish I could've gotten to know her before she was taken from us too soon, but I would never blame her. She did the best she could with what she was given."

"I can't believe she was able to be with my father as long as she was, but I'm grateful she did it, because I can't imagine even one of my brothers not being here. The powers that be say there's always a reason for everything, and I guess even in great suffering, beautiful results can be found."

"That's very true, Brandon. There are sometimes great gifts beneath the rubble. I wouldn't want anyone to go through what your mother went through, and I wish she could've come to us when you were still young. But then again, you might not have turned out as good as you have if life hadn't thrown challenges your way," Katherine said.

"There were times I wasn't too happy about those challenges, but now I realize they truly have shaped me into who I am and who I want to be. It's easy to get lost in this world and just want more and more. But at the end of the day, I like the journey I've taken in life, and I look forward to what comes next."

"I love that attitude," Katherine said. "I don't ever want to leave this world. I'm just so happy right where I am. But I also know that when I go, my family will be just fine. I expect all of you to miss me, but I don't expect my passing to hold anyone back."

"There should never be talk about passing during the holidays," Brandon told her. He couldn't imagine this world without Katherine in it. He couldn't imagine what Joseph would do without the love of his life. Joseph loved his family enormously, but his wife was truly his other half. Without her, he wouldn't be whole.

Brandon glanced across the table again and looked at Chloe. Would he feel that way about her in a year or ten years or fifty? Would she be as essential to him as the air he breathed or the food he ate? He hadn't ever thought he'd want someone or something that badly.

But seeing the pure love Joseph and Katherine shared made him want that. He wasn't going to go so far as to say Chloe was his entire universe at this point in their relationship. But he would admit he could see them reaching that point.

"She is different from any other woman I've ever known," Brandon said.

Katherine looked over at Chloe before meeting Brandon's gaze again. "You are a match. That's been clear from the first time you met."

That surprised Brandon. "Really? I thought she was cute and funny when I first met her, but I wouldn't have thought we were a match," he told Katherine.

"That's because you see with young eyes," she said, chuckling. "I hate sounding like my husband, and I will deny it if you ever say I've said this, but I think he does have a gift," she whispered. "He sees people's souls. He can tell who should be together and who shouldn't. Now, if he knew I was saying this, it would give him free rein to meddle as much as he wanted. But I've yet to see his meddling end in a bad way."

"You know he's meddling?" Brandon asked in shock.

Katherine laughed, the sound drawing Joseph's attention. He gazed at his wife with that look that told Brandon he saw no one in that moment but his true love. She sent a kiss through the air before turning back to Brandon and talking in a hushed tone that couldn't possibly be heard above the mayhem at the table.

"Oh, Brandon, my husband doesn't get away with nearly as much as he thinks he does. Of course I know he meddles. But since the results speak for themselves, I only pretend to put up a fight. It's the same with his cigars. If I said it was perfectly okay, he might smoke himself into an early grave. But if I make it difficult for him, then he only has one once in a while. That's all part of a good marriage."

Brandon laughed as he wrapped an arm around Katherine and gently squeezed. "I can only hope that I have half as good a marriage as you and Joseph," he finally said.

"Don't you dare settle, Brandon Anderson. You reach for the sun, and don't stop until it's consumed you. Along that journey, you'll sit upon stars and talk to the man in the moon. There will never be a dull moment, and there will never be anything you can't achieve. How sad would it be to settle for half a marriage when you can have it all?"

"I don't think Chloe does anything in half measures. I think meeting her and never giving up has been one of the smarter choices I've made in life."

"I would have to agree with you on that. But at the same time, I'm pretty impressed with all of the choices you've made. You're a very talented and successful businessman at a young age, and you love your family. The same can't be said for too many people. Keep on making more and more goals, and when something doesn't go the way you want it to go, then try another way. I see too many people give up when things don't go in the direction they originally planned. It's those who try again and again that rule the world."

"Is that how you and Joseph did it?" he asked with a laugh.

"I think Joseph and I have done as well as we have because we've always put family first. And I think we've done so well because family doesn't always mean blood. We surround ourselves with great people, and that makes us greater."

"I couldn't have said it better myself," he said. "I've had a lot of amazing Christmas mornings, but this has to top the list. To be here with Chloe, my brothers, their spouses, my nieces and nephews, and all of my newest family members has made this day incredible. I'm going to hate to see it end."

Katherine gave him that serene smile again. "Never dread the ending to a day, Brandon, because that just means a new adventure is about to begin. If we spend too much time in the past, we don't look ahead to the future."

"You know, you should've been a counselor," he said.

"I have enough family members to counsel. I don't need to do it for a living," she said with a laugh.

"Are you going to take up all of my beautiful wife's attention?" Joseph said. He stood and moved over to them.

"Now, Joseph, you know I love to move around the table and visit with everyone," Katherine said after he'd leaned down and kissed her.

"Yes, but you've been gone for too long. It's not Christmas dinner without you by my side, your delicate hand on my leg."

"I love you, Joseph," she said as she stood.

He pulled her against him and kissed her again, making the table go silent as everyone looked at the couple who'd brought them all together. He leaned back the slightest bit, his eyes looking completely dazzled.

"You are my world, Katherine," he said as he cupped her cheek.

"Merry Christmas, everyone," someone called out, making Katherine blush.

Brandon knew beyond a doubt when Joseph and Katherine placed their arms around each other and gazed into each other's eyes the rest of the world fell away. They loved their family, but they still easily got lost in one another's embrace. They were the ultimate example of true love.

Katherine went hand in hand with her husband to the head of the table, and Brandon moved over to Chloe. Without a word, he kneeled down beside her and kissed her, making her blush as much as Katherine just had.

"Thank you for sharing this day with me," he whispered.

"Thank you for inviting me," she replied.

The conversation around the table restarted, and Brandon sat next to Chloe, his hand entwined with hers for the rest of the meal. He hoped they were still doing that in another fifty years.

CHAPTER TWENTY-NINE

It was always tough when reality set back in after the holidays. There was so much excitement leading up to them and then a great big crash after. She'd had a beautiful Christmas with Brandon and her friends and then a mellow New Year's where she'd shared a kiss with Brandon at midnight.

Now it was time to get back to work. Luckily things were always a lot calmer at the restaurant in January, as people were recovering from spending too much money in December. That gave her time to do changes there if she wanted and allowed her extra time on other projects.

Right now she wanted to finish the veterans kitchen. She was no longer denying that she was in a relationship with Brandon, but she absolutely refused to use the *boyfriend* word. It drove her crazy.

She wasn't some high school girl with a crush. She was an independent woman who just so happened to be falling in love with a very strong, beautiful man. She wondered if she'd ever be able to admit that to him, to tell him she was in love with him. She wasn't sure, since she was having a hard enough time admitting it to herself.

But he didn't get frustrated with her. That was a good thing. Her appliances had arrived today, and she'd been at the kitchen driving Noah slightly crazy with wanting everything to be perfect. Brandon was off running an errand because she wanted special lighting below the counters so when a person walked by, the lights automatically turned on. But he didn't complain, just said he was on it. As a matter of fact, he didn't complain about any of the extra little things she wanted to do there.

She really did believe the kitchen was the heart of any home, and she wanted this one to be a great big beating heart. There were lights in cupboards and below. There were special slide-out drawers and hidden nooks and crannies. If a kitchen had all the bells and whistles, then it was a haven that was fun to explore. She wanted this place to be filled with volunteer chefs from around the world so the veterans wouldn't just eat, but eat in style.

They'd get all the help they deserved at the facility and would enjoy their time there. In this facility, they wouldn't wait for hours on uncomfortable benches. They wouldn't complain about any wait time, for that matter, because waiting would be a joy, as there were going to be so many activities for them to do.

She might only be planning the kitchen for this facility, but now that she was on board with the project, she was learning about all of the things they were doing. The activities list kept growing and growing. And what was even more amazing was the endless line of volunteers. There might have to be a wait list for people to be able to volunteer. What a joy that was.

And today was the best day of all because now she'd get to see the appliances installed and running, and soon she'd be able to do her first meal in the state-of-the-art kitchen. She couldn't wait. She was going to make it a group event with all of them there. All of the Andersons, the community, and of course her besties had put a lot of time into the project. She'd barely done anything. She was just glad to have had even a small part in it at all.

"Chloe, is this good?" Noah asked for the tenth time. He had all of the cabinets lined out and the counters sitting there ready to go. She walked around the kitchen, eyeing it from different angles. Noah's men were standing there holding their breath as she took her time critically eying it all. Noah just smiled.

He should have been scowling at her, but he was managing to keep it under control. She was sure that was why Sarah loved him so much. He truly was a good man, just like all of his siblings were.

"It's perfect, Noah. Thank you so much for doing it over and over again. I just have a vision, and I can only seem to see it one way," she said with a shrug.

"You're the chef, so your wish is my command," he assured her. "You heard her, boys. Let's get this hammered into place before she changes her mind," he shouted.

The men moved fast. It was actually quite amusing. Maybe they hadn't been as patient as Noah had been. They weren't going to give her a chance to change her mind again. She'd actually lost count of how many times that had happened in the past week alone. Of course, she could be assured that she hadn't been the only picky person on this project. Everyone wanted it to be just as perfect as she did.

"We'll have this all ready to go by tomorrow," Noah said.

She looked at the appliances, which were still in boxes, and sighed. "Not tonight?" she said.

Noah laughed heartily while shaking his head. "You do realize Brandon and his crew will be here all night to get all the plugs finished up just so you can have them installed tomorrow?" he told her.

"Oh," she whispered. "I didn't realize that. I could wait another day so they don't have to do that." Now she was feeling bad.

"Not a chance of that happening. All of us love seeing how excited you are for this. And I don't think there's anything my brother won't do for you," Noah added with a wink.

"It's not like that," she told him, hating that her cheeks were flushing.

"Of course it's like that," Sarah said as she entered the huge room. "Brandon is head over heels for you. It's good to make him sweat a little." She walked over to her husband and gave him a kiss.

"Did you make me sweat?" Noah asked.

She laughed again. "You say that like it was in the past," she told him with a laugh. "I still do it all the time. Have you forgotten so soon?"

"All I can remember is how good you always make me feel," he told her, making Chloe laugh this time.

"I see being a smooth talker runs in your family," Chloe said.

"It's not smooth when it's true," Noah said.

"Oh my gosh, Brandon says the same thing. Do you guys have the same handbook?" Chloe asked.

Noah laughed as he snaked an arm around his wife's back. "We're just very wise men who like to keep our women happy," Noah insisted.

"That is true, brother," Brandon said as he joined them in the kitchen. "A happy wife means a happy life."

"You are wise men indeed," Sarah said.

Brandon's arms were full of wire, but he moved over to Chloe and leaned down, giving her a quick kiss on the lips. "I have everything we need to get this project done," he assured her.

"You really don't have to work all night," Chloe said, again feeling bad. But even feeling bad, she didn't want to protest too much. She was ready to see it all completed.

"Are you kidding? My men *love* overtime. I can't take it away from them now," Brandon told her. "They've assured me they need the extra wages to pay off the credit cards from the holidays." He was laughing as he said this. It seemed Brandon only hired the best of the best, and they were just as much of family men as he and his brothers were.

"Joseph isn't going to be happy. We've got to be way over budget by now," she tried to reason.

"We've been over budget from the start," he said. "But in the end that's not what anyone will be thinking about as they look at this phenomenal facility. They'll just see how perfect it truly is."

"Okay, let's have a grand kitchen opening on Friday. Everything will be installed, and I'll make a meal for us all," she said. "I can't wait to test out the appliances."

"That sounds like a fantastic date," he told her. "I'm going to have to insist you take your adorable booty out of here for the rest of the night, though."

Her feelings were hurt as she looked at him. "Am I already driving you crazy?" she asked, hoping her voice sounded teasing.

He dropped everything in his arms and pulled her to him. "You drive me crazy whether I'm with you or not, and that's in a very, *very* good way. But my men are sweating around you, because if something is off by even a centimeter, you are on it," he added with a laugh before kissing her hard.

"I guess I do get slightly controlling sometimes when it comes to the kitchen," she admitted sheepishly.

"Slightly?" Sarah gasped. "That's *slightly* an understatement." She laughed hard at her own joke.

"That's just mean," Chloe said, but she wasn't offended. She was a good chef *because* she was so picky. "Now I'm electing you and Brooke to help plan a menu. Let's get lunch and decide."

"Mmm, now you're speaking my love language," Sarah said. "We'll see you boys later."

Sarah gave her husband one more scorching kiss before joining Chloe and walking from the room.

"This is a great start to a new year," Sarah said when they were out of earshot of the men. Chloe smiled big.

"Yeah, it's pretty great," she said.

"Are you going to admit to being in love with Brandon yet?" she pushed as they climbed into Chloe's car.

Chloe shook her head. "Not yet," she said.

Sarah laughed. "I won't even push you, because I remember feeling the exact same way when it came to Noah. I was terrified. But I'll tell you that when I finally did allow myself to love the man, it made me the happiest woman on this planet. I now look back and think about how much time I wasted fighting against it."

"I don't know. I think Brooke would fight you on that statement," Chloe told her.

"Well, that should tell you right there that being married to the Anderson men makes us pretty dang euphoric."

"It's a little soon to be talking marriage," Chloe pointed out.

"You've known him for nearly three years," Sarah said.

"But we've only been this intimate for a few months."

"Well . . . technically that's been over a year as well," Sarah reminded her.

Chloe blushed. "I guess that's true. I'm still scared that all of these fuzzy emotions will disappear. I am a control freak, and I like my life done a certain way. What if after all the love hormones die down, I'm suddenly not happy? What if I miss my independence? I think Brandon does care about me. Will I feel I can't leave him, then, or be a true monster? Will I be giving up my own independence and my own happiness because I don't want to hurt him? I am happy with him right now, but what if that changes and I'm no longer happy?"

Her words stopped Sarah from what she'd been about to say as she seemed to think about Chloe's comments and questions. She finally shrugged.

"That could happen, Chloe. But just know if it does, then you have two best friends who will support you no matter what. And as much as I know about Brandon, I think it's more than clear that it would break his heart if you were to leave, but it would break it even more if you were to stay at your own expense. Take it a day at a time. Enjoy being in love with him, and worry about what you're going to feel later. If your feelings start to change, you can talk to him about it. If you don't want to talk to him right then, you can talk to Brooke and me."

"I'm scared I won't be able to," Chloe said.

"Because you think Brooke or I would judge you?" Sarah said, her eyes widening.

"No. I'm afraid I'll judge me."

This made Sarah laugh. "Oh, darling, it's way too late for that. You've been judging yourself for a very long time. But you have Brooke and me to help rein you in when you're getting out of control."

"I guess that's true," Chloe said after a bit.

"Let's have lunch and plan a menu, and I won't push you on the subject of love for at least a day or two. If you want to talk about your love story, you can—if not, then we'll just be three besties having a great meal, planning another great meal."

"That's the story of my life," Chloe said.

Though she said it, it wasn't exactly true. The story of her life was shifting and changing. Now Brandon was a huge part of her story, and if she was fully honest, she'd admit he wasn't going anywhere . . . maybe not ever. She might have fears, and she might feel trapped sometimes. But the alternative was to live without him. And that scared her more than the other options.

Maybe she already was trapped. Maybe it was too late to do anything about it. And maybe that wasn't such a bad thing.

CHAPTER THIRTY

Chloe let out a nervous breath as she thought about the evening to come. She'd been to some lavish events, but they hadn't been something she'd enjoyed. She remembered being young and having her parents get her all dolled up as they'd opened a new restaurant or held a big book-signing event.

Everyone had always looked at her, and she'd been expected to act a certain way. It had been nerve-racking. Now the eyes weren't on just her parents—they were on her and the job she'd done. Of course, it wasn't just her work. The kitchen might be the heart, but the entire facility was on show for this soft opening.

What if she screwed everything up and made an utter fool of herself? She'd been driving all the workers crazy with her need for perfection. But what if it wasn't perfect enough? Ugh. If she could get out of her head long enough to enjoy this night, it might go a lot more smoothly for her.

To add to her anxiety, her relationship with Brandon was going almost too perfectly. You'd think that would have given her assurance, but it was even scarier. It meant that she was constantly waiting for the other shoe to drop. She was waiting for it all to go wrong. She was also desperately trying not to think that way anymore. That was the old her. The assurances from her best friends did help her, but it was truly hard to change her ways. She'd thought a certain way for a lot of years, and it wasn't easy to switch tracks and think in a new light.

So instead of going into full-on panic mode, she sat in her kitchen and sipped on some hot tea as she tried motivating herself to get on with her day and get ready. While she was still having an internal conversation, a knock sounded on her door. She groaned.

There wasn't a chance she was up for visitors at the moment. She also knew who was there—and they wouldn't go away. No way, no how. Sarah and Brooke were her lifelines in any storm, and as much as she sometimes wanted to hide from them, the world would be such a dark place if they ever did allow her to do just that.

"The door is open," she reluctantly called. Sarah was the first to walk in, with a huge smile on her face. Brooke was right behind her. Chloe couldn't help but smile at them. As much as she didn't want visitors, she didn't mind her besties there. They loved her even when she was in the worst mood possible—which never lasted when they were around.

"We have a surprise for you, Chloe," Brooke said.

"Yep, a big surprise," Sarah added. They were practically bouncing on their feet in front of her. It really was pulling her from her thoughts.

"I can't imagine what you two have up your sleeves," Chloe replied. She didn't trust the twinkle in her besties' eyes.

"We have a full day of pampering scheduled for us. I know, I know—it's not spa time yet, but since it's the soft opening for this place we've all put our hearts and souls into, we have to get pampered like royals first," Brooke said. "There will be a lot of people and a lot of smiling. We need to make sure our cheeks are soft, or we'll get wrinkles."

"I don't have time for that," Chloe said as she mentally went through her checklist that never seemed to end.

"Too bad, because I have a feeling Brandon has something planned tonight, and you need to look your best," Sarah said. "And all work and no play makes you suck."

Chloe laughed before she felt heat spread in her cheeks. "What plans does he have?" she asked, ignoring the work comment.

Brooke laughed. "We're just hearing rumors that he's seriously hooked on you."

"I'll admit things have been pretty wonderful with us, but it's too soon for anything big," she said. Was it, though?

Sarah seemed to answer her unvoiced question. "You've known each other for years. You've just fought the attraction. When you know something, you know," Sarah told her. "And since when have you ever considered what anyone else has to say about anything relating to you? You've always been your harshest critic. It's what you feel inside. You have to stop waiting for perfection, because it's the imperfections in life that make it interesting. Yes, people will fail us, even those we love the most, but they don't do it out of spite. It happens because perfect is impossible to achieve. The great thing is that perfection would be boring. That would leave no challenges and no room for improvement. When we reach every single one of our goals, where do we go from there? People like us always need to be striving for something else. Strive for forgiveness in yourself and others, and let go of the straight and narrow. Enjoy living on the wild side a little bit."

"I don't know how to let go. I don't know if I can. All I know for sure is that I like how everything's been between Brandon and me. I don't want to do something that will damage what we have right now."

"What do you have?" Brooke asked.

That made Chloe pause. "I don't honestly know how to answer that," she said after a bit.

"Maybe you have real love," Sarah offered.

"I've been trying to avoid the word *love*. I don't like to use it without meaning. And I'm so scared that if I do use it, I will think it's a mistake and run."

"Do you really think it would be without meaning?" Brooke asked. "I know it's seriously scary to think of love and romance, because of the pain it can cause, but you can't judge new relationships on the unrealistic goals you've always made for yourself or that your parents made for you. Also, you have to allow yourself to be vulnerable in order to have the sweet rewards that can be gleaned from just that."

Chloe nodded. "It's worked out great for the two of you, but I always circle back to that. What if things don't work out, and then it makes it awkward with all of us?"

"Nothing would ever come between us," Sarah insisted. "Not ever. And we want you to be happy. We'd never suggest you do anything that gives you less than everything you have never even dreamed of having. We use the word *perfect* way too often. I do it all the time. But seriously, I don't want perfection. I want messy and real and extraordinary. You can never get that with perfection."

"I second that," Brooke said. "If things hadn't worked out for Sarah and Noah after I was already with Finn, then we would've figured it out. We will with you as well. There are five of them, so if we had to take one out, they'd come back from it."

The ridiculous words made Chloe laugh. "We have vowed to always help each other bury the body," Chloe said.

"If the government ever listened to our conversations, we'd probably be arrested," Brooke said. "But that would just be a new adventure we could do together."

"And at least we'd be together," Sarah added.

"As long as we're always together, we can get through anything," Chloe said. She'd had messy before. Maybe she just hadn't realized it was. And as she thought more about it, she realized those had been some of the freest moments of her life. Why was she still trying to live in this bubble she didn't want to live in?

"So that means you need to live your best life possible and not worry about how it affects the future or our relationship. We're a triad, and nothing will ever break that," Brooke assured her.

"I know this, but there are some things in life worth taking a risk for and other things that aren't. I need to have more faith in myself. It's a very hard cycle to break," Chloe said.

"You need to have as much faith in yourself as the two of us have in you," Sarah said.

"And I think Brandon has that same faith in you," Brooke added. "You can't fake the way he looks at you or talks about you. Even if perfection is boring, you're perfect for him and to him."

"I can't imagine living my life without you guys. I can face anything or any situation as long as you're by my side. Maybe I've been changing more than I've realized. A lot of me wants to run and hide, but the other part is happy where I am. It's such an odd sensation to feel pulled in multiple directions."

"Is that a marriage proposal?" Brooke asked with a laugh.

"Sorry, I'm taken, but we'll still grow old together," Sarah said.

All three women laughed, and Chloe was truly glad to have them. She'd been nervous about the event that night, and now she felt foolish for ever feeling that way. She was a strong woman, and she didn't allow fear to hold her back.

Being with these two women also reminded her that she'd had long-term relationships in her life that had worked out. Maybe a friendship was different than a romantic relationship, but it did prove that relationships could last—even when you saw the worst of those you loved the most.

"Okay, let's get beautiful," she said to the girls.

"We're already beautiful. Let's get made up and knock our men's socks right off their feet," Brooke said.

"Amen," Sarah added.

Brooke pulled out a bottle of champagne, and though it took a few moments, she got the top popped while Sarah grabbed glasses. She poured them and held hers up. The girls joined her.

"We're positively gorgeous, independent, and loyal women," Brooke started. "Because we believe in ourselves, in family, and in values."

"And in taking care of ourselves and our loved ones," Sarah added.

"And that we all deserve a little pampering once in a while," Chloe said.

"Hear! Hear!" They clinked glasses and had a drink.

They finished their champagne, then Chloe put on some sweats and a comfortable T-shirt. She'd be spending the rest of the day in a spa robe, so there was no reason to get dressed up.

The next six hours were exactly what the doctor ordered. The girls giggled, drank wine, and had masks placed over their entire bodies, their hair waxed, their nails done, and their skin treated luxuriously.

It wasn't often that they went all out, but the results were fantastic. At the end of their pampering, Chloe looked in the mirror feeling like an entirely new woman. Her skin was silky smooth, her hair soft and teased, and her smile permanently locked on her face.

She actually felt beautiful, and she hadn't even put on her dress yet. She wasn't sure if she would've made it to the event in one piece if it hadn't been for her friends. Sometimes she forgot who she was. That was why it was important to surround herself with people who could remind her. Her strength was always there. Sometimes she just couldn't manage to find it.

By the time she'd finished with all the pampering and had gotten dressed, she was wondering if she'd be able to recognize the person looking back from a mirror. But as she looked, her eyes filled with tears. The spa hadn't overpowered her with layers of makeup but had high-lighted her eyes and lips, letting her natural glow shine through. Her hair was placed on top of her head, with several strands curling around her face and shoulders. Her gown cascaded over her body, hugging her curves and then flaring into a full skirt that was perfect for being swirled around a dance floor.

Her besties stood by her side, looking stunning as usual. They linked arms as they smiled at their final results.

"Thank you so much for today," she managed to get past her tight throat.

"Don't you start crying and ruin all of this hard work," Brooke said, sounding suspiciously close to tears herself. "We have a gala to go to," she finished. "It's so nice to be a woman for a while—separate from being a mother, an employee, and even a wife. We do lose ourselves in the many roles we play. Those roles are amazing, and I wouldn't trade them, but I like finding myself again with the two of you."

"I couldn't have said it better," Sarah said.

"Let's go surprise our men," Chloe said.

The three of them glided from the house to where a stretch limo awaited them. Chloe had no doubt she'd see a smile on Brandon's face. Did she want more than that from him? She was thinking that she just might indeed.

CHAPTER THIRTY-ONE

Brandon stood with Finn, Noah, Hudson, and Crew. It was always nice when he was with all four of his siblings. It wasn't often, as they were all busy. But this soft opening for the place they'd all worked hard on was the perfect chance for them to come together and appreciate what they could accomplish as a family and as a community.

"Where in the world is Chloe?" Brandon asked. "I wanted to pick her up, but she said she was coming with Sarah and Brooke."

"You know how those ladies are when they get together," Finn said with a laugh. "I wouldn't be entirely surprised if they got to talking and forgot the time. They might not make it here at all."

"Yeah, I've seen that happen before," Noah chimed in.

"So you're saying your wives would rather have an evening without you?" Hudson said with a smirk.

"Maybe they're already regretting their marriage vows," Crew teased.

"If you guys ever settle down, you'd know what a real relationship is like. My marriage is nice and cozy," Finn said, not goaded one bit.

"Yep. I thought being in a relationship with one woman was the end of everything. I was so wrong," Noah said.

"I've never been happier in my life," Brandon added.

"Not you, too, Brandon. Didn't we all vow eternal bachelorhood at one point in our lives?" Hudson asked.

That made them all laugh. "I think we were preadolescent," Finn pointed out. "It doesn't count then."

"I have to admit I'm a little jealous of what you have. It's pretty impressive," Crew said, seeming extra thoughtful that evening.

"Does that mean you're next?" Brandon asked with a smile.

"I think you're next if your constant attention to the door is any indication," Crew pointed out.

"Oh, I'm done for," Brandon said, not even slightly embarrassed. "I'm in love. I'm just waiting for the perfect moment to give Chloe this." He pulled out an impressive diamond ring from his pocket.

Crew and Hudson whistled while Finn and Noah smiled. "You did good," Finn approved.

"Mine's better," Noah said.

That again made them all laugh. They'd been competitive their entire lives, and it wasn't going to stop with marriage and becoming fathers. They'd compete at who raised their kids better and looked the best being a father. No dad bods for them. It wouldn't ever get to the point that it became harmful to their relationships, though, or to where they didn't love their nieces and nephews as much as their own children. But friendly competition was good for the soul.

"We'll see whether Chloe takes it or throws it back in my face, then know whose is better," Brandon said.

"I can't believe you bought a ring. I guess you have fallen," Hudson said. He seemed a bit panicked.

"What's the matter?" Noah asked.

Hudson's face grew pale. "It's like a marriage flu," he finally said without any humor. "Three of you have succumbed to it. I'm a bit worried I might be next."

There was a pause before his brothers laughed heartily, even Crew, who was supposed to be the most rational of the family. He was a psychiatrist, after all.

"You don't catch a marriage bug," Crew finally said. "If you don't want to get married, then don't do it. People take marriage far too cavalierly. I think there'd be a lot less divorce if couples took more time getting to know each other. Marriage shouldn't be done impulsively."

"Do you think I'm being too impulsive?" Brandon asked.

Crew thought for a moment, then smiled. "No, I don't. I've been watching you and Chloe dance around each other for a couple of years now. I think I might win the bet."

Brandon's eyes narrowed. "What bet?"

Crew smiled. "You had to know we'd be betting on how long it would take, especially when Joseph paired you up with Chloe."

Brandon should've been annoyed that anyone would dare play matchmaker on him or that any bets would be made. But he was so in love with Chloe he couldn't find even an ounce of irritation.

"I don't care," he finally said. "I'm too happy to care about how it began or who had a hand in it."

"What are you happy about?" a loud voice asked.

"Are you eavesdropping?" Brandon asked Joseph as his huge uncle joined their circle.

"It's not eavesdropping at my own party," Joseph said with a stern look. "I know your mama taught you better manners than that."

Brandon could've drawn this out and teased his uncle more, but he was in too good a mood to do that. Instead, he beamed at his uncle.

"I was just telling my annoying brothers that I don't care how Chloe and I came together—I'm just glad we did."

Joseph's grin was brighter than the sun as he clapped Brandon on the back. "I'm very glad to hear it, boy," he said. He then looked around the crowded room. "Where is Chloe?" He paused and looked some more. "It appears *all* of your women are missing."

This made the brothers laugh. "We were wondering that ourselves," Finn said. "But they're together, so it could still be a while."

"Yes, I remember those days. My Katherine still makes me wait on her, and let me tell you, the wait is always worth it," Joseph assured them.

"Yes, it truly is," Noah said.

"The music is beginning in a few minutes, so the second they enter, you can parade them around the dance floor. I plan on doing that with Katherine any minute now. There's no place I enjoy being more than in my wife's arms."

"I don't think she can fit you in her arms," Finn pointed out.

"Well, it's a good thing my arms are big enough to carry us both," Joseph said. He looked over their heads, his eyes finding his wife. Brandon had definitely noticed over the years that Joseph was always well aware of his wife's location.

"If my love is even half as strong as yours when we're in our last days, I will call it a success," Finn said.

Joseph lost his smile as he glared at his nephew. "Are you saying I'm in my last days, young man?"

Finn laughed. "Not at all, Uncle. I think you're immortal," Finn said as he held up his hands in surrender.

"Very good retreat," Joseph told him.

"They're here," Brandon whispered, his eyes glued to the door that the three women had just stepped through.

Maybe it was his imagination, but it felt as if the entire room stopped speaking, and the world stood still as Chloe, Brooke, and Sarah moved forward. The world *should* have stopped at their presence. He'd certainly forgotten how to breathe, let alone how to speak, at the sight of Chloe.

She was stunning, unlike anyone he'd ever seen before. He'd been around the rich and famous, even royals, and the world's most elite on a regular basis, but her beauty outshone them all. She had such a pureness about her it was simply breathtaking.

She moved forward in a shimmering silver gown that curved to her body before flowing out at the floor. She was free of jewels, her hair the only accessory she needed. She had a confident smile on her lips, and her teeth were gently biting into her bottom lip. He wanted to replace her teeth with his lips, to brush her pouting mouth with his tongue. He wanted to take her somewhere private and, at the same time, show her off on his arm.

She filled him with so many emotions he wasn't sure which he should act on. But that was one of the reasons he loved being with her. She was unpredictable and beautiful, and she stimulated him in so many ways. She was his—and he was most certainly hers.

He started moving forward before he even knew what he was doing. He couldn't stand to be away from her for even a moment longer. He could only assume his brothers would be doing the same as him.

They stopped in front of each other, their eyes connecting, and all felt right in the world. Tonight would be the night. He had no doubt about it.

"May I have this dance?" he asked. Chloe looked at him with a deep blush on her cheeks that fascinated him. She was confident, there was no doubt, but she was humble as well. He loved every aspect of her personality.

"There's nothing I'd like more," she quickly replied.

He took her hand and led her to the floor. The music had barely just begun, but he'd pull her into his arms whether the band was playing or not. He couldn't bear to not hold her for a second longer. The sigh that fell from her lips as she snuggled against him nearly dropped him to his knees.

They finished the song and kept dancing into the next one. When she leaned back and looked at him, he knew he wasn't going to spend another night without her. Some might try to tell him to give it more time, but he knew where he was supposed to be.

With her. Always with her.

"You take my breath away," he told her. They stopped moving, just standing there in the middle of the dance floor, not caring if anyone was looking at them. This moment was for them and only them.

"I can say the same about you. That tux looks pretty dang hot on you," she said.

"I can clean up okay," he told her. "Though I definitely prefer my jeans."

"I prefer my sweats," she whispered. "But I'll have to admit it feels nice to get all dressed up once in a while."

He leaned down and kissed her, unable to stop himself. It seemed he wasn't able to keep from touching and kissing this woman on a minute-by-minute basis.

"You do realize you've completely taken my heart, don't you?" he asked, pulling her closer.

"That scares me a little," she finally said.

"Why would it scare you?" he asked.

"Because I've never had a successful relationship. What if this fails?" she said. "I grew up knowing everything had to be perfect—everything I did had to be right. What if this all goes wrong? What if it's too messy or complicated? There are so many people involved. I could fail them all."

He was quiet for a moment as he looked at her, loving her even more than he had five minutes earlier. She was everything to him. She would be for the rest of his life. He'd help her see that. He'd help her see that even her perceived weaknesses were actually strengths.

"For one thing, you have had two very successful relationships," he told her as he turned her to look at her two best friends, who were currently dancing with their husbands. "They love you and would die for you. That kind of loyalty isn't inspired in many people."

She smiled as she looked at him, her eyes filling with tears. He cupped her cheek. "And for another, I, for one, am glad you haven't had a lasting relationship with another man, because then you wouldn't be here with me. You are loyal, passionate, and loving. And the fates have somehow smiled upon me and brought us together. We've been together long enough for you to know how in love with you I am," he said, looking deep in her eyes. "Just look at me, and see if you can find an ounce of deception in my words. I love you. There isn't anything I won't do for you—ever. Give us a chance to truly shine together, and let me show you what my love means. Let me show you how messy can be perfect."

Chloe's eyes filled the rest of the way, and tears flowed down her cheeks as she gazed at him. Hope sprang into her expression, and he knew he was doing the right thing. It was all about timing and speaking the truth.

He dropped to his knee and pulled out the box that had been in his pocket for weeks. He'd looked at the diamond a thousand times. Her eyes widened as her lips parted. He was barely aware of the music stopping or the eyes that were all on them. He didn't register Joseph's huge grin as he fist-bumped his brother George.

"Chloe, you've brought joy and hope to my heart. I can't picture my life without you. Please, take away my suffering and marry me," he asked.

She didn't take her eyes off him. And he didn't look away from her. He wanted her to see the truth in his eyes. Besides that, he was holding his breath as he waited for her answer. She was either going to trust him or not. But he knew he wouldn't give up, even if her answer wasn't yes on this night. They were meant to be together, and he had no doubt that wasn't going to change.

After what felt like an eternity, she nodded as the tears continued to flow. Brandon jumped to his feet and pulled her into his arms, then lifted her high off the ground and locked his lips to hers. She fell into his kiss, and he knew this was truly the best day of his entire life.

He wasn't sure how long their kiss went on before he noticed the sound of applauding around him. He reluctantly pulled from Chloe, whose cheeks turned scarlet as she realized they weren't alone. Both of them had completely tuned out the rest of the world for this precious moment. Brandon took her hand and slipped the ring on her finger, the gem sparkling brightly in the perfectly lit room. He turned toward the swarm of people, his lips turned up so much his cheeks were beginning to ache.

"She said yes," he said. Their friends and family erupted into applause all over again. His brothers came over and clapped him on the back before giving him hugs while Sarah and Brooke engulfed Chloe in a group hug and squealed.

All the air was sucked from Brandon's body as Joseph enveloped him in a hug so tight he was wondering if he had a few cracked ribs when his uncle let him go.

"You've done very good, son," Joseph said.

"Yes, I have," Brandon agreed.

Chloe looked up, and their eyes met again. They pushed past all the people offering their congratulations and fell into each other's arms again. He couldn't quit smiling as they gazed at each other.

"I love you, Brandon," she told him. It was the first time she'd spoken the words, and that was when he knew how powerful those three words truly were.

"I love you, Chloe," he said, then kissed her again. The cheering of their friends drew them apart. "Is it time to leave yet?" he asked.

She laughed with pure joy. "Not a chance. I just got engaged. I'm going to enjoy my five seconds of fame as the belle of the ball tonight."

"As you wish, my princess," he said with a bow that had her laughing.

He might have been joking, but he truly did mean the words. There wasn't anything he wouldn't do or give to this woman. And their journey together was only just beginning.

Her mother stepped up to her, a smile on her face. "You look absolutely radiant," her mother said.

Chloe wrapped her arms around her mother in a messy, hard hug. "I feel amazing," she said. "I love him."

"That's more than obvious, darling. I'm glad you have found yourself. I know I haven't always communicated in the best way, but your father and I both want you to get all of your dreams."

The words obviously shocked Chloe. Brandon knew her mother had never said anything like this to her before, and he was sure she didn't know how to reply.

Her father saved her from having to do so. He took Chloe from her mother and gave her a hug.

"Your mother couldn't have said it better. Watching you this past year has made us realize we've made many mistakes in life. One thing we got absolutely right was in having you and seeing the beautiful, talented woman you've turned out to be. We're very happy for you."

"Thanks, Dad," she said. Brandon knew she'd always called her parents by their formal names of Mother and Father. He was glad to see that tight hold loosening. Formalities had been instilled in Chloe since she was a very young child.

"Mr. Hitman, can we ask you some questions?" a reporter said as she pushed her way in, having zero issues with any sort of boundaries. Before Chloe's father could say anything, the woman continued. "This veterans facility is making news all across the globe. Will you be hosting some cooking shows in the fabulous kitchen to bring more awareness to the project?"

A camera crew was on the edges of their group, their lenses focused on Chloe's famous father. Chloe smiled proudly at the man she'd been lucky enough to grow up with. She was obviously in shock when he spoke.

"Tonight is all about my daughter and her soon-to-be family, who have put their hearts and souls into this project. My daughter, Chloe, designed this kitchen and will be the one hosting some cooking shows here. I couldn't be more proud of her." He turned and winked at Chloe. "The show is all yours," he finished. Then he took her mother's hand and moved out of view of the cameras.

Tonight was a night of firsts for all of them. Chloe's parents had told her they were proud of her. And then they'd given her the credit she hadn't known she'd wanted, but Brandon knew it meant a lot to her. She was proud of this project he'd had to drag her into. She looked at Brandon, who smiled down at her.

Then she faced the cameras and smiled. "Let me tell your viewers how best they can help . . . ," she began.

This journey they were on was only just beginning. He couldn't wait to see where the road would take them next.

CHAPTER THIRTY-TWO

Three months later

"I can't believe this day has arrived. It seems to have taken forever and yet gotten here in the blink of an eye," Brandon told Crew as they got ready. His other brothers were in and out of the room. It all seemed a bit of a blur.

"I can't believe she hasn't wised up and left you," Crew said with a grin. "Of course, it's not too late. You might be standing at the head of that aisle with birds chirping."

The smile fell from Brandon's face. "I don't even know how I'd handle that," he admitted.

Crew laughed. "That was a very bad joke. It's more than obvious how the two of you feel about each other. Nothing will stop this marriage from happening."

"I've never loved someone like this. It's both awing and terrifying at the same time. I don't know how people get through the loss of loving this much and then losing the person."

Crew patted him on the back. "Maybe I'll find out what it feels like someday—to love, not to lose," he clarified.

Brandon assessed his brother. "You've changed a lot over the years," he told him.

"Yeah, I have. I think we all have," Crew said.

"Is there something that's made the change?" It was nice for Brandon to focus on something other than himself. He was nervous—but not to be marrying Chloe. That was the best decision he'd ever made. He was just anxious to say *I do*.

Crew shook his head and gave Brandon a crooked grin. It might've worked on someone who didn't know his siblings as well as Brandon did, but they couldn't easily fool each other. But before they could delve further into it, Crew clapped him on the shoulder again.

"We've got to set aside all of this sappy stuff. Today is a happy day. You're marrying the perfect woman for you—hell, for most men," Crew said, quickly pulling himself together.

"I agree with you on that. Just know if you ever need anything, I'm always here for you, just as you've always been there for me and the rest of our brothers," Brandon said.

"You've already proven that time and time again," Crew responded.

They didn't often hug, even though there was no shortage of love, but right then Brandon hugged his brother. He was grateful for Crew and for all of them. Just as they parted, Finn, Noah, and Hudson walked in.

"What's going on in here?" Noah asked.

"We're just being reminded why we're so lucky to have the family we have," Brandon said.

"I can easily toast to that," Hudson said. "Not to get too sappy, but since you started it, I can't imagine a better life." He paused, and none of his brothers interrupted. "We've been blessed time and time again. We were saved from our horrific father without inheriting any of his traits, were given the most amazing mother in the world, and now have this extended family. We should never forget that we have so much more than so many others. I know I do sometimes, but I never mind being reminded."

"I'm thankful for Joseph and thankful for everything. There's nothing in this world I couldn't handle as long as I have you guys there and, of course, now my beautiful wife and kids," Finn said.

"I love that the women we've been lucky enough to marry have added so much to this family, taking nothing away. I didn't know life could be this good," Noah added.

"To family, to friends, and most importantly to Brandon and Chloe. May their marriage be as strong today as it will be in fifty years. And may we all be there for one another the rest of our lives," Crew said.

They grabbed their beers and clinked them together. It was just another blessed day in a slew of many blessed years.

Chloe tried to catch her breath as she stared in the mirror. She had a moment alone as Sarah and Brooke ran out to grab a few items they'd forgotten. She never needed time apart from her friends, but it was nice to catch a few breaths. It all felt so unreal.

The wedding had taken only three months to plan. It could've been done even faster if Joseph had gotten his way, but she'd enjoyed planning the wedding and hadn't wanted to give up a single moment of it.

The one terrifying thing of marrying an Anderson was the fame that came from it. Everyone wanted to know what it was like to be in the exclusive Anderson family and empire. She'd graciously done a few interviews, as it was now expected of her. Brandon had promised her things would slow down after they were wed. He was going to take her on a monthlong honeymoon to a private island, away from cameras and reporters. She could barely wait.

She'd grown up in the spotlight, and she didn't want anything to do with it anymore. But you made sacrifices when you loved someone. And the truth about that was that it wasn't even sacrifice when it was done out of love. You just adapted to a new situation.

She knew there was a flurry of activity going on outside her suite door, but none of that mattered for one moment in time. Getting her ready for the wedding had taken two days, and she missed Brandon desperately. She hadn't seen him much the past week. Knowing he'd be waiting at the end of the long aisle was the only thought that would get her through the walk.

There was a knock on the door, and she let out the air she hadn't even known she'd been holding. She was more than ready to meet her fiancé at the head of the aisle. But she wasn't quite ready to face the crowd of people who'd be watching her take her walk.

"Sorry that took so long," Brooke said. "But we forgot your something old in the car."

Brooke and Sarah came into the room and pulled out a very, very old friendship bracelet. The string color had faded, and the first sight of it made her fear disappear and a smile fall on her lips.

"I lost mine before we were out of grade school," Chloe said.

"I don't know how I kept mine all these years, but when I got married and was going through all my personal stuff, I found it, and I knew it would be your something old when you got married. We've been best friends since grade school. We'll stay that way for eternity," Brooke said.

She stood and rushed to her best friends, then threw her arms around them.

"We're going to mess up your dress," Sarah said in a scratchy voice.

"I don't care. I can't imagine having any of these special moments in our lives without the two of you," Chloe said. "I also can't believe I'm the last to marry. I definitely would've thought it would be Brooke, and yet she was the first."

"Trust me—I know!" Brooke said. "I was so set on never marrying. But I guess all it took for all of us was to find the right man."

"I can't believe it was brothers," Sarah said with a laugh.

"We should've always known it would be, but in the real world three magnetic brothers for three best friends just doesn't exist," Brooke said.

"It's a good thing we don't live in the real world, then," Chloe said.

The three girls laughed before Sarah grabbed their wineglasses. "One last toast before we're all three officially married. To the past, the present, and the future. We've done the first two together—let's do the last as well."

"Always," Chloe and Brooke agreed.

Another knock sounded on the door before their driver opened it. "Your carriage is waiting."

"I feel like I can't breathe," Chloe said as she gripped Sarah's and Brooke's hands.

"This is just day one of the rest of your life. You can have a magical day, and then in ten years you'll look back and realize this was just one moment," Brooke replied.

"That's so true. Every momentous occasion seemed so big at the time, but there's always something bigger around the corner," Chloe told her with emotion crackling in her voice.

"Now, don't start getting all emotional and ruining your makeup," Sarah said with tears in her own voice.

"The next event will probably be big," Brooke said with a laugh as she rubbed Chloe's belly.

"Oh, I can't even think of that right now," Chloe said, almost horrified. The thought of a child was a bit terrifying. Kids were a heck of a lot of work.

Brooke and Sarah laughed, and she realized she must look as scared as the thought made her.

"Okay, I'm ready," she finally said. The girls led her from the room, down the long staircase, and out the front doors. Sitting at the curb was a beautiful horse-drawn carriage, with a footman holding open the ornate door.

Several people had to help her inside because of the long train of her wedding dress. She'd been intimidated by all the silk and lace when she'd first seen the exquisite gown, but it floated on her, and she could barely feel the yards of fabric draping her body. It was exceptionally made.

The top had thousands of sparkling beads weaved throughout the fabric. The gown hugged her tightly down to her hips, where it then cascaded in a full skirt. Before the train had been attached, she'd twirled in a circle, loving the layers of silk arcing out, reminding her of when she'd been a little girl and had dreamed of being Cinderella. The buttons up the back of the dress had taken a half hour to fasten. She smiled, thinking Brandon would be frustrated when it came time for the gown to come off.

Her long hair was mostly up in a bun, with several strands curling down her neck and shoulders. They'd even attached sparkling gems throughout. She knew she'd glow when Brandon took her in his arms on the dance floor.

The carriage started away from the resort, continued down the road, and rounded a corner, then entered the wedding venue. She looked out the carriage window and smiled gratefully at where she was heading.

After another ten minutes, the carriage arrived at the trail that led down to where Brandon waited. The door opened, and the driver was there to help her from the carriage. She took his hand and stepped onto the red carpet rolled out before her.

Brooke and Sarah helped straighten out her dress before stepping back and smiling.

"You're stunning, Chloe."

"Thank you," she said, once more fighting tears. They helped her step forward, but she halted. "One second," she said as she took in some soothing breaths. This was the moment she'd never thought she'd want, and it was the greatest moment of her life. It was odd how things worked out.

"Take all the time you want," Brooke said. "You're worth waiting on."

Those words were all it took. "I'm ready," she said. She beamed at her best friends. They stepped in front of her when someone handed them their flowers. The music began, and then they were gliding forward.

She continued down the scenic path, everything a blur, not even seeing the people who were all standing and watching her every move. Once she caught her first sight of Brandon, it took everything in her to not rush forward, straight into his arms. He looked so stunning in his military uniform, badges proudly displayed. His smile caused butterflies to stir in her already-nervous stomach.

Though he turned her legs to jelly and her stomach inside out, she also felt a calming deep inside her from knowing he was going to be her husband in just a few moments. She finally arrived at the stage, where he took her hand in his and led her to the altar.

The ceremony went by quickly, and they repeated their vows, unifying them as one. They were pronounced husband and wife all in a blur of words and actions. All she could do was look at her husband's face in awe that he was truly hers for the rest of her life.

"Are you ready to run away?" Brandon whispered.

His words made her smile. "I'll go anywhere with you," she said.

He kissed her again, much to the pleasure of their guests. They walked down the aisle, and Joseph stepped up to them, a suspicious shine in his eyes.

"Do you get emotional at weddings?" Brandon teased his uncle.

Joseph didn't seem to mind one little bit. "Though I didn't have the pleasure of watching you grow into a man, I have gotten to see you now, and what a fine young man you are. I couldn't be more proud of who you are," Joseph said in a surprisingly quiet voice.

Then he turned to Chloe. "I knew from the moment I met you what a fine woman you were. I'm so glad to have you be a part of our family," he added.

She didn't try to hold back her joy as she threw her arms around Joseph and hugged him. "Thank you for all you do and for never giving up on anyone," she replied. Brandon gladly took her back into his arms when Joseph released her. She was safe and happy and right where she should be.

Joseph turned the two of them toward the hundreds of people watching, a big grin on his face. His happiness was quite infectious.

"Meet Mr. and Mrs. Brandon and Chloe Anderson," he said to all present, and a roar of approval exploded all around them. She beamed as she thanked everyone. Then Brandon pulled her back to him and softly pressed his lips to hers, making her tremble when his tongue slipped out to rub against her bottom lip. She'd never get over how he made her feel. Each kiss was like the first time ever.

They pulled apart when they heard some throats clearing, and Chloe felt her cheeks glow with embarrassment, but the kiss had been well worth it. Then Joseph led them to the reception. The area had been transformed into an incredible fairy tale, and Chloe hoped it would never end. She laughed as she cut the cake with Brandon, and he kissed away the extra frosting. Cameras snapped and questions were asked, but she floated along in her own perfect bubble.

When it came time for her first dance as a married woman, she glided into his arms, happy her long train had been removed hours before. There was still too much material separating them, but soon they'd be alone.

"Words can't express how happy I am to have found you. You've brought so much joy into my life, and I know we'll be happy the rest of our lives," he whispered as he spun her around the romantically lit dance floor.

"Brandon, you're the prince I didn't even know I was looking for. I love you today and always," she promised.

They danced for several more songs and stayed long enough to appease the crowd before they finally slipped away to begin their honeymoon.

CHAPTER
THIRTY-THREE

Chloe woke up with Brandon's hand softly caressing her hip. She stretched out her arms as his hands became more insistent on her body. They'd been on their honeymoon for a week, and she didn't want it to end anytime soon. She turned into him, and they made love as the morning rays seeped through the open windows.

"I love you, Chloe," he mumbled as he nuzzled along her neck.

"I love you, Brandon," she replied, feeling content.

"What would you like to do today?" he asked.

"I remember you promising me a boat ride," she replied. "We'll never get out of this room if you keep kissing me like that, though," she said with a giggle. She couldn't seem to get enough of him.

"Ah, I think staying in bed sounds just about perfect," he replied.

"But I'm starving," she told him before jumping from the bed and walking across the room. She enjoyed the groan escaping his lips as she swayed her hips, moving away fully naked.

"You're killing me," he said with a smile.

"I wouldn't want that," she said and then firmly closed the bath-room door. She quickly showered and dressed for the day. They'd barely left their cottage since arriving. They were on a beautiful private island,

and it was a shame not to do some exploring. There was only a limited staff on hand, which gave them endless hours of alone time. If their friends and his brothers could be there with them, she'd stay forever.

They had a quick meal, then walked hand in hand toward the beach, where his boat was docked. Before long the sails were raised, and they were floating across the smooth sea. She loved the feel of the wind blowing through her hair. After an hour of sailing, he anchored the boat and started walking toward her. She knew the look in his eyes well.

She gladly fell into his arms and let him seduce her with nothing more than his skilled hands and masterful mouth. He turned her to liquid in only seconds.

"How about a swim?" he asked as he nuzzled her throat.

"I could certainly use some cooling down," she told him, her body already responding to him like they hadn't been making love for a week straight. She loved how every time he touched her, she felt something new and exciting. He made her feel things she didn't know were even possible to feel.

He started pulling her clothes off, taking his time kissing and licking his way along each newly exposed piece of flesh. She was a quivering mess by the time he removed her last piece of clothing, yet he was fully clothed still.

"Your turn," she said, beginning by sliding her hands under his shirt and slowly lifting it up and over his head. She ran her hands along the smooth muscles of his flat stomach and defined pecs. He was so perfect, with his tanned skin and light sprinkling of hair. Everything about him was appealing.

He groaned when she leaned her head forward and took his nipple into her mouth. She gently bit down on the dark skin before rubbing her tongue over the spot soothingly. He pushed his hand through her hair, then pulled her head tighter against his body. She freed herself from his grasp and moved downward, licking along his stomach, enjoying the slightly salty flavor of him.

After undoing the button on his shorts, she slowly pulled down the zipper. His arousal was pushing against the fabric, straining to get free. She was more than happy to oblige him. She slid her hands inside the denim, running them along his muscled rear, her own breathing matching his excited gasps.

Soon, he was standing before her, gloriously naked, his erection only inches from her face. He tried to bend down, and she shook her head. She'd never before tasted a man the way she wanted to taste him. She tentatively leaned forward, flicking her tongue across his pulsing head. His entire body jerked, and a moan rumbled from his chest.

"Chloe, I can't take much more," he said through gritted teeth. His loss of control gave her courage she didn't know she had. Slowly, she moved forward and took him into her mouth. He was smooth, solid, and tasted good against her tongue. He gripped her head in his hands, his legs shaking as she moved along his length.

"Enough," he growled and pulled her to her feet. He quickly wrapped his arms around her back, pulling her body flush with his, pushing his arousal into her stomach. Her beaded nipples brushed against his chest.

He kissed her deeply, swiping his tongue inside her mouth, catching her cries of pleasure with his own. His tongue slipped out, rubbing along her bottom lip, and she couldn't help but squirm, trying to get closer to him even though they were already pressed together.

He pulled away from her, the warm air caressing her skin. She reached for him, ready to have him sink deep inside her, but it seemed he had other plans. He took her hand and walked toward the edge of the boat. She barely had time to plug her nose before she figured out what he was doing.

He wrapped his hands around her and jumped off the boat, and both of them landed in the warm seawater. She came up with a look of shock.

"What are you doing?" she asked him incredulously.

"I've wanted to make love to you in this sea since we arrived," he told her. He pulled her tightly against him again, and her confusion was forgotten as he stroked her passion immediately back up.

He grabbed her legs and pulled them around his body as he continued kissing her. He pulled his mouth away only to trail his lips down her throat and finally capture her straining nipple, gently nipping her aching flesh.

He ran his hands along the curve of her backside. She could feel his thick shaft pushing against her tight passage, begging for entrance. She was more than willing to accommodate his request. She pushed her hips forward, no longer able to wait even a second longer to have them joined as one.

He thrust inside her, quickly moving in and out of her heat. He'd been teasing her all afternoon, and she wasn't going to last very long. He took turns lavishing each of her breasts while he pumped into her faster with each thrust. When he reached between their bodies and rubbed his thumb along her swollen flesh, she jerked in his arms and tensed as her climax washed over her.

"Brandon," she cried out in pleasure, only seconds before he tensed, and she felt his release pumping deep inside her. He brought his head up, taking her lips in a gentle kiss as he held her tightly to him, spilling his seed deep inside.

"Ah, I'll never be able to swim again without this image in my mind," he said with a chuckle.

"Mmm, it may not be a problem, considering my legs aren't going to work long enough for us to get back into the boat. We may have to just stay in the sea permanently," she said with a laugh.

"Sounds good to me," he told her. Her legs were starting to get a bit sore, though, so she finally released her grip around his hips and pulled back. He protested the movement.

"Okay, I'm getting some energy back. Swim with me to the sand," she said before pushing off and swimming toward the shore. She'd never sunbathed in the nude before, but her honeymoon was full of firsts, so it was one more thing she could add to her list. Her brow wrinkled as she realized other people could be about.

"Is this area private?" she asked.

"Yes, I brought you here so I could have my way with you," he answered. She chuckled at his attempt at a wicked laugh. He wasn't very good at playing the bad guy.

They spent the rest of their day alternating between lying in the warm sand, swimming, making love, and eating wonderful food his private chef had prepared. By the time they got back to their cottage, she was completely depleted of energy, but the day had been well worth the exhaustion.

Her last thought before falling asleep was she hoped she didn't wake up back in the real world to find out the last year or so of her life had been nothing more than a dream. She couldn't imagine how cruel that would be.

She really had gotten her Cinderella story. She hadn't dreamed of it, but that didn't mean fairy tales didn't come true. Plus, if she was dreaming, she never wanted to wake.

EPILOGUE

Joseph was kicked back in his favorite chair, sipping on a bottle of scotch, smoking a cigar, and wondering what he was going to do about his nephew Hudson. The boy was withdrawn, pulling away from his family and his friends.

And Joseph couldn't get him to say why. He didn't know what was happening. Joseph didn't like being left in the dark. It was far too unfamiliar of a place for him. Now, Crew was another mystery altogether as well. That boy had made significant changes in his life the past few years, and Joseph couldn't seem to keep up with him.

Were both of his nephews trying to confuse him? That would seem about right. He wouldn't put it past either one of them. The kids all knew he was meddling in their lives. But instead of being grateful that he'd helped them find the loves of their lives, they were complaining. That just showed how ungrateful kids could sometimes be. Maybe his last two nephews were trying to outsmart him. He laughed at the thought. That wouldn't go too well for them at all.

His door suddenly burst open, making Joseph jump in his chair. He wasn't easily startled, but a door slamming against the wall was enough to make him sit up. He looked at the person standing there, then let out a breath of relief.

He'd thought for a moment Katherine had gotten home early and was about to bust him. It was a nice day, and he knew he should've gone outside to puff on his cigar. But he loved his good chair.

"What in the world are you doing?" he asked the man standing there. "You nearly gave me a heart attack."

Damien Whitfield glowered in the doorway, not moving forward. His fists were clenched, and he looked as if he was trying to form words. Joseph had known this was coming. He'd been waiting to see how long it would take.

Maybe it was boredom, or maybe it was a need for adventure. But whatever it was, he could've circumvented this entire scene—but what was the fun in that?

"You have a *lot* of explaining to do," Damien said.

"You're the one who walked away several years ago, saying you wanted nothing to do with this family," Joseph pointed out.

Damien took several long breaths as he tried to tamp down the rage that was shining in his eyes. Joseph hadn't seen that look in a family member's eyes in a long time. But Damien had been put through the wringer time and time again. His heart broke for his nephew.

"I guess because I decided to walk away, I didn't deserve to know imposters had come along, making up some fictional story," Damien said.

"What makes you think you know what the story is?" Joseph said.

He had to admit he'd been hurt when Damien had walked away— very hurt. But now he was feeling bad that he hadn't reached out to him when he'd discovered what had happened. It had taken Joseph two years to get to the bottom of it, which meant he'd been sitting on the information for over a year now.

Joseph was never afraid of facing anything. But he was horrified at the monstrous acts his uncle had committed. That man had been a plague most of his life, and even in death he was still hurting people.

Damien finally moved forward. He didn't sit, but at least he stepped inside the room instead of standing there at the doorway, where he could disappear again in the blink of an eye.

"I deserve to know what's happening," Damien said.

"Then have a seat. This is going to take a while . . ."

AUTHOR'S NOTE

I can't believe another book is finished. It seems like just yesterday that I was finishing my first book, but it's been over ten years, and now I'm losing track of how many titles I've completed. What a blessing it is to write books for a living. It's more than a job—it's a passion. I love what I do. I'm so immersed in my fantasy world that when real life doesn't go the way I'd write it, I'm always shocked. Being an author is the greatest experience I've ever had.

This is book three in a new branch of Andersons, and I don't think I'll ever let this family go. I love them! I love the relationships within this fictional family so much that they feel real to me. Whenever I put them through some tough situations, there's a part of me that feels guilty about it. The gleeful-author part of me rubs my hands together and wonders how much torture I can put them through. I talk to friends and family about these characters as if they're real. It's pretty great to live in a fantasy world 90 percent of the time and have no one looking at me as if I'm insane. They nod their heads and agree. I was talking to my bestie about doing something awful to one of my characters, and she called me a monster. I love it! I love that these characters become as real to those who follow them as they are to me. I love that I dream about them and continually think of what I can do that will be different and entertaining.

As is the case with all of my books, I don't do it alone. I have help from my family and friends and from my amazing editors. I never worry about how bad a first draft is, because I know I'm going to jump on the phone with my editors, and we'll get it all worked out. I think if an author attempts to write a book alone, that story will be the same over and over again. We desperately need the help of others to mix things up and to bring a different perspective to a story. I do spend a lot of time alone writing, but I love to be surrounded by book-loving people while editing and storyboarding. Every single person has a story inside that needs to be told. It's up to us as authors to care enough to listen. Thank you to all of you who share with me, inspire me, and make me a better writer. I truly couldn't do it without you. My stories belong to all of you because without you, I'm just another person with a story that needs to be told but would never make it to the end.

With love,

Melody Anne

ABOUT THE AUTHOR

Melody Anne is the *New York Times* bestselling author of the popular series Billionaire Bachelors, Surrender, Baby for the Billionaire, Unexpected Heroes, Billionaire Aviators, and Becoming Elena. Anne loves to write about strong, powerful businessmen and the corporate world, and this allows her to do what makes her happiest—living in a fantasy world 95 percent of the time. To date, Anne has sold more than seven million books and has been an Amazon Top 100 bestselling author for three years in a row.

When not writing, Anne spends time with family, friends, and her many pets. A country girl at heart, she loves her small town and is heavily involved in her strong local community. For updates and news, follow her blog at www.authormelodyanne.blogspot.com, subscribe to her newsletter at www.melodyanne.com, check out her official Facebook page at www.facebook.com/melodyanneauthor, and follow her on Twitter @authmelodyanne.